# Marked Men

Michael C. White

University of Missouri Press
Columbia and London

University of Missouri Press, Columbia, Missouri 65201
Printed and bound in the United States of America

5 4 3 2 1 04 03 02 01 00

Cataloging-in-Publication data available
from the Library of Congress

ISBN 0-8262-1294-8

∞™ This paper meets the requirements of the
American National Standard for Permanence of Paper
for Printed Library Materials, Z39.48, 1984.

Design and composition: Vickie Kersey DuBois
Printer and binder: Edwards Brothers, Inc.
Typefaces: Arbitrary, Bellevue, Century Schoolbook

This book is dedicated to KBW—
again and forever.

# Contents

# Acknowledgments

Some of the stories here originally appeared, some in slightly different form, in the following magazines: *American Way, New Letters, The Advocate Newspapers, Redbook, Mid-American Review, Beloit Fiction Journal, Colorado-North Review, Permafrost, Four Quarters, Oxford Magazine,* and *The Nebraska Review.* The author gratefully acknowledges and thanks each of these magazines.

# Marked Men

# Marked Men

Pop and Toby are still at it when I get back. I'm barely in the kitchen door when Pop says, "Their *Nebelwerfer* launched six rockets at once. Plus they had a sweet little number called the *Panzerfaust*. Knock the stuffing out of our Shermans."

"You're comparing apples and oranges, Pop. NVA and VC didn't dig in. They didn't need armor. It was guerrilla warfare."

"Nobody dug in over there. That was the problem."

Toby looks at me, shakes his head. Then he grabs for the bottle of Chivas on the table and pours himself another drink. "Anybody with me?"

I tell him I'll pass.

When I was out walking my old neighborhood, I'd hoped they would have brains enough to give it up and go to bed. But I should've known better. Not those two. Before I left—the reason why I left—they'd been telling war stories. It's what they argue about now when they get together. A few drinks and Pop's back taking Anzio, while Toby's on patrol in some place like Quang Tri. All this stuff about assaults, body counts, ambushes, snipers, fear in your gut, tracers buzzing over your head. M-1's and M-16's. Krauts and gooks. Last time we got together, for Pop's sixty-ninth, they argued over what was worse, desert heat or jungle heat. Pop went on about how in Tunisia they used to fry eggs right on the tank turrets, while Toby said if you wanted heat, if you really wanted to scramble your brains, just try humping it through the Delta with a sixty-pound pack and it's a hundred and ten out.

After a while you want to tell them to knock it off. You want to tell them, who cares? When Toby got back in '71, you couldn't get him to say anything about *over there*. And Pop, the only thing he'd tell you was the time they shot some Arab's cow and one of the guys in his outfit, a butcher from

Cleveland, cut it up and they all had steaks. That was WWII for me—Pop eating steaks in the desert somewhere. But now it's different. Give them half a chance and you're going to get a belly full of war, whether you like it or not.

"Run into anything out there?" Toby asks me. My brother has melted into his chair. His head is tipped back against the wall, his eyes glowing reddish like a deer's jacklighted in the night. Pop is sitting across from him, playing solitaire and not having much luck. He stares down at the cards the way a lost man would stare at a road map, trying to figure out just where he'd made the wrong turn.

"What was I supposed to run into?" I ask.

"You tell me. You're the one on night patrol."

*Night patrol,* I think. "I just needed some air."

"Yeah, air. There's plenty of that in here," he says, darting a look at Pop, who's concentrating on his game. "Sit down and take a load off, little bro."

"No, I should hit it. We want to get an early start tomorrow."

It's four hours back to Long Island, where we live. We'd come up to my parents' house in western Massachusetts, like we do for a few days around Christmas every year. But we want to leave early, beat the holiday traffic on the Throg's Neck. Stace has to be back for work on Monday, and though I'm on semester break I still have a ton of exams to grade. Besides, two days home is about all of home I can stomach anymore. Pop is hard to get along with now. He's always jumping on my son, Joel, for the least little thing, or complaining about the neighbors not taking care of their yards. He's getting old and cranky, starting to fray at the edges. And my brother's not much better. He drinks way too much, has crossed over the great divide separating a fun drinker from a full-fledged alky. He goes on and on about his ex-wife's new boyfriend or how much he hates his latest job. He's depressing to be around for longer than ten minutes.

"What's the big rush, Bry?" Toby says.

"Got to leave early tomorrow."

"Lighten up, will you. The professor's on friggin vacation."

"Stacey isn't," I say. Gutlessly, I blame our having to leave early on my wife when I'm the one who really wants to be gone.

But I make the mistake of standing there for another moment looking down at Pop. I know I should just head upstairs to my old room, where my wife and son are already in dream land. It's late, after midnight. Ma's in bed, and Toby's girls, who he has for the weekend, are wrapped in sleeping bags in the den. Despite the walk in the cold night air, I feel groggy from too much booze and too much food, and too much talk, and I'd like nothing better than to drop into bed. But something about Pop catches my attention. He looks different, not just older, more shabby and careless about his appearance. There's something about him I've not seen, or at least not noticed, before.

"Humor an old fart for five minutes," he says, looking up at me suddenly. His eyes are loose, swollen under his thick reading glasses. I shake my head but without conviction, and before I know it he's already pouring me a drink in somebody else's coffee mug and kicking a chair out with his foot. The leftover coffee turns the Scotch a rich dark honey color. "Park it, Bry," he commands, turning me into a little kid again. So I sit. I figure Stace can drive tomorrow while I sleep.

"The Wasniewskis move?" I ask, trying for neutral territory, for safe, high ground. "I saw a different name on the mailbox."

"Move?" Toby says. "Where the Christ've you been?"

"Hell, that crew's been there three, four years already," Pop adds. "They never heard of a lawn mower, that bunch."

My father downs his juice glass of booze, winces out of habit, pours another. He's beyond troubling himself with sipping, or with the amenities of water or ice. He's too old for such subtle distinctions. And if we weren't here I doubt if he'd even bother with a glass. How many times did I come home late from a night out with friends and catch him sitting here alone drinking straight from a bottle of Wild Turkey? His face is a raging brush fire of broken capillaries, the stern, bony nose the only brace against sagging flesh. With his heart attack last year he's supposed to go easy on the sauce, but when Ma's not around he cheats. Out in the garage he'll sneak a smoke now and then too. He keeps a pack of Luckies behind the water heater, a pint in his tool box. The Chivas is OK because it's a present from a guy he used to work with at Pratt & Whitney and therefore is condoned. Besides, it's the holidays so Ma has cut him some slack. But Pop's attitude is, What difference does it make? What's he saving it up for?

"The Wasniewskis? Try like eight years, Pop," Toby says.

"Can't be," he counters. I watch him throw an eight of clubs on a nine of spades, wait for him to catch his mistake, then see that he's not going to. "Hank just retired a couple of years ago. They can't be gone that long."

"Take my word for it," Toby says. "At least eight."

"I never noticed," I say, sipping the coffee-flavored booze.

"No offense, little bro, but you always did have your head up your ass. Or should I say, up your nether ye?" Toby smiles at his literary allusion he's made for my benefit.

"I don't get back up here that often," I say.

"The Absentminded Professor. Remember him in Little League, Pop?"

"You never mind. Bry was a good little ballplayer," my father says, not looking up. As usual he takes my side against Toby. I was always the fair-haired son: good in school, the one who went on to grad school, the one Ma can brag about to her bingo friends as being "a doctor of English," the one who stayed married, stayed off the booze, made something of himself. Toby, on the other hand, was the black sheep, the one who flunked out of college and got drafted, the one who screwed up his job, his marriage, his life, the one about whom Ma usually says, as a kind of loyal afterthought, "And my other son's doing good, too." Toby's the "other" son.

"Yeah, but he always had his head in the clouds," Toby says. "I remember you yelling at him, 'For crissakes, Bry, get in the goddamn ball game.'"

"I never said any such thing," Pop says.

"Sure you did. I was there."

"Don't tell me what I said. I ought to know what I said. Bry had a good arm on him. And he was a good little hitter too. I remember."

"Oh, Christ. I'm not saying he wasn't good, Pop. I'm just saying he was kind of flakey. No offense, bro. But you know what I'm saying, right?"

I figure it's easier to nod than to argue, so I nod.

"And look who's talking," Pop says to Toby.

My brother pauses, tips his head back trying to get an ice cube stuck in the bottom of his glass. He taps the bottom, and finally the ice comes loose and clinks against his teeth.

"I remember this guy in our unit," Toby says, crunching on the ice. "Horace *T.* Pelky. He never wanted anybody to forget the *T* part. This guy was certifiably fucked up. Not a bad guy but he wasn't firing on all eight, if you know what I mean. An airhead. Just like you, Bry."

"I manage," I say.

"Sure you do. You get by just fine. You got the Ph.D. and all those horny college chicks eating out of your hand. And nobody's trying to take that away from you. But you get by with that here."

"What's that supposed to mean?"

"It means it's a different set of rules here. You can go out for your little stroll and step in a pile of dog shit and that's cool. Nothing happens."

"What?" I say.

"What I'm talking about is you can be an airhead over here, and they pat you on the back and hand you a degree and everything's fine and dandy. You don't have to pay the consequences."

I don't have any idea where he's going with this, but I nonetheless feel myself being sucked into something I want no part of. I tell myself, *It's late. Much too late to get into this.* Yet I find myself saying, "What consequences, Toby?"

"Over there, bro."

*Other there,* I think. So that's it.

"Where?" I ask, though I know exactly where he means.

"Nam. Always consequences there. We're talking a whole 'nother situation. Different playbook. Over there, you fuck up just once—don't watch where you put your foot, open your mouth the wrong time—yo ass is grass, muhfucker. They cut your balls off and hand 'em to you on a platter."

"Watch your mouth," says Pop, who's been quietly playing his cards. "This isn't a barn."

"What I'm saying is what passes over here, wouldn't cut it over there, my man. I'm talkin' 'bout one narrow margin for fuckin' up. Sorry, Pop."

When Toby gets on this kick, he starts in with this phony black talk. He's really a blue-collar white kid from the suburbs, but for Nam he has to become this ghetto dude, he thinks. Tough, supercool, like one of the bro's I've heard him mention. When he came back from a vets rally in Hartford a few weeks ago, he talked about guys with names like Curtis, Monroe, somebody he referred to as Sweet Henry J. The brothers.

"But I'm not *over there,*" I explain. "I'm right here. I didn't go to Nam and I wouldn't have either."

"Lucky for you. Over there, something you take for granted, say like putting one foot in front of the other, becomes this big deal. It can mean the difference between coming home first-class and coming home in baggage with a toe-tag on. That's the difference, little bro," Toby says.

I think about saying something. I could tell him how I'd made my choice, how I'd protested against the war. How that's all in the past anyway, and he has to move on. I could say that to him. But Toby's more than half-ripped and there's no sense arguing with him when he's like this.

Pop, who's been pretty quiet, snorts.

Toby looks over at him. "What's your fuckin' problem?"

Pop says, "Can't you go two words without a *fuck?"*

"Sure, I can go two fuckin' words without a *fuck*. See, no fuckin' problem."

"You think everything's so funny. That what you learned over there? To be a disrespectful gutter-mouth?"

"No, that I picked up over here. But I learned the real meaning of the word *fuck* over there. Since we got it but good."

Pop sips his drink. He's looking at me when he says, "A conflict."

"What are you talking about?" my brother asks.

"A conflict, not a real war."

"It was a war if you were there," Toby says.

"Huh. We lost more men in North Africa and Italy alone than in your whole damn *conflict*. And we weren't up against some little punks wearing black pajamas and eating rice. We faced Panzer divisions."

"You don't know what you're talking about, Pop. The VC were fighting before you were born. Before Hitler was born."

"Rice farmers."

"Tell me about it. They were breast-fed on war. Sucking tits filled with war while Uncle Sam was trying to bugger the hell out of them. And before us the French. And before the fuckin' French—"

"I told you to watch your filthy mouth. What if one of the girls hears you?"

"They're sleeping, Pop. And besides, they've heard it before."

"I have no doubt of that."

"Don't worry. Gonna give yourself a heart attack you don't watch it."

Pop stares across the table at Toby. I can see the big vein in my father's forehead, like a blue earthworm, moving beneath the skin. He slowly picks up his cards. Then he starts laying them down again, but this time it's not solitaire. It's not any game I know of. He arranges half a dozen cards in an arc across the table. Then he lines up several below the arc.

"Kasserine Pass," he says. "February 19th, 1943. We were right here, trying to defend it. Part of the First Armored Division. We'd been in Tunisia only a few weeks. Raw kids. What the hell did we know about war? We came up against Rommel's Afrika Corps and his Tenth Panzer. Hardened troops. Fighting since '39. They hit us at night. Rommel figured he'd take us on, instead of the Brits who'd been in Africa a while and knew what was up. That kraut kicked the living daylights out of us. I was never so scared. Every time one of those twenty-one-pounders hit something, I thought the earth would open up and I'd get swallowed. That was a war."

Toby looks over at me and mouths the words "Audie Murphy."

"We fought the best fighting machine the world ever knew," Pop continues. "And kicked their ass, too. We didn't come home with our tail between our legs expecting sympathy and handouts."

"Here we go," Toby says. "The Pop McNally Story."

"Stupid souse." Pop gets up from the table. He undoes his belt and drops his pants down around his ankles. A pale scar, the one we used to ask about as children but have had no interest in for years, slithers across his knee. "A pin is all that's holding it together."

Toby pretends he's playing a violin.

"They took out six pieces of shrapnel," my father explains. "One of those kraut 88's hit a Grant in front of us. Killed two guys in my unit. I still remember. Battle of Kasserine Pass. February 19th, '43. Rommel was trying to keep the krauts from losing Africa. He damn near pulled it off, too."

My father stands there in the middle of the kitchen with his pants down. His calves, big and pale as plucked chickens, are knotted with purple veins. In his hands he's holding something invisible, a carbine maybe, and looking through the kitchen window as if he expects the Germans somewhere out in the night. It's hard not to smile, the sight of him standing there in his yellowed Fruit-of-the-Loom's, his knees wobbly from too much Chivas—going on about some desert battle half a century ago.

I'm hoping Toby still has enough sense to give it up, to see that Pop is just a tired old man with a bad heart and caught in an old battle with his pants down. But Toby's just as bad now, perhaps even worse. He unlaces one of his boots, takes it and his sock off, and puts a foot up on the kitchen table. The toes are puffy and deformed, several of them have no nails, just scaly pink stubs. Though it's been almost twenty years, he still has problems with his feet. The skin peels away in white, rubbery layers.

"Jungle rot," he says. "They still freakin' hurt. I don't even go to the VA anymore. They can't do fuck so what's the use."

"Take your feet down from the table," Pop says. "We have to eat here. And if you can't keep a civil tongue in your head, there's the door."

"I'm just making a point."

"What point? A little skin ain't the same as taking a direct hit from an 88."

"Don't give me that crap. Charlie had his RPG's and chicons," Toby says, getting up from the table. Still with one boot off, he hobbles over to the fridge and starts poking around inside. Finally he settles on a drumstick, some left-over stuffing and potatoes. "They had this mine called a bouncing betty. Where'd Ma put the gravy?" he asks.

"Look, why don't you," Pop says.

"It had two charges. The first one put it up about waist level. Then the second one went off. A real sweetheart. Cut you in half."

"That's why your feet hurt," Pop says. "You're carrying too much weight."

I don't know exactly when this all began, when these two got into this war thing. With Pop it might've started a year ago after he'd had the heart attack. It turned out to be only a mild one. Outside his hospital room Toby said to me, "This was just to get our attention, you know. The old fart will bury both of us. Mark my words." But it scared us. Probably scared Pop more than anybody. Maybe that's when all this really started. Ma would call me when Pop wasn't around. She'd say, "He hardly sleeps anymore, Bryan. He just walks around the house all night."

"Try sleeping pills," I suggested.

"Three o'clock in the morning he's sitting at the table, writing all these names down on a piece of paper."

"Names?" I asked.

She told me they were the names of dead soldiers. Men he fought with in the war. Pop had never been the sort to talk much about it. Some men did—talked about it all the time. Mr. Wasniewski, our former neighbor, was always telling stories about the war, about the time he was shot. His son Walter and I used to go through a scrapbook he kept down in the basement. It had pictures of him in uniform, his Purple Heart, other medals and souvenirs. Mr. Wasniewski had a Luger he'd taken off a dead German, a heavy, blue-black gun he kept in his bedside bureau. Like it was nothing, some trophy he'd won. When I'd tell Pop about something Mr. Wasniewski had told us, he'd say the guy was just a big bullshitter. With Pop, it was different. You got the sense the war wasn't something he was proud of or ashamed of either. It was just something private, finished business for him. Something he'd tucked away and covered with mothballs, like his old uniform.

But in the last few years Pop has started going to these reunions, gatherings for men who fought in the war. Last year, on the forty-fifth anniversary of the capture of Monte Casino, he flew to Lincoln, Nebraska. That's all he talked about for weeks afterwards. On the phone he went on about his "comrades in arms." "Bry, you never fought so you don't know what it means. But I tell you, it's something else to see all your old buddies. Guys who saved your butt." Ma says he brought back addresses and that he writes letters to these men, as if they're long-lost relatives. When he gets word that one of them has died, Ma says he's in a lousy mood for days. I don't pretend to understand it.

Right after he got back from Nam, Toby got a job doing refrigeration work for a company in town. He married Jen, a girl he'd dated in high school, had two kids right away, and it was like he'd never even been to war. He didn't belong to any of those vet groups, didn't say much about it at all. And he didn't sit around feeling sorry for himself. When he saw some vet in a TV cop show go bananas and start killing people, he'd just say it was bullshit. Pure bullshit, he'd scoff. He said it wasn't like that at all. He said they were making a big deal out of nothing. Even before he came home, in his letters, he didn't say much about *over there.* I was in high school then and he'd write to me about what he did on R&R, some joke they played on a guy in his platoon. He made it almost sound fun, like the football camp he used to go to. Toby, who's big like Pop, used to be a pretty good linebacker. He'd wanted to play for Boston College but he flunked out his freshman year and went to Vietnam instead. When he came back his feet gave him problems and he no longer cared much about football. And he came back skinny, too, built more like a runner than a football player. I remember that was what shocked me the most when we picked him up at Logan. I almost didn't recognize him. His cheekbones stuck out and his head looked too big. Something over there had whittled him down, had cut away all the baby fat and even some of the muscle, too. If you tried to get him to talk about the war, he'd just say, "It was all nothing but a circle jerk, Bry. Everybody pulling everybody else's meat."

Three years ago he and Jen split up. That's when things started to fall apart for him. He began to drink and kept it up until he was doing it in a big-time way. He gained back all the weight he'd lost, became actually fat, smoked two packs a day, got into doing coke and who knows what. The guy looked like hell. He'd had a good job in the front office of his company, but he started calling in sick and after a while they canned him. He was forty-one, alone, unemployed, and his life was a mess. He used to visit Stace and me a lot then because he didn't have any other place to go. When he was coming, it got so we had to hide the booze. Over a weekend he'd knock off a case of beer and a half-gallon, plus a few joints or some coke if he could lay his hands on it. In those days he was hard to be around. Sober, Toby's the nicest guy you'd want to meet. But when he gets ripped he turns nasty and he was ripped a good part of the time now. A couple of times he said things about me or Stace and I don't know why I didn't send him out on his ear. But he's my brother, so I let it slide. I knew he was going through a rough time.

About a month ago he took a trip down to Washington, to see the Memorial. Up until then he'd been doing OK. He'd joined AA and seemed serious about putting his life back together. He'd gotten another job, one he seemed to like, and had a new girlfriend named Maria. I thought maybe he was over the hump. We'd invited him and Maria down to our place for Thanksgiving. We were sitting in the den talking, having a good time. It was like the old days with Jen. Then Stace said something about how it was good to be with family for the holidays. And Toby gets quiet all of a sudden. He's just sitting there staring off into space. I knew something was up. Pretty soon his eyes get watery and the next thing we know he's crying. It was terrible. This big, fat, middle-aged guy balling his eyes out. Of course we all thought it was on account of his girls being with their mother for the holidays. She was engaged to some guy Toby couldn't stand, and he hated the thought of the girls living with him.

"I got an idea," Stace said. "Why don't you bring Suzy and Paula down here for Christmas?"

But Toby looks up at us and shakes his head. After a while he stops crying enough to talk. He tells us he was thinking about this guy from Nam. Horace T. Pelky.

"This real dopey redneck kid from some place like Arkansas. I ran into his brother when I was down in Washington," Toby says. "Horace T. was supposed to get his DEROS just after the first of the year. But on Thanksgiving day we're out on recon, and the stupid fuck steps on a mine. Must've been one of those big chicons," Toby says. "It's plastic explosive sitting on top of a fifty-gallon drum of gasoline. Could knock a twenty-ton track right on its ass. You get the picture. There wasn't much left of old Horace T. I'm not shitting you. The poor bastard was there one minute and—*like that!*—gone the next," Toby said, snapping his fingers. "You can't imagine what can happen to the human body." Somewhere along the line Toby's crying had turned to laughter. Like it was suddenly the funniest thing he'd ever heard. Stace and Maria and I are all looking at each other, wondering if the guy had flipped out. Then he says, "Get this. First Sarge had us on our hands and knees looking for something of old Horace T's—a finger, a toe, anything. I mean, you had to have something for Dust Off to pick up. And you know what some guy in our unit says? I swear to God. True story. He says, 'How in the hell are we going to tell the difference between Horace T's pinky and his pisser?' And we all bust up. I mean, we're howling."

Stacey and Maria got up and went to bed. Afterwards I said to him, "What the hell's the matter with you?"

"What do you mean?" he said.

"Why do you want to go and say stuff like that? We're having a good time and you got to spoil it, you stupid asshole."

And Toby said, "It happened, man," like that made it all right, like anybody really wanted to hear that crap just because it happened.

Pop has left the kitchen and gone to the bathroom. Toby's tearing into his drumstick and wolfing down his potatoes. With a slice of bread he's mopping up the cold gravy.

"Why don't you let up on him?" I say.

"Fuck him. He deserves it. I'm sick of his war hero bullshit."

"He's an old man. Let him talk."

"An old bullshitter, is what you mean."

"He won't be around long," I say.

"Give me a break, would you. He's got you buying that line. Mark my words, bro—he'll bury both of us. He'll be dancing on our graves." He reaches across the table and grabs the bottle and pours himself another glass.

"Don't you think you ought to ease up on that?" I say.

"You sound just like Jennifer."

I'm about to say maybe she had a point, but I sense Pop standing in the doorway. When I turn, I see he's holding a sheet of paper. He doesn't say anything for a few seconds, just stands there staring at the paper. I wonder if he overheard us.

"It was so black out," Pop begins, "you couldn't see your hand in front of your face." Toby and I look at each other, then at Pop. He's into something now, deep into it, so far in it scares me. And I recognize what it was I noticed in him before, the thing I couldn't quite put my finger on: he's dying. That's it. I don't mean now or a month from now. But dying nonetheless. I can see it so clearly—the drawn flesh around his mouth, the hollowness of his stare, how it's not really Toby and me he sees when he's looking right at us. I wonder why I never noticed it before.

"What was so black, Pop?" I ask.

"That night."

"What night?"

"You couldn't see anything. Except for a tracer now and then. We were all dug into foxholes on the side of this hill. Fifty, sixty miles from Rome. A place called Carroceto. We'd fought our way up. North Africa. Sicily. The Italian coast. It was black out. Then the flares would go up. Every night, like clockwork. And you knew the krauts were about to drop the kitchen sink on you. So this night the flares go up and we're getting ready for a barrage. But we look out, and guess what's out in the middle of the field?"

"Sophia Loren," Toby jokes.

Pop glares at my brother but keeps talking.

"This little wop girl in a long, white dress. She couldn't have been more than eight or nine. She's got her dress lifted up to her face. We thought because she was afraid, you know. She's walking toward us. I keep watching her, we're all watching her. Just waiting for her to get it. We figure, no way the krauts are going to let her walk over to our lines. Her dress is so white, like she's a ghost or something, and everybody in the whole valley can see it. But she made it. She really did. The cutest little Italian girl you ever saw. And guess what she's got in her dress?"

"Raviolis," Toby says.

"You want to hear this or not, you stupid souse?"

"Yeah, I want to, Pop," I say. "What'd she have in her dress?"

"Figs. In her dress she's got a pile of figs and she gives them all away to us. The damndest thing I ever saw."

There's silence for a time. I can hear the sink dripping water, going *tick . . . tick . . . tick.*

"So?" Toby says finally.

"What do you mean, 'so'?"

"What's the point? Who gives a flying fuck if she had figs in her dress?"

Pop takes a couple of steps toward Toby likes he means business, the way he once did when we were little and we knew we were in trouble. I stand quickly and get in front of Pop, cut him off.

"Get out of my way, Bryan."

"Easy, Pop," I say. "Watch your blood pressure."

"You let me worry about my blood pressure. That stewed brother of yours better watch his big mouth."

"Toby didn't mean anything. Did you, Toby?"

My brother looks at me, wags his head. Finally he says, "You know I never mean anything, little bro." He pours himself another drink. Then with the bottle still in his hand he says, "How about you, Pop? Want me to grease your slide?"

"To you, everything's a goddamned joke."

"Not at all, Pop. You say you're living on borrowed time, I believe it."

Toby pours Pop another drink. He's about to pour me one too, but I put my hand over the cup. "Not for me. I got to go to bed," I say. Yet he pours anyway and it spills over my hand, onto the table. The alcohol is cool, making my skin tingle.

"Christ, you don't want to waste twelve-year-old booze," Pop warns us. "What was I saying?"

"The little wop girl with the fig newtons," Toby says. "How you saved us from the Huns."

"No. I mean before Bry came back. What were we talking about?"

"Marked men," Toby says. "Marked *bleeping* men, Pop."

"What?" I ask.

"Pop and me were talking about marked men," Toby explains matter-of-factly. "Guys you could tell were gonna get nailed."

"Cut the crap," I say.

Toby shrugs.

"He's right—for once," Pop says, looking out the window again, into the darkness. "It was something in their eyes. They got this look just before and then . . . *bingo.*"

"Bingo?" I said.

"The next day, two days later, a week—they'd get it. Killed. I swear, it never failed. You could spot it a mile off. You ever see those pictures of saints? That halo and that long-distance look. Well, that's the look they had."

"So what about the little girl?" I ask skeptically. "Did she have that look?"

"Her? Christ, no. She's probably got a dozen kids and weighs two hundred pounds now. Not her. The funny thing was she gave everybody in my unit a fig. Except one guy. Walt Trewell. A truck driver from Philly. When she got to him she'd run out. He said, 'What about me? Don't I rate a fig?' Everybody laughed because Walt was a joker. Always joking around. For the next couple of days we needled him about it, but you could see the fig business stuck with him. He got that look, I swear to God. He started seeing way off, for miles. A few days later we were marching through a small village just outside of Rome. We'd secured it, supposedly."

"Secured," Toby adds. "I've heard that before."

"A sniper bullet hit him right here." With his thumb Pop makes a mark on his forehead the way the priest used to on Ash Wednesday.

"A coincidence," I say.

"Don't tell me about coincidence, Bry. I saw it time after time. They'd get that look and then bingo."

I shake my head. "I don't buy it, Pop." I look over at Toby, waiting for him to jump in but he doesn't. He smiles at me instead, then says, "Got to agree with the old man, little bro. You could smell it on them. Their body would smell a certain way. Even their piss. A sour smell, the way piss smells when you're taking penicillin. I'm sure there's a scientific explanation for it. Maybe it was fear. Maybe the dinks could smell it on you like it was aftershave. Some biochemical reaction. Who knows? But they'd get it and then *sayonara.* Every stinking time."

"Jesus," I say. "You're both nuts."

"Something to it, bro."

"Cut it out."

"Really," Toby says. "But you had to be there. Ain't that right, Pop? You had to be there."

Pop leans against the stove, folds his arms across his large belly. "Christ, it got so I wouldn't even look at myself in a mirror. I didn't want to know if I had it. Ignorance is bliss, they say."

He walks over and drops the paper he's been holding onto the table. It's heavily creased, as if it's been folded and unfolded many times. It's curved, too, and you can tell he's been keeping it in his wallet. Because of this it's hard to read. Yet slowly I make out that it's a list, the sort my father makes out when he goes grocery shopping with Ma. This one, however, is a list of names. Dead men, I think suddenly, remembering what my mother told me. We all stare at it. No one moves for several seconds. It's as if something, a piece of the moon, say, has fallen from the sky and dropped in our midst, and we're too stunned to move or say anything, almost afraid more will fall. We have no words for this. Just silence. Then my father leans over my shoulder, close enough so I can catch the stale odor of his underarms, see his nostrils rimmed with white as he strains to suck in another mouthful of air. With his thumb, the same one he touched his forehead with just a minute ago, he touches one name. "There," he says. "If you don't believe me, read it." I do: it says Walter Trewel. The guy who didn't get the fig. I look up at my father, about to say something, but I see that he's staring hard at Toby. And when I look at my brother I see that his eyes are closed, as if he's finally had enough of this.

## Disturbances

What I know of death is how hard we work to deserve it and how little we appreciate it when it finally comes.

"Doc, you there? Sorry to wake you," comes Cecil's voice, thick-tongued, urgent. What I imagine an unmilked Holstein sounding like if a cow could talk.

The bedside digital clock says, in letters so red they hurt the night eye, 2:13. A dream, something about Willie, is still close by. In fact, I have to rub my eyes before I'm sure he's not beside the bed, awakened from some childhood terror. *A fox was chasing me, Dad,* he'd say. Always a fox, never a wolf or monster. He'd crawl into our bed, his small heart chugging away, a vague smell of urine lingering about him even at eight. He used to wet the bed and wake shivering in cold sheets. A long time ago.

"Yeah," I manage finally into the mouthpiece.

"Got one for you, Doc."

Cecil's the county sheriff, and when he calls at night like this it can only mean one thing. He wants me to go out with him and pronounce somebody. Maybe some trucker who was hauling logs over to Knoxville when his brakes gave out. Or a woman who'd picked up the wrong guy and now some fisherman's Rappala had snagged her creamy thigh. Or some old fart, like me, a foreman at the Champion plant till they closed down last year and moved to Mobile, who decided one night to shut the garage door, start up the Buick, and put on a Waylon Jennings tape. I'm the medical examiner, part-time anyway. Two weeks a month and whenever Rob Neinhuis, the other doctor in town, a young Duke fellow with a growing practice and seventy-five thousand in loans, goes on vacation, which isn't often. By day I'm a GP. Stomachaches, ear infections, croup: the minor disturbances of people desperate to keep on with their lives.

"How?" I ask.

"Twelve gauge in the chest. From about ten feet."

I see the sternum caved in, the heart and lungs a red pulpy mess. At ten feet there won't be powder burns but the skin will have little blackened pieces of the wadding embedded in it. The pupils will be the size of pennies, and staring up at you as if you'd just said the most remarkable thing. And of course blood—a slaughterhouse. It won't take a medical degree, but somebody has to sign the papers.

"Who?" I ask.

"Some kid up near Wolf Lake. His old lady did it. It was her that called in. I'll pick you up?"

"You're sure about him, right? I mean, we're not in a rush?"

"Hell no, Doc. Darryl said when he got there the sucker was already cold. How long, he couldn't say. That's your territory, Doc."

"OK, give me ten minutes. Better make that fifteen."

"I'll have coffee," Cecil says.

"Strong," I say, as a joke.

"Come on. Gimme a break."

Once out of bed, I feel the grudging coldness of the house. Not wanting to wake Tess, I dress in the dark, my joints stiff with arthritis that's gripping me like epoxy. I head off to the stove in the den, poke the embers awake, fill it with more beechwood, and turn the damper. So the house is warm when I get back. There'll be coffee—good coffee, not Cecil's dog piss—and eggs and a paper, and the house will seem like another planet that I've just touched down on. I might even be able to grab a catnap before I head in to the office. Though I don't need much sleep anymore, I hate getting out of bed much before six. I usually like to lie in bed for an hour, in the dark, next to Tess, and sort of get used to the idea of being alive all over again.

I go back into the bedroom and kiss Tess's dry mouth, which always tastes of cider flavored with nutmeg. It's a ritual. What if something were to happen to you, she says. What if it were you out there instead? I grab a big warm handful of breast at the thought. Not passion but the clinging to what we know. Her thirty-two years as a doctor's wife have taught her to sleep through such disturbances, and she clears her throat, moans softly but continues on her way.

In the hall I put on my coat and gloves. As I pass Willie's room, I peek in, a habit I've not been able to break after all these years. I can remember wandering the house at night when I couldn't sleep, a sentry standing guard. I used to like knowing that until dawn nothing could happen, nothing touch us, the demons of the night only imaginary: like those foxes. I watched over Willie's sleep like a miser guarding his hoard. I'd bend over him, watching his eyes flicker beneath lavender lids, views into another world, a child's world. Willie was drafted in '71 and entered the world I knew all too well. He didn't die in Vietnam, as some of his classmates did. He never reached it, in fact. He died of meningitis while he was still in boot camp in Kentucky. Two other kids from his unit caught it but only Willie died. The army doctor said Willie developed meningococcal meningitis, turned septic on them in four hours, and there wasn't a thing they could do. He felt pretty bad about it, the army doctor. Especially after he learned I was a doctor, too. But that's how it is with meningitis.

I grab my bag—a formality tonight but there's always paperwork—and head out to wait for Cecil's cruiser. Overhead, the stars are little slivers of glass that would cut if you were dumb enough to handle them. The night's blue cold is softened only a little by the sweet odor of burning beech. Down in the valley I can see Waldroop's chimney shooting a line of smoke skyward. There's a light on in the kitchen, and I picture the old man sitting there reading about the Etruscans and Carthaginians, about old battles and invasions. That's what he does late at night. "Did you know, Doc," he once told me, as if uttering the deepest of humanly secrets, "Hannibal's elephants were just for show? Served no tactical purpose whats'ver. But they sure scared the bejesus out of those Romans."

In a few minutes Cecil pulls down my long dirt drive, the flashers turning slowly to proclaim this official business. As I get in the cruiser, he hands me coffee in a Styrofoam cup.

"Here you go, Doc," he says, backing out of the driveway. The fence and behind that the rhododendrons flash red, then white, then red again from the cruiser's lights.

"Thanks."

"Hope it's strong enough." He looks over at me and then does a double take—our tired joke. "You finicky old fart, you."

"How's Rosie anyway?" I ask.

"Got something. Coming out both ends. I told her she should see you."

"Have her to wait till she's not contagious."

"Listen to him. Tell you the truth, I don't feel so hot myself. Achy. Right up in here, Doc," he says, grabbing his neck. "I'm getting too old for this."

"You?" I say, because I have a good ten years on him.

"Least you got a choice, Doc. You don't have to do this. Me, this's what I get paid for."

"I like a night out with the boys now and then."

"Yeah. How's Tess?"

"She's fine. Sleeping."

"Hell, where we all should be," Cecil says, not selfishly, but thoughtfully. As he backs onto the main road and drops the shifter into drive, he says, "Why can't they just *go to bed?*"

"That's not always the safest place either," I say, but Cecil doesn't hear me, doesn't want to.

"Why in the good Christ do they have to be up at this hour?"

"Some people can't sleep."

"Why not play cards or read then? Or fuck? They could still do that, couldn't they? If they were busy fucking they'd be too worn out for all this other craziness. Now tell me what's wrong with that, Doc?"

"Nothing," I say. "Sounds like you're on to something, Cecil."

"You damn right. I ought to write a book. *How to Fuck Your Troubles Away.* How's that sound?"

"You could hit all the talk shows, Cecil."

"Yeah. Maybe put out a video," he says, and we both laugh uncomfortably at our almost total freedom, like a couple of teenagers out for a few in the old man's car, a little frightened almost with our options. But that's just an illusion. We don't have many.

I sip my coffee. Cecil makes it strong, metal-tasting, like a dentist's bit in your mouth. Exactly the sort of thing you need to get out of bed on a night like this and go look into somebody's dead eyes.

We sit silently for a while, watching as the road snakes its way up to Wolf Lake. Cecil's fifty, short but compact as a woodchuck in August, with a full red beard starting just below his glasses. He stares intently at the lit tunnel of road ahead. It's the way some men stare into their drinks, others at naked women they can't ever possess. Even less than I do, Cecil doesn't like this business. People dying on him on cold, black nights. People getting out of bed and loading shotgun shells into guns, forcing us out of bed, too. The motives behind such events, more so than the events themselves, are an exasperating puzzle to him. And yet he's not a timid or a naive man. When we used to hunt together, before my arthritis became too bad, I saw him reach his arm up to the elbow in a still warm buck and tear out its steaming entrails, just like that. And in his own way, he's seen as much as I have the gnarled shapes men's souls can take: those of drunks, thieves, child molesters, rapists, a murderer or two. What I picture him happy as is a gardener, his fingers in the soil. A job with answers you could touch, prune, snip, even dig up and transplant if you didn't like them. Cecil's a friend and he knows I know he's in the wrong line of work.

"Darryl's got the girl out at the place," Cecil explains. "She's not saying squat except she did it. Pretty cut and dry. I'll drive her over to Raleigh tonight."

"She called it in, you said?"

"Yeah. Said she shot him and then said she didn't think their truck would start. Told me I'd better come out. She even gave me directions, said most people couldn't find the place. How's that for consideration?"

Cecil looks over at me, smiles out from behind the mask of beard. His eyes are glassy and wet-looking, like dogs' eyes in the dark, waiting for a friendly hand, for reassurance. The greenish light of the cruiser's dash makes him look gnomish, old, much older than I.

When we get up near the lake—a slick black mirror between stands of hemlock and white pine—Cecil turns up a steep hardscrabble road. The rear wheels slip and growl over the stones. At times the rear axle bottoms out and there's a terrible scraping noise.

"They keep promising a four-wheel," Cecil says, meaning the town. For these mountain roads you really need one, too. The car lurches forward, bucking like a horse under you. Sometimes the tires spin free and let out with a catlike snarl. After a while, the road levels off and we reach a clearing. In the cruiser's headlights a shabby green trailer covered with asphalt shingles sits at the far side against some pines. There's a pick-up truck, a couple of cars without wheels or doors, and the other cruiser Darryl came up in. From a doghouse beside the trailer a pair of red eyes glint out at us, but the thing doesn't bark at all. It just stares inquisitively, wondering what's up.

Cecil shuts the engine off, gets out, and stands next to the car. I finish the last of my coffee. As I sit there another moment, I try to firm up the muscles in my stomach. It's something I do. Like when I have to tell a woman that the lump in her breast might be trouble. I'll sit in my office for a minute trying to make my flabby middle tight and hard. So I can say what I have to. It's one of the tricks they don't teach in med school.

Outside, I can see steam rising up around Cecil as he takes a leak.

Funny how whenever we go out on something like this, it seems Cecil has to go. A sympathetic release. I guess it's like my stomach exercise. I tighten up and he relaxes.

I get out and follow Cecil's wide sloppy butt up to the trailer. As we get near, something like a sick animal's baying cuts through the night. High-pitched but hollow-sounding, like a screech owl only fainter.

"What the hell?" I ask, but no sooner are the words out than I realize what it is. "There's a baby in there!"

"Yeah. That's why Darryl didn't bring her in. She was nursing, so he let her finish. Then she wouldn't let him take the kid from her."

"Jesus." As soon as Cecil opens the door you can smell the raw odor of coagulated blood: a trapped, secretive smell like the insides of a turkey. Darryl's leaning against the refrigerator, smoking a cigarette.

"Hey, Doc," he says, almost cheerfully. Darryl is mid-twenties, tall, pasty-looking from too many night shifts. He's got long hair, which Cecil doesn't mind, and he looks more like a violinist than a deputy sheriff. He tried to get into diesel repair and when that didn't work out he took the test for a job as a deputy.

"She's finished but he keeps crying," he says. "Isn't paragoric supposed to work?"

On a couch in the tiny living room a young girl sits rocking a crying infant. She's Indian, full-blooded Cherokee, with long hair that's pulled back in a single tight braid like a black snake, and eyes as hard and impassive as chestnuts. She doesn't look at any of the people now standing in her house. She stares straight ahead, at a beer bottle sitting on its side on the small kitchen table. Near it is a single plate of food, half eaten, hardened into cement. Methodically she rocks the baby back and forth. It continues to cry, though it doesn't have its heart in it. The cry is weak, not from the lungs, a premie's shallow whimpering. The kid looks about three months old—a girl, I'd guess, despite what Darryl said. She's solid, with pudgy hands and a perfect dark circle for a face. Her eyes are wide and clear and brown, and from time to time she looks around at the strangers surrounding her.

"Where?" Cecil asks Darryl.

Darryl indicates with his thumb toward the back of the trailer.

"Why don't you see if you can get the baby quieted down, Doc. I'll take a look."

While Cecil heads down the hall, I go over and kneel down in front of the mother, who's all of sixteen.

"Better watch it, Doc," Darryl advises. "Be careful."

"How old's your baby?" I ask the mother.

She remains silent, looking over my right ear. Her eyes don't move, don't even blink. Her skin is pock-marked from a bad case of chicken pox. I've never seen either mother or daughter. They must've gone to the clinic on the reservation, if they've ever been to a doctor at all. Way back here in these mountain hollers there are still people who are born, live, and die without ever needing my services. Then, still not looking at me, she says, "She'll be four months the eighteenth."

"*She*. Shoot, no wonder she was pissed at me," Darryl says.

"Did she take enough milk?" I ask.

"Yes, I think so. She's usually a good eater. I don't know tonight."

As I go to touch the baby, the girl draws back, curls around the baby to protect it.

"I'm not going to do anything, miss. All right?"

"You need you a hand, Doc?" Darryl asks.

"No, that's OK." Then to the girl, "I just want to help."

"It's my baby. You understand, mister?" She makes eye contact for the first time, and I know she'd claw my face before she'd let me take her baby.

"I'm a doctor," I say, holding up my bag. "I just want to take a look. Make sure she's all right."

"She's mine," the girl repeats. "Don't think you can pull something on me. I know what's going on."

"I'm not going to pull anything. I just want to see if your baby's OK. Does she have a fever?"

"I don't think so. She doesn't feel hot to me."

"Can I see? I just want to help. Give you my word."

She stares hard at me for a while to make sure I can be trusted.

Slowly I reach out and touch the baby. Maybe a little hot but nothing serious. Other than being exhausted, the baby looks healthy enough. In fact, well cared for. She has the mother's black hair but the features are different, the eyes softer, the chin more prominent.

"She might still be hungry," the girl offers. "She nursed for a good long time but I don't know as she got much."

"You want to try again?" I ask.

"Is it all right?"

"Why don't you give it a try?"

She opens her shirt front and takes out a small, tired-looking breast and positions the baby's mouth against it. The baby finds the nipple and begins sucking hungrily on it. But after a couple of minutes she stops and begins to cry again.

"I don't think she's getting anything," the girl says, looking at me. "I don't know if I have any milk."

"Have you any formula?" I ask.

"No. I have some powdered milk."

"Let's try that. Where is it?"

"In the cabinet over the refrigerator. There's a bottle in the sink."

I fix the milk, then wash the bottle out. I fill the bottle up and put it in a pan on the stove. While it's heating I go back over and kneel down in front of the girl.

"Is she teething?"

"She might be."

"Let me take a look?"

She props the baby up and lets me poke a finger around in her mouth. In the front I feel two small nubs, about to break through. I open my bag and take out some benzocaine, rub a little along her gums. She puckers her face at the taste. While I'm at it I get out my stethoscope and take a quick listen. Then I percuss the chest, ascultate the lungs. She seems in good health. It might be the first checkup she's had.

Cecil comes back into the living room then. "Hey, Doc. See what you think." Then to Darryl he says, "You Miranda her?"

"Of course. There's the gun over there. I didn't touch it. And I bagged the shell. Double-ought 12 gauge."

I get up and walk over to the bedroom. Just inside the door, as if he was about to head out, a tall thin guy lies on his back. His legs are bent and one arm lies under his body at a sharp angle. His shirt and the surrounding floor are covered with blood. He isn't Indian. He has reddish hair and a face that's the nothing color of trout that's been frozen too long in a freezer. That's what he looks, frozen. Not serene. Christ, they *never* look serene. More like the discouraged look of somebody who finished second in a race, just relieved it's finally over. The baby has his chin, which is long and sharp with a little bump at the end.

I put on some gloves, then go through the motions of checking for vital signs. The blood feels greasy like kerosene. In the middle of his chest, there's a hole I could put my fist through. With the stethoscope, I listen for a heart that's no longer there. I look at my watch and jot down a couple of things in a notebook, for court. He's cold to the touch already. Just technicalities. With that my job's done. They'll ship the body to the state medical examiner's in Raleigh for the whole nine yards. I'm just here to stamp his ticket and say when he left.

Out in the living room Cecil's trying to convince the girl to give the baby over to him.

"You don't want your baby in a jail cell, now do you, miss? You wouldn't want that," Cecil says, reaching for the baby.

"I told you, get away," she says, hissing at him and curling into a ball on the couch. She appears ready to snap at Cecil if he tries anything.

"Come on now. Be reasonable. You need to come with us," Cecil says, holding out a pair of handcuffs, as if as enticement. Finally he turns to me. "Whyn't you try, Doc?"

"Me?"

"Maybe she'll listen to you."

I sit down next to her on the couch. "Do you have any relatives you could leave the baby with?"

"None I'd reckon I'd want to."

"How about any friends? Anybody at all? Just for tonight?"

The girl shakes her head slowly.

"Well, you can't bring your baby in a jail cell, miss," Cecil says. "You just can't do that."

"They'll take the baby away and put it with protective services," I say. "That's what they'll do."

She doesn't say anything for a while. Finally she says, "Here," and shoves the baby at me. "You take her. OK?" It's part command, part request. Then she gets up and offers her wrists so Cecil can put the cuffs on her.

Later, after Darryl has left with the girl for Raleigh and the ambulance has come for the body, Cecil and I get in the cruiser and drive back down to the main road. It's still dark, though now the night shapes are slowly becoming articulate. I can't remember when the baby stopped crying, but it lies quietly now in my arms, sleeping, its mouth forming a tiny full triangle.

As we pull into my driveway Cecil says, "I hate to ask you, Doc. But would you mind taking her? Just for a couple of hours and then I can bring the kid over to the shelter in Waynesville."

"Why can't you keep her?"

"Hell, with Rosie's sick and everything. And what if something should happen? I'd feel a whole lot better if she was with you."

Cecil stares at me with his sad collie eyes. When he says thanks, I know already I've agreed to do it. He reaches under his seat and takes out a pint of Old Grand Dad. He passes it to me and says, "Cheers, Doc." I take a short nip, then tack on another to make it count against the cold. It slides down my throat making a noise like someone yelling in a cramped space.

"Cheers," I say.

"I'll owe you one."

"You bet your sweet ass you will. A weekend with Rosie at Willow Pines," I say, grabbing my bag and getting out of the car. The baby's still asleep in my arms.

"With room service," he says, backing out of my drive.

Halfway up he sticks his head out and calls, "I'll have a bottle of Dom Perrignon sent up for the two of you lovebirds." In a minute he's gone and the mountain I live on is quiet and dark again. Down in the valley Waldroop's light is off and I picture his dreams full of spears and fallen Etruscans. The wine dark sea.

Inside, I think about bringing the baby into our room, putting her in bed with us. Just to see the expression on Tess's face in the morning. That would be something. But I decide against it, so as not to wake my Tess and have to explain everything right now. In the morning, I will. Instead I bring her into Willie's room and pull the covers back and lay her on his bed. I can't remember the last person, except for myself, who's slept on this bed. Sometimes on hot summer nights when I can't sleep I'll get up and come and lie in here, on top of the covers. The window faces out on a small creek and there's always a nice breeze. For a time I couldn't bring myself to set foot in here. I just couldn't do it. But then things quieted down, like they do even with death, and it was just another room, his room still, but nothing painful about it. Just a good place to sleep and sometimes I even dream of him here. Not bad dreams. We talk sometimes and sometimes he'll just be there, quiet, like he often was in life. Tess says he had the most beautiful hands, long and slender, not effeminate but well shaped. Hands that would've done something important, though we cannot say what. He didn't have a chance to do anything important. I don't remember his hands all that well. He was a good kid and I miss him even after all these years. There's not much to say beyond that. Some men, I guess, would've devoted their lives to finding a cure for meningitis but what I do is lie on his bed now and then, and whisper that it's all right to him, over and over again, until I fall asleep.

Soundlessly, so as not to wake anyone up, I slide in beside the woman's baby, in between the cool sheets with all my clothes still on, even my boots which have mud on them, and I know there'll be hell to pay for that tomorrow. I wrap the covers around us and try to get the warmth back in my old bones. I find myself thinking, not of Willie, who I know is safe and beyond harm, nor of the baby's father, who is also beyond harm, and not even of the baby, who is just a solid ball of heat against my chest. What I think of is that woman. Sitting in some drafty cell, her breasts slowly filling up with milk until they ache, the ache turning slowly to a rock-hard pain, and finally, when she can't take it any longer, maybe doing something like pumping her breasts and letting the milk run down the drain. And I see her hard black eyes not so much as shedding a tear. That's what I see now.

# Ray's Shoes

"I want you to talk to him, Steve," Ali says above the noise of the sander.

I put my hand to my ear, pretending I don't get what she's saying.

*"Talk,"* she repeats, louder. *"To Ray."*

I've come into the barn to get the garbage cans for our Saturday dump run. Ali's sanding a student desk she picked up at school. Sawdust billows up around her, her hair and eyebrows are covered with the stuff. It makes her look stagy-old, like someone in a school play. Out in the driveway, Bonnie and Mike wait impatiently in the truck.

"We going or what, Dad?" Bonnie calls.

"Hold your horses," I say. Then to Ali I ask, "What about?" though *Why me?* is what I'm thinking. It wasn't my idea she look after Ray's kids.

"Tell him it's not working out. Tell him I'm tutoring a new student. I don't care. Anything."

She bullies the sander across the desk, punishing it for her mistake. It's covered with old graffiti: obscenities and oaths of love side by side. *JM x ST* is written inside a lopsided heart. Another—*Mrs. Gunderson eats pigeon shit*—fades under Ali's assault.

"This was only supposed to be temporary," Ali says. "He needs to start thinking about other arrangements. He'll have to when school starts."

I say yes, but she doesn't hear me because of the noise.

"Don't you think it'd be easier coming from you." It's not a question though. She shuts the sander off and looks up at me expecting resistance. When she doesn't get any, her momentum takes her further. "Damn it all, Steve." She hasn't adjusted for the sudden silence and her words are loud enough to startle both of us. Sort of like when you were at a dance back in high school and trying to talk to a girl and the music suddenly stopped and you found yourself shouting at her. Even Bonny and Mike stare at her.

"Mom?" Bonnie calls.

"Nothing. I just banged my finger." Then whispering, she says, "He's getting too . . . too *cozy.*"

"What on earth does that mean?"

"He just is. You know what he asked me today? He asked if I liked to go out dancing. *Dancing!*"

Ali stands there, sweaty and covered with sawdust, waiting for me to say something.

"So what?" I ask.

"He makes me uncomfortable, that's what."

We've been through this before. For a couple of weeks now, she's been saying Ray is beginning to get on her nerves, make her uncomfortable. When I ask why, she's vague. When I ask why she doesn't do something about it, she gets mad. I can't win.

"I don't know how much more I can take," she says. "And I don't want to hurt his feelings."

"But you want me to."

"Don't put it like that. I just think it'd be easier coming from you. Man to man. Promise me, Steve, you'll talk to him. OK?"

I tell her I will. Only after she starts the sander again, I add, "When I get the chance." Like I said, this was her idea, not mine.

Ray Warner lives a mile down the road, just past Nine Mile Lake in an old farmhouse that needs work. He and his wife moved in about two years ago. Ali, a reading teacher, had gotten to know Mrs. Warner a little since she'd been working with their older daughter, Dede. In May, the woman died of a brain tumor. The last few months she was in and out of the hospital, so it was Ray who'd pick Dede up after school, talk with my wife on the phone about her progress. Ali had Dede over a few times to tutor, but it was more just to get her out of the house, to help the Warners, than it was for her reading problems.

After Mrs. Warner died, Ali would drop off casseroles, extra work for Dede. She'd tell me how the kid came to school looking sloppy, her hair uncombed, pants that could've used an iron. When you bumped into Ray in the Stop and Shop, he looked like someone trying to change a flat tire and not knowing where to start. Lost is what he looked like.

"The guy's got his hands full," Ali said. When school let out, she invited him over for dinner one night. A decent and kind thing to do, but that's Ali for you. It was then she offered to look after Dede and her sister for a few weeks.

"Thanks, Ali. But I couldn't do that," explained Ray, a small, stocky man, with no neck and stumpy forearms, built like a wrestler. He's a couple of years younger than us, early thirties, I'd guess. He runs his own landscaping business. He takes care of other people's yards, yet his own looks like a tornado hit it. Tree limbs and piles of leaves, newspapers and rusty engine parts lie everywhere. You drive by and you'd think some helpless old lady lived there. Not a landscaper.

"Why not? I'm off," Ali said.

"I don't know," said Ray, glancing at me across the dinner table. "I'd hate to tie you up like that."

"No problem, really. At least for a while until you can find somebody. It'll give Bonny and Mike somebody to play with. Besides, I could work with Dede."

Ray finally agreed but made it clear it was only until he could work out something more permanent, a couple of weeks at most. Later that night, I asked if Ali knew what she was getting herself into.

"Only for a couple of weeks," she said. "Until he can get things sorted out. The poor guy needs some help."

Ray would show up in the morning in his dump truck to drop the girls off. Dede, seven, and Kristen, five, were about the same ages as our two and the four got along well together. They played in the fields behind our barn, and Ali would take them to the lake for a swim. I didn't see Ray much. I'm an electrical contractor and this summer I'd been doing a development out near Pittsfield, an hour's drive away. Mostly I heard about him from Ali.

Since she wouldn't take any money, Ray brought her things to show his appreciation. He heard she liked the Beatles so he showed up with this ten-album collector's set. I'd come home and Ali'd be rocking out to "I Wanna Hold Your Hand" or "Here Comes the Sun," like she was back in high school. Sometimes Ray would bring plants, rhododendrons and azaleas, things he had from his landscaping work. He even planted them for us. I didn't mind. I'm not one of those men who gets possessive about his yard. I could care less, to tell you the truth. If he wanted to plant things around the place, let him was my feeling.

"He pruned the Chinese maple today," Ali said late one evening several weeks ago. We were at the kitchen table. "He said all the growth was going straight up." I said that was great, like I cared about where the growth was going. I didn't look up from the estimate for a job I was pricing. This summer we couldn't go four sentences without Ray's name coming up. Ray said this or Ray said that. Ray said we should put mulch around the rose bushes. Ray thought we might have a problem with grubs.

"He's such a nice guy," she said. "I just wish there was something else we could do."

"These things take time."

She was quiet for a moment. Then she asked, "What would you do?"

"I think you're doing all you can."

"No, I mean if it'd been me? If I died. If you were in his shoes?"

"Oh. Have some fun, I guess. I wouldn't be worrying about mulch, that's for sure."

"No, cut it out. Be serious."

"I don't know."

"It could happen. You could be in Ray's place."

"I know."

"Really," she insisted, and I finally looked up. She was staring at me. Two years ago, during a routine checkup her doctor found a mass in her stomach. It took several days before they were able to biopsy it and find out it was something called a desmoid tumor, which just happens to be benign. Pure luck. But for those few days it was hell. I'd be in somebody's cellar hooking up a two-twenty-amp breaker and start to thinking. And once you get started like that there's no stopping. Your mind just sort of takes off. It was only when I'd nearly screw up, almost touch a hot wire to a ground, that I'd snap out of it. So I knew, all right. I knew what she was talking about. The *what if* of things.

At first, Ali was glad to do what she could. She'd talk about how Ray was managing, what he should do next. It was the way she'd talk about some kid at school who was foundering. Ali would make a plan for her student, with all these steps for improvement. That's how she spoke of Ray.

"There's this support group for young widowers. It meets once a month at the high school," she told me. "Maybe I could mention it to him."

"He has to work it out on his own, Ali."

"But what about when school starts? What's he going to do then?"

"That's his problem, not yours, hon. You're doing enough already."

Ali gave him the names of some women who looked after kids. He had one sitter, a high school girl, for a couple of days but that didn't work out. And he talked about his mother, widowed herself, coming down from Maine to stay with them. But August rolled around and he was still dropping his girls off at our house. They weren't the problem. His girls were nice kids, well-behaved, sweet. That wasn't it at all. It was Ray. He'd hang around in the morning or stay late when he picked them up. Sometimes he'd still be there when I got home for supper. "Geez," he'd apologize on seeing me. "I didn't know it was so late." But how could you blame the guy? He just wanted to talk—about the kids, his job, things he'd have talked to his wife about. I don't imagine it was so hot going home to fish sticks and an empty, unclean house, which is what Ali said it was. A mess. Clothes all over the place. Dust and dirt.

"I know the poor guy's lonely," Ali would say. "It's just that . . . "

"Just that what?"

"I can't sit around talking to him all morning. I have things to do."

"Tell him you're busy," I offered.

"I try to. But he doesn't take the hint. Like this morning. We're sitting at the kitchen table yakking and I got up and started vacuuming. You'd think he'd get the message? Instead what he does is follow me around. From one room to another, trying to talk over the vacuum. What am I going to do—tell him to hit the road?"

"Yes."

"Mr. Sensitive," she called me.

About a week ago, Ali and I were moving the bedroom furniture. Every so often, usually when something's bothering her, she gets this bug to rearrange things. Therapy, I guess. I go out and slice golf balls, she plays chess with the furniture. This night we'd lugged the bed back and forth across the room several times already. Nothing seemed to suit her.

"OK, before I break my back. You want to tell me what's up?" I asked.

"Nothing's the matter." She grabbed one end of the bed by herself and started shoving it another way. "Are you going to help or what?"

"Not until you tell me what's wrong."

"Nothing's wrong." Finally I sat down on the bed and waited. After a while she said, "He cried today."

"Ray?"

"I was hanging clothes and we were talking. He told me I used the same fabric softener Jenny did. That's when he started crying. Bawling like a baby. Right out there in the yard. It was awful, Steve."

Ali didn't look at me for a while. She smoothed the covers on the bed. She put her hand to her mouth and squeezed her bottom lip. Then she said, "He was so pathetic looking. I didn't know what to do. So I held him. You know what I kept thinking? What if Mrs. Jantzen saw us?"

"Don't worry about that nosy old bitch. You were just helping out."

"I know. That's what I told myself. And afterwards he apologized. But *I* felt uncomfortable."

"He'll come around."

"Yeah. Three weeks and I go back to school, Steve. Then what?"

At the dump, Mike helps me throw the garbage into the "scruncher," as he calls it. Sometimes Dave, the garbage man, lets him push the button that operates the thing. My son likes all that power, to be able to crush things. He says it's wicked fun.

"Hi, Steve," a voice calls to me. I turn to see, who else but Ray Warner.

"Hi," I call back.

He's alone in his dump truck. He gets out, grabs a box from in back. Then he walks over and heaves it in. We stand there for a while talking about the Sox. How Clemens blew a 2-0 lead the other night against Detroit. How they could use a good short reliever. Safe, guy sort of things. I ask him where the girls are and he says, awkwardly I sense, at a sitter's. I think of telling him Ali's taken on a new student, that she won't be able to look after the girls anymore. Sorry, I'd say. I could easily slip it in.

But just then Mike yells, "Look, Dad!" He points down at a bike someone's thrown away. A two-wheeler, something we've been promising him for months. The front wheel's bent a little but it could be replaced. "Can I have it?" he asks. I look over at Dave and he nods, so I reach down to grab it. That's when something else catches my eye. It's the box Ray threw in. It's filled with shoes. Women's shoes. There are all sorts—

pumps, open toes, wedges, espadrilles, loafers. The box gets crammed into the slot along with the rest of the junk, crushed into oblivion. When they're out of sight, Ray says good-bye, gets in his truck, and takes off. I think, *Jesus*.

On the ride home, Bonnie asks me, "Can't Mr. Warner get another wife, Dad?"

"Yes. If he wants to. Someday, I suppose."

"How long does he have to wait?"

"Nine months," Mike blurts out.

"That's for a baby, silly," Bonnie says. "How long for a wife?"

"It depends. First he'd have to find somebody he loves. And loves him back. That usually takes some time."

"Oh," is all she says, wading as far as she dares into the murky waters of adulthood.

Two days ago I stopped home just after noon. Ali was at the kitchen table with Dede. The other three were running through the sprinkler. It was one of those muggy August days, the sort that drains me and leaves me with a headache.

"You're home early," Ali said.

"I finished roughing in one place but the drywall fellows didn't show up. Thought we could go out to Bigelow Hollow." It's a secluded lake on the Connecticut line where we sometimes go for a picnic and a swim. The water's always cold enough to loosen your fillings.

"Fine," she said, but I could see from her expression things weren't. As I started washing my hands, I noticed in the sink plates with egg yoke and hollandaise sauce on them. Ali just about never makes eggs.

"Who had the eggs?" I asked.

"Ray made eggs Benedict," she replied, smiling awkwardly.

"He made them?"

"He showed up with all these groceries and just started cooking. Wasn't *that* nice?" Ali said, the irony in her voice barely going over Dede's head.

"My Dad used to make breakfast . . . when Mom was

alive," Dede said, embarrassed. "I liked the home fries best. He made them nice and crunchy."

Dede chewed on a strand of her dark hair. She was quiet for a while. "Mrs. Tipaldi?" she asked finally. "Is my Dad going to be OK?"

"Why, of course he is, honey. He's going to be just fine. Listen, how about if we call it quits for today? You can go out and play with the others."

When she was outside, Ali said, "He sat here all morning talking."

"Yeah?"

"Yeah. He talked about Jenny, me. He said I have beautiful hair. Like hers."

I started doing the dishes, my back to her. I figured I'd keep my mouth shut, let her do the talking, let her take this thing wherever she wanted.

"I know I must sound selfish. I know it's part of the grieving process. I *know* all that." When I didn't say anything she said, "Aren't you going to say anything?"

"Like what?"

"I'm upset and you don't even give a damn."

"That's not true. I just don't know what you want me to do."

That's when she first brought up the idea that I could talk to him.

"Me?"

"It might be easier coming from a man."

"Why would it be easier coming from a man?" I thought how men don't talk about those things. Feelings. Sadness. Loss. We don't have the language for it. We're like chimps when it comes to that sort of thing.

"It just would. He needs to make other arrangements."

I did my best to put off talking to Ray. The way I figured it, in a couple of weeks Ali'll be back in school and he'll have to make other arrangements anyway. I'm the sort who thinks most problems, if you just leave them alone and don't pick at them, will work themselves out eventually.

One evening we're in the den listening to *Abbey Road,* from the set Ray got her. Ali's sitting on the floor, her narrow back to me. She's flipping through a magazine, not reading it, just using it as a prop. Her hair, newly hennaed the color of a red oak leaf in the fall, is still wet from her shower. I think how Ray Warner's right, she does have beautiful hair. I try to recall the last time I'd told her that. And I think how if I were in his shoes it'd be easy, really easy. What I mean is to fall for Ali. Finally I ask what she's been avoiding all along: "Do you think he's in love with you? Is that what's the matter, Ali?"

"Who?" she asks, pretending not to know.

"Who're we talking about here?"

"We weren't talking about anybody."

"All right. Who *weren't* we talking about then?"

"Ray? Are you crazy?"

"Isn't that what's been bugging you?"

"No. It's . . . just that he counts on me too much. It's not healthy."

"Then I'm wrong? That's not it?"

"He just expects too much. I know it was my idea to watch the girls. But . . . " Ali doesn't finish her thought. She flips through some more pages while the Beatles sing "I Want You."

Finally she turns toward me. She looks about to cry but doesn't. She's not the sort that cries easily. It takes something really big to make her cry.

"I only wanted to help. I didn't want things to get all fucked up like they are."

The next night after dinner, I walk down the road to Ray's house. I've put it off as long as I can. I figure I'll walk though, so it'll give me time to think. The twilight's cooler, but the hot tar smell continues to rise off the pavement. Over the lake a pair of ducks skim inches above the surface, moving with the precision of planes in an air show. I don't know what I'll say to him. I still don't even know what's going on, except that his wife is dead and mine's uncomfortable having him around anymore. I am as well. I'm not a jealous person, but I feel possessive suddenly, ready to protect what's mine.

I ring the doorbell, realize it doesn't work and knock. Soon the door opens and Kristen's standing there in her pajamas, a candy cane snagged in the corner of her mouth like a fishhook.

"Hi, Kristen," I say. "Is your Daddy home?"

She nods shyly and opens the door wider for me to enter.

Just then I hear Ray calling. "Kristen, who's that?"

"It's me. Steve."

"Hey, Steve. I'm up in the attic. Kristen, show him the way up."

She takes my hand in her sticky one and leads me up two flights of stairs to the attic. It's hot up here and smells like a rug that's just been beaten. The only light is a naked overhead bulb in the middle of the room. Ray's sitting on a suitcase, with Dede on the floor beside him wearing a floppy hat. In the weak light I can see several boxes in front of him. One has Christmas things in it. Another's filled with clothes—mostly blouses and slacks and sweaters.

"Look at all this junk, Steve," he says, smiling and spreading his arms wide. "I think it grows all by itself."

"What're you guys up to?" I ask.

"We're gonna have a sale," offers Kristen.

"A tag sale," Dede adds. "And we get to keep the money."

"OK, girls," Ray says. "It's getting late. Let's do the teeth."

"Oh," Kristen whines. "Five more minutes. Please."

"We don't have school, Dad," argues Dede. "We're on vacation."

"School's almost here again. We got to get back in training."

"Just one more candy cane, Dad?" Kristen begs. "Please please please."

"All right. One." They reach into the box of Christmas things and grab a couple of candy canes. "Now go. Make sure you brush or you'll have rotten teeth. I'll be down in a minute to tuck you in." After they leave he says, "Those two. Give 'em an inch and they'll take a mile."

"Mine are the same way."

"I guess I haven't been so great in the discipline department lately."

"It's not an easy job."

"Let me tuck them in. I'll be right back," Ray says.

He's gone for maybe fifteen minutes. I sit there, glancing around, wondering what's the best way to break the news to him. Should I beat around the bush or just tell him straight out? When he returns he says he's sorry, that Kristen always wants a story before bed. I tell him I understand. He sits down and there's an awkward stretch of silence. He stares down into the box in front of him.

"Ray," I begin. But just as I do, he reaches into the box and holds up a long black dress. It looks like silk, gathered at the waist, dressy. It's hard to picture Ray being with someone who would wear such a thing.

"It kills me to get rid of this stuff," he explains. "Some of it's almost brand new. I got her this and she wore it like once. She was more a jeans person, you know what I mean?"

I nod, listen as Ray's callused hands catch on the sleek material.

"Oh, now and then she'd get dressed up. She liked to go out dancing. I was never much on it. Two left feet." Ray looks down at his shoes, clunky work boots with big steel toes. "But I liked to watch her. She moved real good. She was a good dancer. We'd go to a wedding or something, and she'd get somebody to dance with her. A cousin or somebody's husband. It didn't mean anything. And like a jerk I'd sit back and watch." He stares at the dress for several seconds. "It should've been me out there, Steve. But I was afraid I'd make a goddamn fool out of myself. You know what I mean?"

I nod.

"Do you like to dance, Steve?"

"Now and then," I say. "I'm not very good."

"It doesn't matter. Take my word for it." He looks at the dress again, turns it in the light so it shimmers, sways as if someone were inside it, moving sinuously. "You don't think this would fit Ali, do you? I bet she'd look good in this."

"No," I reply.

He glances at the dress again, then says, "I didn't think so. Just that I hate to see it go to waste. It's a nice dress."

"It is," I agree.

"It would look good on somebody."

"It sure would."

We sit there for a while, held in a palm of silence, smelling the carpet odor of things put away for too long. The roof creaks with night noises. Bugs knock against the vent. We are two men together in an attic looking at a dress, wondering why things are the way they are. When the silence has run its course, we head downstairs. Funny, but he doesn't ask me why I came and I don't volunteer anything. But he knows. He *knows*.

At the door, he says, "You tell Ali thanks for me. Say I didn't mean to impose. Tell her . . . just tell her that." I say I will.

When I'm out at the road he yells, "Don't forget, Steve. You take her dancing. If you don't know how, you just make it up as you go along." He tacks on an awkward laugh. I say goodnight and he shuts the door.

For a moment, I stand there in the cooling night air, looking into Ray's house, watching the lights go out one by one until it's dark. Finally, I turn and head home as quickly as I can, feeling the blood pounding in my neck.

# Burn Patterns

They had been riding only a few minutes when Hough spotted the snake poking out from her down vest. He thought maybe the fat girl was just playing some kind of joke, that it was one of those rubber things you won at carnivals. He saw only the narrow little head, yellow with rusty diamond patterns, the liquid-black eyes, glossy as charred wood after a fire. The girl he'd given a lift to sat quietly across from him, one hand guarding her backpack, the other holding the snake behind the head. Hough stared at it for several seconds before saying anything.

"That for real?"

"Yeah," she replied. "Why?"

"Why!" Hough exclaimed, shaking his head. "Jesus Christ. I'm not in the habit of giving rides to snakes."

"I put him inside my shirt when it's cold. He just goes to sleep."

Hough shivered, felt a tingling sensation down in his testicles. "That thing's not poisonous, right?"

"It's just a corn snake."

"I'm not up on my snakes. They're not poisonous?"

"You kidding?" she said, smiling condescendingly, showing grayish teeth. "There's only four poisonous snakes in the U.S. You got your rattlesnake, copperhead, cottonmouth, and coral," the girl recited, as if she were naming state capitals in a contest. "Your coral are the worst. They're neurotoxic. That means it hits the nervous system. You go to sleep."

"You a snake authority or something?"

"I read a little."

Hough shifted a little toward his door. He didn't like the idea that something like that, a damn snake, had invaded his car. "It can still bite you, can't it?"

"Only if you don't know what you're doing. See that?" she said, showing Hough the flap of skin between the thumb and forefinger on her pudgy left hand. "Sucker got me there once."

"That's reassuring," he said.

"It was my own fault. I was putting a mouse in his cage and I got careless. They don't see too good."

It was just his luck to pick up a snake charmer out in the Pennsylvania mountains. He considered stopping and letting her out, saying he hadn't bargained for any snake. Yet it was a good ten miles to Wilkes-Barre and what was the chance she'd be able to hitch another ride out here? Maybe the thing was supposed to establish ground rules, he thought. A young girl hitchhiking. Don't try anything funny, pal, or I'll sic my snake on you. Still, he didn't like it.

"You ought to be careful with that thing," Hough advised. "Most people don't want any part of snakes."

"That's their problem."

A tractor trailer blew past then, its wake shoving Hough's company car, a small Citation, sideways like a bully. The car hit a patch of black ice and fishtailed, the tires spinning momentarily out of control. Hough felt his stomach drop away. But he was used to this sort of driving. This was his territory. He turned into the skid and the car straightened out, continued down the long mountain grade.

"Look who wants to be careful," the girl said, glancing over at him.

"Don't you worry. Twenty-nine years without an accident," he said, trying to show her he was all right, that she had nothing to worry about. "Do me a favor, would you. I'd feel a whole lot better if that thing was out of sight."

"Your car."

Instead of stuffing it back into her vest, however, she slowly pulled the thing all the way out, the way you'd pull off a belt. Its size took Hough's breath away. It was almost a yard long, its middle as thick around as his forearm. The tail curled up like a sea horse's, the head lethargic and dull. She then lowered the snake into the backpack on her lap. It seemed as stiff as a piece of heavy-gauge wire, and she actually had to bend it and stuff it into the backpack.

"How come you got that with you, anyway?" Hough asked after the snake was out of sight.

"You don't want to know," the girl replied, though she said it in such a way that suggested she wanted very much to tell him. "I'm trying to find it a good home. Know anybody might be interested?"

"Not off the top of my head."

"Actually, they make pretty good pets. They're not as much bother as a cat or dog. They only eat like once a week."

Hough looked over at the backpack to reassure himself there was no way the thing was getting out. "You from around here?"

"*Here?*" she said, looking out the window. "You couldn't pay me enough to live here."

"To tell you the truth, it's not my favorite place either. Where are you from then?"

"Seattle," replied the girl.

"You're a long way from home."

"Everybody's a long ways from some place, right?"

With that she looked out the window.

Hough was an arson investigator for an insurance company in Massachusetts, and his territory was the Northeast. But he didn't like working Pennsylvania. The driving was always iffy, the roads icy and rutted, and nearly always covered with fog. Out in the boonies here, if your car broke down, forget it. You could go for miles without running into a service station. And there wasn't a decent restaurant or motel once you got past Wilkes-Barre, just truck stops and redneck diners where the locals eyed you as though you'd just walked into their private kitchen. Besides, the country itself was ugly, raw and unfinished-looking, with huge mounds of evil-looking black coal and long stretches of forest where the trees just seemed to have given up and died.

He'd picked up the girl just south of Scranton, as he was pulling back on the highway after stopping for gas. She stood at the bottom of the entrance ramp, her gloveless thumb stuck out, a challenge, as if daring someone to stop. He thought she was older at first, but as soon as she got in the car he decided she was more like eighteen. What had thrown him off was her size. She was a *big* girl, must've been close to six feet, and heavy, big-bellied, thick-thighed. Hough himself was no shrimp, went well over two hundred pounds, but he felt actually puny with her beside him in the car. She wore a florescent, orange down vest, the sort hunters wear, which only made her size more pronounced. Like a highway road sign. She looked sloppy, the way fat kids often do, but this one looked as if she hadn't come near a bar of soap in a week. She even brought into the car a hard, musky odor. Her long brown hair was greasy, and her nails dirty. Hough thought street person, only the girl was younger than he was used to seeing, and she didn't have that floating look street people had. This kid seemed focused, grounded in a way homeless people weren't.

Now and then he'd pick up a hitchhiker, especially if he had a long drive. He wasn't supposed to, it was a company car and against policy, but who would know? He liked to talk, that's what everybody in the branch offices said about him. Hough could talk your goddamn ear off, they said, but good-naturedly, fondly. At forty-six, he'd been on the road for nearly twenty years and talking came in handy, especially in his job. He could strike up a conversation as easily with a witness to a fire as with the guy sitting next to him in a diner. People trusted him, would tell him things they wouldn't to a cop or fire marshal. Sometimes he'd even talk a waitress into coming back to his motel room and sharing a six-pack. Amaranth, the town he was headed for, was a good six-hour drive, and conversation along this dreary section of highway would help pass the time. Besides, it was cold and raw out, the gray sky looking as if it were getting ready to snow. He felt sorry for her standing there in the cold. Hough wasn't heartless.

Yet the snake business gave him second thoughts. He didn't need to pick up some weirdo. He had enough headaches of his own. His new boss back in Worcester, this hot-shot kid with an engineering degree from MIT, expected a report on his desk by the end of the week. From what Hough had gathered over the phone, the Amaranth fire sounded suspicious. Which meant there'd be people to interview, pictures and lab samples to take, research at the town clerk's office. The usual on a suspected arson case. He wanted to get there before it snowed and covered the site, or before kids started picking through the debris, making his job harder. And he didn't need to go looking for trouble. Maureen used to say he had a nose on him like a beagle: couldn't keep it from sniffing around in other people's garbage. Maureen said a lot of things.

He glanced over at the girl. She hadn't said a word for exactly five miles—he'd been watching the odometer. She sat with her head against the window, drawing something in the mist her breath made on the glass. Even more than the snake, the silence made him uneasy.

"By the way, I'm Hough," he said. It was the sort of name that invited people—friends, coworkers, strangers, even lovers—to use it alone, as if it were a first name.

"Like in 'I'll huff and I'll puff?'" the girl asked.

"Right. You're looking at the original Big Bad Wolf," he said, smiling.

When she didn't offer her name he asked, "What's yours?"

"Little Red Riding Hood."

"No, come on. Really. I'm giving you a ride. Least you could do is tell me your name."

She hesitated for just a moment, then said "Rosemarie." The way she said it, a little too pleased by the sound, Hough had a feeling she'd just made it up. In his work he got used to people lying to him. You even came to expect it. It was one of the few things you could count on: given the chance, people would lie to you. They might not even mean to but they did. It was part of the situation that someone who worked for an insurance company found himself in. If you knew that you were ahead of the game.

"That's a pretty name," he said, going along with it. "Where you headed, Rosemarie?"

"Virginia?" she replied.

"You know what they say about Virginia, don't you?"

"No, what?"

"That it's for lovers."

She squared around to look over at him. She had tense, brown eyes under thick brows. "What's that supposed to mean?"

"Nothing. It's just what they say in those ads."

"Let's get one thing straight, Hough. I'm only interested in a ride. Period."

"What do you think I had in mind?"

"I just wanted to make sure we're working from the same playbook."

*Playbook,* Hough thought. She was something else, this fat kid. He considered saying he wasn't that hard up since he left Nam. He'd been over there in the early days—'64, '65—before things heated up. Once, in Saigon, he'd gotten so drunk he agreed to some pimp's offer to get laid for five bucks. What the hell, he thought. It's all the same when you're drunk. The woman he woke up beside in the morning had no teeth, dugs withered as an old hound dog's, and looked ancient enough to be his grandmother.

"You got folks in Virginia?" he asked, trying to change the subject.

"Yeah."

"I thought you said you're from Seattle?"

"Is there a law against having family in both places?"

"Don't get all bent out of shape," he said. "Just making conversation."

She wrapped her arms around the backpack and slumped down in the seat. They drove in silence for about ten minutes and Hough started looking for an exit to dump the girl. He didn't need this. A fat kid with a snake and an attitude. But damned if the next thing he knew she wasn't snoring. Sound asleep with her face mashed against the window like a loaf of white bread. Weird kid, he thought. One minute she was worried about him having his way with her and the next she was sleeping next to him, peaceful as can be. He glanced over at her. She had light, freckled skin, soft and creamy, the way some fat girls have nice skin. Her features weren't unattractive, full lips, a straight, firm nose, though everything about her was big, even her earlobes. A heavy oafish girl, one he could imagine had had a rough time in school.

As he drove along, he pictured coming home and telling Maureen about the girl with the snake. He wasn't sure he even missed her anymore. Not really. More the way you'd feel the absence of something familiar, like a couch. The only time he felt much of anything was when he'd wake up at night in some motel room. And even then it wasn't so much *her* he missed as the sense of connection she'd lent to his life—the routines, the shared patterns, knowing the lights would be on when he got home, that her robe would be on her side of the closet. "Guess what she had inside her shirt?" he'd have said to her, and he could just picture that cynical look Maureen had made into an art. But then, of course, she'd want to know why he'd picked her up in the first place, a young girl, and just how he'd managed to see it if it was *inside* her shirt. Maureen was jealous like that, especially in the years following the accident. She seemed almost to look for fights: questioned him if he got home late, grew suspicious if he didn't call exactly when he said he would. Of course, the booze hadn't helped. He could tell she'd been drinking as soon as she asked who he had with him in the room. "Who's there, Hough?" she would ask. "Who's with you?" And yet, for the seven years they were married, he'd never been unfaithful to her once. Not once, though he certainly had his chances. The really funny thing, *she* was the one who ended up running off, with some guy she'd met at her Wednesday night support group for parents who'd lost a child. That was six years ago. The last he heard she was expecting a baby. Forty-two and expecting another kid. Yet he couldn't even hold it against her. At least their split hadn't been complicated by children. That was something to be grateful for. Having married in his thirties, he'd been used to traveling light, thinking only of himself. Now he was once again settling comfortably back into a bachelor's loose patterns, knowing he wasn't stupid enough to make the same mistake twice. The rest of his life alone didn't really look so bad to him. It would have certain consolations. Still, he sort of wished someone were waiting so he could tell this story.

Off the highway, small, dirty-looking towns shot past: tar-shingled tenement houses clustered like a brood of filthy chicks around the domed roofs of Catholic churches. Then more woods and black crumbling mountains. There was a junkyard, just south of Scranton, that extended along the highway for about a mile. At another point, Hough counted six deer stretched out in the snow by the side of the road or in the medium. Trying to cross at night, they froze in the headlights and were smashed by semis. Finally he saw a sign that said *Harrisburg 108 Miles*. He decided he could put up with the girl till then. He'd deposit her safely at the bus station and be on his merry way.

He thought about the Amaranth fireground—a three-family house with a pizza shop on the first floor. He liked to plan out his investigation, picture it in his mind. Who he'd see first, how'd he'd go about finding the point of origin. He'd want to check out the pizza joint, have a look at the books to see if it was in the red. People didn't torch a place that made money. Maybe the guy ran a bookie service out of the back and owed somebody. Then Hough would look someplace the fire hadn't touched, searching for clues there and working backwards. Sometimes they told you as much as points of origin and accelerant residue. If someone had taken their picture albums, say, then you knew something was up. This one guy, a dentist, had removed all of his diplomas two *days* before there was a fire in his office. He told Hough he was having them remounted. It turned out the guy had an expensive mistress he was supporting in grand style and was up to his eyeballs in bills. The insurance money, he thought, was going to save his ass. He was now working as a dentist in the Somers prison in Connecticut. Working for free, hoping for time off for good behavior.

The girl had been sleeping for only a half hour when out of the blue she said, "Where we headed, Hough?"

*"I'm* headed for the Turnpike. You can ride with me as far as Harrisburg. But don't give me any more crap. Or I'll cut you loose right here. Got it?"

"Yeah." She sat up, rubbed her puffy eyes. "My last ride was with this trucker. He got some ideas in his head."

"What do you expect, hitchhiking all alone?"

"I can take care of myself."

"Sure you can. Some wing-nut'll dump you in these woods, they wouldn't find you till the snow melted. If you were my kid—"

"I'm not," she interrupted. She twisted his rearview mirror around to look at herself. She tugged at the skin beneath her eyes, stuck out her tongue. "Ugh. You wouldn't have any mints, would you? My mouth tastes like shit."

"Look in my briefcase in back. There should be some gum."

She reached into the back seat, opened his briefcase, took out the pack of gum. She must've noticed the Nikon and the smaller camera he used for inside shots. "You a photographer?" she asked.

"No. I use it in my work. I'm an arson investigator."

"A what?"

"An arson investigator. I investigate fires."

"Like a cop?"

"No," Hough said. "I work for an insurance company. I don't get into the criminal side of it. Not directly anyway."

"More like a company cop."

"I guess so." Hough looked down at her backpack. "So what's the deal with your buddy there?"

"Jorge."

"That his name—Jorge?"

"Yeah. It's Spanish for George. I was living with this Colombian guy named Eduardo. It was his. He took off and left him with me. Bastard stiffed me for three months' rent. I got evicted because of him."

"So where are you living now?"

"Good question. I was at the Y in Bridgeport for a couple of weeks. But they didn't like Jorge around. I guess it messed up some of the alkies."

"What about your folks? The ones in Virginia."

"My old man *really* is in Virginia. Near Roanoke. Or maybe it was Richmond. Something begins with an *r.* But we don't really hit if off. I've been on my own since I was fifteen."

"How do you support yourself?"

The girl looked over at him. "I don't do tricks, if that's what you mean."

"I didn't say that, did I?"

"But that's what you were thinking, right?"

"I wasn't thinking anything. What do you do?"

"Some waitressing. But I've had my belly full of that. I'm looking for something where I don't have to bust my tail to make minimum wage. What kind of money do you make in this arson stuff?"

Hough smiled. "I make decent money. I'm not rich, but I do OK."

"How do you get into it?"

"First you have to go to school."

"Figures."

"I was lucky. I got in right after I got out of the service. I was a DC II on a destroyer. It's like a fireman. With that I was able to get in without a college degree. But now they expect one. Then you go to arson school."

"It must be interesting."

"It's OK. It's like any other job, I guess."

"You got any smokes, Hough?"

Hough took out his cigarettes, gave her one, and then lit it with his butane lighter. He took out a cigarette for himself but didn't light up. He was trying to stop.

"I saw a rerun of *Columbo* once," the girl offered. "This rich guy was going to burn his own factory to get the dough.

But this old bum was sleeping in back and got cooked. Columbo caught the dude in the end."

"That's just in the movies. In real life it's those actuary kids sitting in front of their goddamn computers, handicapping the odds. I just do their dirty work."

The girl nodded as if she understood what he was saying. "I bet you seen some things."

"A few. Most of my cases are pretty average. Some guy who can't make the mortgage payments and is going to lose his house. Kids setting fires—I get quite a few of those. They'll get pissed at their parents and try to burn their house down. A few weeks ago I got this lady who didn't like the color of her rug so she set it on fire."

"You're kidding?"

"No, really. She bought this rug, hated the color and figured she'd buy another one with the insurance. The fire got out of hand. Mostly it's regular people who think they can burn their problems away."

"You ever catch a murderer, Hough? Like Columbo?"

"Once," he said with a self-deprecating laugh.

"Tell me about it."

Now she was all chatty and wanting to talk. Weird kid. Hough was figuring maybe she was on drugs.

"There was a fire about ten years ago. It was in all the papers. I was one of the people on the case."

"What happened?"

"It's a long story."

"I'm not going anywhere."

Hough usually didn't talk about his cases with people outside the company. It wasn't a smart thing to do. You never knew who you were talking to. But he didn't see how it could hurt in this instance. Who was she going to tell, this Rosemarie?

"This guy died in a fire at his ski lodge in upstate New York. An overturned kerosene heater. We saw a lot of them back then, in the seventies, during the energy crisis. The place was wood frame, no smoke detectors, twenty miles from the nearest hydrant. Damn thing went up like a bonfire. The guy never made it out of bed. The fire marshal spent half an hour on the case and called it accidental in his report. But I took one look at the burn patterns on the stairs and you knew an accelerant had been used."

"What's that?"

"Something to get a fired started. Like kerosene. Somebody had poured kerosene on the floor in the husband's room and down the stairs."

"I bet it was his old lady. Am I right?"

"You want to hear this or not?"

"Go ahead."

"It turned out it *was* the old lady. She had something going on on the side. With the mechanic that worked on their Mercedes. The husband finally got wind of Mr. Mechanic and was going to divorce her. They had a pre-nup and she was going to get shit. So she decided to get rid of him and collect the life insurance at the same time. It was like a half mil plus a couple of houses, stocks, a boat. She was looking to do all right for herself."

"Sounds like a movie."

"Yeah."

"How'd you catch her?"

"Wasn't too hard. The mistake every amateur makes is thinking the fire takes care of everything, leaves no trace. But that's not the way it works. Take the burn patterns."

"The what?"

"The patterns a fire makes in something. They're like fingerprints. This one you could tell somebody set because of the way the floor was charred where the kerosene touched it. The old lady had poured kerosene all over the floor and then lit a match. Pfft. There goes hubby. Then the autopsy showed he had enough sleeping pills on board to coast through an earthquake."

"Where's she now?"

"Last I heard she was up at Attica. Doing twenty-five to life. A real sweetheart."

"Want to know what I'd have done if I was you?" the girl said. "I'd've cut a deal with her. Had her split the money with me."

"You're crazy, you know that."

"Really. If you played your cards right you could've been all set, Hough. Been sitting on some beach somewhere sipping pina coladas."

"I'm a Scotch man."

"Whatever. You get my point."

"She was way out of my league. I'd have been next. That's the way she operated."

The girl shrugged, seemed to quickly lose interest in the subject. She slumped down in her seat, put her thick knees up on the dash. "We need to stop pretty soon, Hough. Mother nature's calling."

"I'll start looking."

The girl said, "That's what my mother used to always say. *Mother nature's calling.* So it didn't sound so bad. Like nice ladies didn't need to piss." The girl held the cigarette poised in front of her mouth, watching the smoke curl upward. "She was real big on being a lady. She was raised in Mississippi. One of those southern belle types. Whenever she'd go out she'd wear these like white prom gloves, you know. Even if it was just to the grocery store."

"Nothing wrong with being a lady," said Hough.

"The old man used to say she thought her b.m.'s didn't stink. Said she thought she was too good for him. I remember she used to have this Hummel collection. You know, those little figurines. Any time anybody'd come over she'd bring them into the living room for tea and bore the crap out of them for a couple of hours with her collection. That was her pride and joy. The old man couldn't stand them. They were like her, he used to say—too fancy and not worth a dime. Every time they'd get into a fight, he'd take a couple and heave 'em. She was always gluing the things back together. Well, right before the old man hit the road for good, he took a hammer to all of them. They were worth like thousands of dollars but he busted every last one on her. She cried for days,

I swear. Hardly missed the old man. Whenever I think of her I picture her kneeling on the floor picking up these little arms and legs, and crying like they were real. Pretty weird."

"She live out in Seattle?"

"She don't live nowhere now. She's dead," the girl replied, blowing smoke straight into the air.

"Sorry to hear that."

"I got over it. How about your old lady, Hough?"

"My old lady?"

"Yeah. Who's the mechanic works on her car?" she said, smiling.

"That's good," Hough replied with a laugh. "I don't have to worry about that. I'm not married. My wife and me split up a few years back."

"Why?"

"Jesus. Now who's asking all the questions?"

"Just making conversation," she said. She smiled so her cheeks slid up and nearly pressed her eyes shut.

"A lot of reasons. I guess she needed things I couldn't give her."

"Like what?" she said, glancing down at his lap.

"Not *that*. For one thing, I was on the road a lot, and she needed somebody around more."

"Any kids?"

Hough looked out the window. He saw a buck frozen in the snow, its legs sticking straight out. Half its rack was broken off.

"One," he replied.

"Your wife get custody? My old lady got me."

"No. Our daughter died when she was two."

"That sucks."

"Yeah. It was a long time ago though. I don't think about it much anymore. By the way, I'm getting kind of hungry. How about you?"

"Sure."

Hough turned off at the next exit. At the bottom of the ramp he followed the signs for a restaurant. The place turned out to be a log cabin with a giant fiberglass bear guarding the entrance. One of the bear's paws was broken off, and white fiberglass splinters dangled from the stump like spaghetti. As they got out of the car the girl had her backpack in her hand. Hough had almost forgotten about the snake.

"You're not going to bring that in."

"He'll be cold out here. I'll keep him zipped up. Don't worry. I do it all the time."

"Well, just make sure it stays put. I don't want any trouble."

Inside, various animal heads—deer and bison and moose—looked wearily down from the walls, their smoky eyes glazed with far-off visions. Several customers, in orange hats and plaid hunting jackets, stared suspiciously at them as they came in.

"Welcome to the Klan," the girl said, well above a whisper.

"Just be quiet," Hough warned.

She told him, "You go get us a table while I hit the head."

A woman who seemed much too old to be a waitress led Hough to a table that had syrupy stuff all over the surface. When the woman put the menus down they stuck to the surface. She told him she'd be back over when his daughter was ready to order.

When the girl came back she dropped a pack of Salems, the brand Hough smoked, in front of him.

"A present," she said.

"You didn't have to."

"I know. Geez, don't they even wash these tables?" she said, rubbing her hand over the surface. "Gross."

The old woman came over again and took their order. Hough ordered an open-face turkey sandwich while the girl got two cheeseburgers, fries, a side of slaw and potato salad, and a strawberry milkshake. The woman had difficulty writing it all down and had to have them repeat everything.

"Where'd they dig her up?" the girl said as the woman shuffled off on spindly brown-stockinged legs to the kitchen.

When the food came, the way she wolfed it all down Hough guessed she hadn't eaten in a while. She was done before he was halfway finished. She noticed him staring at her.

"When I was six I weighed eighty pounds," she said. "My mother always thought it didn't look feminine. She used to cart me to this doctor for fat kids. I had a screwed-up pituitary gland. That's the thing says how big you're gonna be. Mine was supposed to straighten out. I'm still waiting," she said, stuffing a french fry into her mouth.

"You look all right," he said.

"I know what I look like, Hough. It seems to bug everybody else though."

After a while she said, "I got to make a call. When Granny comes back get me a piece of pecan pie and some vanilla ice cream. If they don't have pecan I'll take Boston cream, OK. No apple. I hate apple."

Hough figured he'd have to pick up the tab but he didn't mind. He could put it on his expense account. Besides, he was starting to warm up to this weird kid he'd picked up.

She was gone for a long time. After she got back he had a cup of coffee while she worked on her dessert. When the bill came he tried to pick it up, but she grabbed it first.

"Relax, Hough. I always pay my way. It's easier that way. No *quid pro quo,* you see."

Hough held his breath as she unzipped the backpack and put her hand in. When she pulled it out she had several rolls of quarters. She plunked two rolls down on the table and cracked open another and left a pile of quarters for a tip.

"The old broad can use it," the girl said. "Get herself a hearing aid."

"You rob a bank or something?" Hough kidded.

"No. A hardware store," she said, grinning. On the way out she stopped and fed quarters into the candy machine, loading her pockets with M&M's, Milky Ways, and bags of peanuts.

They drove. It had gotten completely dark out and beneath the headlights the road glistened in spots with ice. Now and then the car would hit a patch and Hough could feel himself losing control, like in a falling dream. He was tired now and didn't look forward to several more hours behind the wheel. He decided not to push it. He'd stay over in Harrisburg and then go on to the fireground in the morning. He looked forward to a couple of Scotches, then a warm bath and dreamless sleep.

"Mind if I ask you something, Hough?" the fat girl said. She had a bag of peanuts up to her mouth and was shaking it like a salt shaker into her maw.

"What?"

"How'd your kid die?" He glanced over at her. "Just curious."

"She drowned. We used to have this little pond out in back of our house. You could hear the frogs at night in the summer. Cassy—that was her name—used to like to throw rocks in it. It wasn't more than a couple feet deep. But she was just a little kid. She wandered away from the house and fell in. End of story."

"Wasn't anybody watching her?"

"My wife was home. She went in to get the phone. She wasn't there more than a couple of minutes. When she came out she found our daughter floating face-down."

Hough could still picture the pond in his mind, the wild lilies growing along its bank, a child in a pink outfit with rose patterns, floating within arm's reach. He could have lifted her out without even getting his feet wet, she was that close to the world of the living. At least that's the way scene came to him in dreams. He'd been on the road when it'd happened, and of course had no way to know for sure. That was what he'd pieced together.

"That's terrible, Hough. Must've been hard on your wife."

"It was," Hough replied. "I don't think she ever got over it. I kept telling her it wasn't her fault. That it was just an accident. It didn't do any good. I heard somewhere like fifty percent of couples break up after the death of a child. That's what happened to us."

Hough could feel his eyes begin to swell. It was stupid, to do that all these years later, in front of this girl. He bit into the soft skin on the inside of his mouth until he tasted blood. The pain he felt was exquisite, a bright flickering light in the center of his brain. He seldom talked about this, and then it was only to strangers, never, of course, to people he knew. He tried not to think of Maureen now, her having another child, getting a second chance. It was too much. It was just too much.

"It must be hard to lose a kid."

"What can you do?" Hough said. "Things happen. I try not to dwell on it."

"I can understand that."

Hough looked over at the girl and she held his stare for a couple of seconds.

In Harrisburg, Hough got off an exit near the river. He pulled into a gas station-convenience store and stopped.

"What are your plans?" he asked the girl.

"I don't know."

"How about if we found you an emergency shelter."

"No way."

"Just till morning. They might be able to help you out. Get you hooked up with social services."

He thought about asking if she wanted to stay with him, in the room, have a warm shower and a good night's sleep. No obligations. No *quid pro quo.*

"I don't need any help, Hough. Honest. I can take care of myself. I'll just get out right here."

"Least let me give you a ride to a bus station. Look, here's a twenty," he said, handing her some money. "You can buy a ticket someplace. To Virginia or wherever."

"I don't need it."

"Take it, for crissakes. It's cold out. And it would make me feel better."

The girl finally accepted the money.

"I'll go inside and see if I can find out where the bus station is," Hough said. "All right?" The girl nodded.

He got out of the car and went inside. The guy behind the counter, a young black kid, didn't know where the bus station was but he got out a city map and spread it on the counter. As the kid was going over the map, Hough suddenly had a terrible thought. He'd left his keys in the car. My God, he thought.

He ran out of the store, half expecting to see it gone. Yet it wasn't the car but the girl who was gone. He hurried over to see if she'd touched his camera or other things, but everything was where he'd left it. He looked around yet the girl was already out of sight. Although he couldn't say why, he felt both relief and a sinking feeling in his stomach.

That night Hough stayed at a Holiday Inn just across the river. He splurged and got a suite. Instead of going out, he bought a pint of Scotch at a liquor store down the street and some Chinese food and brought it up to his room. After he ate he took a long, hot bath and lay in the tub and sipped his drink, staring at the ceiling. He lay there until the hot water and the booze loosened the muscles in his neck. He lay there until he began thinking about Maureen. What he'd told the girl was a lie, he knew. Not exactly a lie, but certainly not the truth. He *had* blamed Maureen for Cassy's death. Of course, he'd never said that, not openly. But there were all those things he hadn't said, the times he could've done something to help her and hadn't. They both knew. *Secretly they both knew he blamed her.* It was true. That was what had eaten away at both of them: not the booze or his being away, not even the lover she ran off with. Those things came later. What came first was the fact that he'd blamed her for the death of their child.

Although he didn't expect sleep to come that night, he was exhausted and dropped quickly off into a place of dark, musty silence, like a cellar. He woke, however, a little after three. He made that out by the glowing hands of his wristwatch. He sat up in bed in the dark room. For a moment he didn't know where he was. He started by eliminating where he wasn't: his apartment, his old house, the bedroom of a woman he'd slept with a few times over the past few years. Slowly he was able to get a foothold. He could make out the edges of the drapes covering the window, the noisy heater that coughed out that distinctive motel warmth, purchased and homeless. He'd had a bad dream, that he knew. Yet he couldn't really recall what it'd been about. Only that it left him feeling cold, vulnerable, empty. He knew it wasn't about his daughter. Those dreams were always remarkably vivid, sometimes even days later. He then realized this dream had something to do with the girl, the hitchhiker.

He turned on the light and got out of bed. He pulled on his trousers and then his shoes without bothering with socks, and finally his jacket. He got his car keys and his cigarette lighter, and he left his room and walked down the corridor to the stairs and out into the parking lot. The night was cold and smelled of diesel fuel and river water. Hough's feet and hands already ached with the chill. He hurried over to his car and, cupping his hands over the window, peered into the darkness within. He couldn't see anything. He unlocked the door and cautiously opened it. Still he saw nothing. There remained the lingering musky odor of the girl. He kneeled on the cold ground, feeling the grit of the parking lot embedding itself in his knees. He flicked on his lighter. He looked under his seat and saw only an ice scraper and a crumpled cigarette pack. Then, squeezing past the shifter, he leaned over and looked under the passenger seat. His heart curled into a ball when he spotted it. There, tightly coiled, its black liquid eyes throwing back the lighter's flame in brilliant, dancing patterns, the thing lay exactly as Hough had seen it in his dream.

# Crossing

As they waited for the last car to drive up into the ferry's huge maw, Margaret found herself taking quick, shallow gulps of air.

"Now don't get hyper on me, Ma?" Kate said a little too loudly and with that patronizing tone Margaret found so irritating in her daughter. She caught an old woman standing nearby glancing at them. The woman was old enough to be Margaret's own mother, yet she waited nonchalantly to board. She wore a beret pulled jauntily over one eye, a stylish black wool cape, and lipstick the color of fresh liver. And she was smoking one of those slender brown cigarettes, the sort Margaret associated with the word *feminist.* For some reason the old woman made her think of Amelia Earhart: not the daring young woman that flew off into the blue yonder but the Amelia who might've returned, grown old, lived to suffer wrinkles and see others leave her.

"You don't have to shout, for heaven's sakes," she said to her daughter, pressing her hearing aid deeper into her ear. "I'm not deaf *yet."* On the ride down it was, "Ma, did you bring your pills?" "Ma, you did shut off the coffee pot, didn't you?" and "Stop *worrying,* Ma. You'll do just fine," as if she were a timid girl needing reassurance before her first prom. Her older daughter was always ready with advice that made Margaret feel stupid and inept.

Yet who was she kidding? She was scared—scared silly. She could hardly breathe for fear, the air around her suddenly becoming as thin as ether. The crossing dominated huge stretches of her thoughts. It seemed filled with, if not actual danger, then certain vague unpleasantries she'd rather have avoided. A stiff wind full of gritty ice particles carved the water out in Long Island Sound into fearsome-looking whitecaps, and closer to shore the greasy smell of diesel made her think of turkey guts. Overhead, seagulls, dangling in mid-air like mobiles, stared down at her with evil gray eyes. Like in *The Birds,* she thought. She pictured one swooping down and pecking at her noggin. No, she wasn't at all certain about this trip. But it was too late to turn back. If she balked at going, she could just picture the long ride back, her daughter's syrupy condescension: "Ma, it's no big deal. Really. Bea'll understand."

"Do you have your ticket?" her daughter asked.

"Yes. "

"And how about batteries for your hearing aid?" Kate asked. This time though she discreetly leaned close to her mother. "You know how p.o.'ed Bea gets when you can't hear them."

"Isn't that just too bad," Margaret snapped, asserting herself.

As if she hadn't heard her, Kate continued, "And when you get on, remember to grab a seat before they're all taken. With the holiday it'll be a madhouse."

"You might think I'm going to Timbuktu, for Pete's sake. Bea's is just . . . over there a ways."

She motioned with her head out toward Long Island, toward where her younger daughter, Bea, lived and was at that moment waiting to pick her up. As if they were playing catch with her: one daughter tossing her, the other waiting to catch her, and in between the dark, cold sea. But over there could've been the other side of the world for all she knew. A flat, suddenly unpredictable world filled with unseen terrors, sea serpents lurking in the dark, cold waters. A person could fall right off the edge if she wasn't careful.

Taking the ferry over for Thanksgiving had been Bea's bright idea. It'd be easier, her daughter had reasoned, than driving the hundred miles around the Sound, fighting the holiday traffic on the Throg's Neck. The ferry would be an experience, she'd called it. She'd been wanting Margaret to come down to visit for a while. To get her mind off *things.* The girls used that word a lot. There were all sorts of things she had to confront. Things Margaret was supposed to do. Or avoid doing. Things she had to put behind her. Or things she had to face up to. Things she had to change and things that she had to ensure remained the same. As if by slight manipulations they could control her thoughts, her moods. To get her mind off things, Bea had made all the necessary arrangements for the trip, including sending her a ferry ticket and having Kate drive her down to the dock. She imagined them on the phone, conspiring, plotting. "If we don't get her out she'll sit in that house and rot. You know Ma," she pictured Bea, the more blunt of the two, saying. They'd plotted it all out like Haley Mills in *The Parent Trap,* that movie she and Don had taken them to see when they were kids. So they'd seen to everything. Except for the crossing part. That she had to do alone.

"It's only an hour over," Bea had said on the phone.

"Yeah, only an hour. Your father couldn't even get me in a rowboat."

"This isn't a rowboat, Ma. It's a big ship. You won't even know you're on the water it's so big. It'll be fun."

Margaret hadn't been so sure, and now as she was about to board she was even less so. This was *not* going to be fun, that's for sure. An oath slipped from her as she dutifully kissed Kate on the cheek: *Why'd you go and do this to me, Don?*

She wasn't sure if she'd actually said it out loud, but Kate, maybe reading her thoughts, replied, "Dad would've wanted you to do things."

There was that *things* again!

"Don't worry about me," she joked. "I'm doing things. Sinbad the Sailor."

Kate gave her a gentle shove and she was moving with the other passengers, up into the cool cavity of the ferry, like stuffing into a huge steel-ribbed bird.

"Bye, Ma. Have a good time," Kate cried. "Give my love to Bea and Mike."

Margaret turned halfway up the stairs leading to the main cabin. Kate stood below waving broadly, the way they did in old movies and on *Love Boat* reruns. There was always that touch of the theatrical to Kate, lovely and sweet and melodramatic Kate. *Wait till it happens to you,* thought

Margaret, and as soon as she did she regretted it. She felt terrible, wishing such a thing on a daughter. Standing below, Kate looked suddenly vulnerable to Margaret, the way she had as a child standing out on a rainy day waiting for the bus. It seemed as if a sudden gust could've swept her off the dock and into the cold Sound, and put Margaret, who'd always felt threatened by water, to some maternal test—like those daydreams she'd had when the kids were little *(What if a man broke in and went for the children? What if a mad dog charged at the three of you, would you throw your body? What if . . . )*

"Love you," Margaret called back with such finality it made her acutely aware of an unfamiliar spot along her throat. It was as if she were using a portion of her vocal cords for the very first time, uttering a totally new sound never heard by human ear. "Bye," she said, feeling tears well up behind her eyes.

Before she disappeared completely into the ferry, she heard Kate call, "I'll be here Sunday, Ma. Check where they keep the life jackets."

Now why on earth would she say a silly thing like that, Margaret wondered.

In front of her, a little boy wearing a green boarding school blazer and a white shirt as stiff as gristle turned and said, "You won't need a life jacket."

"Probably not," Margaret agreed, smiling.

"The water temp's about 34 degrees. You wouldn't last five minutes. Then you're into hypothermia. The heart stops."

"My, aren't you full of facts."

"I take this over every Friday," he said, as if that conferred on him an intimate understanding of one's chances for survival.

Margaret went up into the main cabin and, remembering Kate's warning, quickly found a seat. She then glanced around for signs indicating where the life jackets were stored. The room was filled with tables bolted to the floor and red molded chairs, and on the far side there was a concession where people were already lining up. The place smelled heavily of french fries. She looked out a thick, scratched, Plexiglas window for Kate but her daughter must've already headed for her car. No sense waiting out in this weather.

Margaret closed her eyes. She tried not to think about what the boy had told her, how cold the water was. She tried to picture something calm. She'd recently read somewhere that was a good thing to do to keep her anxieties at bay. A meadow filled with Queen Anne's lace, the sort she and Don had had a picnic in once. But the more she thought of it the more she realized they'd never had a picnic in such a place; there had been a picnic in some field, yes, but the Queen Anne's lace was something she'd tacked on (she found herself doing that a lot lately—trying to make her memories more complete, more satisfying, more *real)*. So she thought of the way she used to feel when she received communion—this complete stillness surrounding her heart. Yet even that image gave way to another—she saw the greedy, menacing eyes of the seagulls swooping down at her, going *cahw, cahw.* Ugly, vile birds.

She opened her own eyes as the ferry heaved slowly forward, resolute as an army marching into some holy battle. They were on their way. Margaret instinctively curled her toes into the soles of her shoes, the way she did in elevators, when walking on ice, or falling in a dream. Trying to maintain her balance.

She decided she wouldn't talk to anyone. Though the room was crowded, her seat was separated by a discreet distance from her closest neighbor, a distance which said she wished to be left alone, thank you very much. If that wasn't enough she got out a book from her overnight bag, the only reading material she'd remembered to bring along. It had the morbid title *Surviving the Death of a Spouse.* Bea had sent it to her with a note: "It's up to you." What was up to her she wasn't sure. A grinning, bald psychologist with the neck of a linebacker had written it. He raised peacocks, the dust jacket said. What sort of person raised peacocks? she wondered. They were really dirty animals. Worse than seagulls. Did he just let them strut around his yard, shitting on the grass and sleeping in the trees at night? And what made him such an authority about survival anyway?

She'd only glanced at the book but had brought it along to show Bea she was taking the preachy stuff the peacock man said to heart. The it-was-up-to-you attitude that her daughter would take as progress. She propped the dopey book in front of her, looked at her watch, and hoped the trip would be swift and uneventful. The first sentence her eyes fell on said: "It's important to maintain patterns of behavior during this time of adjustment. If you're used to eating breakfast at seven, continue to do so." She hadn't eaten breakfast that morning. In fact, she hardly ever ate breakfast anymore. Or lunch either. For supper she'd go up to the mall and eat half a sandwich at Friendly's, down five cups of bottomless coffee, and watch the people walk by in pairs. The mall was made for couples. Lately the food in her mouth tasted like batting she'd stuff into a pillow, to fill it out. Her insides felt like that, dry and coarse, and the skin hung over her bones like an ill-fitting slipcover.

She tried to think of something clever for Bea when she arrived on the other side. Clever and light-hearted. Don had always had clever things to say to the girls. Jokes. Amusing anecdotes about people he worked with. There was a guy named Cosgrove who was always part of the story. But she could never think of them. To Bea, humor meant healthy. It meant alive. And her daughter would, of course, expect some sign that her mother's period of mourning was officially over, that she was now committed to getting on with those things. Kate's method was to patronize; Bea, on the other hand, was like a drill sergeant. She *insisted* on recovery. Demanded it, in fact. *Taking an interest in one's appearance*—Bea had underlined that phrase in Mr. Peacock's survival book. So Margaret had gone out and bought a new pantsuit especially for the visit, a thing as pink and ugly as a diaper rash, so ugly that she'd have no inclination to wear it ever again. She spent most days in her bathrobe. What did it matter? No one saw her except her cat, and she could have gone around stark naked and Rex wouldn't have batted an eye. Cats didn't care about the world; they didn't need it.

She checked her pocketbook again. She'd checked it several times before she left and again on the ride down, but she wanted to make sure she had everything. The ticket was there. Her wallet. The Dramamine. The extra batteries for her hearing aid (she wanted to appear attentive at the dinner table that day, an involved participant). Her keys? Now where were her keys? For a moment she panicked. She'd left them in the front door! Yes, she was sure of it. She pictured her paperboy, a hoody-looking kid named Papagello, opening the door, searching the place for money. She saw him going though Don's drawers, touching his sweaters, the things she hadn't the heart to bring to Goodwill yet. She felt the blood rushing to her cheeks. She would call Kate as soon as she got to Bea's. She'd have her—But then she remembered: she'd already given them to Kate. To water her plants, feed Rex. You idiot, she scolded herself. Her daughters *did* need to arrange everything for her, just as Don had for all those years.

Since his death, almost four months ago now, she found herself at odd moments cursing him for leaving her so ill-prepared, for having concealed from her, however inadvertently or well-intentioned, all those trivial functions upon which existence itself seemed so much to depend: who to call when the burner went out suddenly one night or which lever to pull to get the stubborn lawn mower to obey her as it had him. Even such a simple thing as ordering at a restaurant proved traumatic. Recently she'd gone out with another widow, Jeananne, an old friend of theirs, and when it came time to order she found herself looking to her friend. "What are you going to eat?" Jeananne had asked. Don had always taken care of ordering for both of them, for knowing how much to leave for a tip, what wine to choose, for joking with the waitress. He'd also seen to it that at gatherings she had someone to talk to, that she didn't stand out as the awkward, clumsy introvert she really was. Left to her own devices, she was just as likely to wander off in a corner and read a magazine or talk to the host's dog. Except Don wouldn't let her. But now there was no one to pull her out of her taciturn ways.

Once, a few weeks after Don's death, she was driving home from the dentist's when she got lost—literally, completely, terrifyingly lost. Her mouth hurt from the novocaine and her mind was on other things, she wasn't watching where she was going and suddenly she found herself in a neighborhood she didn't recognize. She tried to stay calm. She drove around for a while hoping she'd see something familiar but the more she drove the more lost she became. Finally she had to pull over to the side of the road. "Where the hell are you?" she cried. Her heart thumped loudly in her chest and she felt she couldn't breathe. She found herself cursing Don for getting cancer, for dying and leaving her alone in such a terrifying, unfamiliar world, one that hadn't seemed so terrifying or unfamiliar when he was in it. She'd closed her eyes and pictured that meadow they'd had the picnic in. After a few minutes she'd been able to calm down enough to make it to a gas station where she asked for directions. But from then on she was more cautious whenever she ventured out of the house, which was not too often.

Now on the boat, she had that same feeling. She slumped down in her seat, pulled her coat tightly around her. Outside, the clouds looked like the various overlapping grays in a chest x-ray. Looking back over the ship's wake, she could no longer see the coast. It was gone, erased by clouds and mist and water. And ahead there was only more water. Cold, endless water. Water whose potential for cruelty almost made her light-headed. She could feel it as a hammer driving her ankles mercilessly into her unsteady shins. She recalled Bea's "You won't even know you're on the water, Ma." Oh, yeah! What was she doing here? Why wasn't she home in her bathrobe, watching TV from the couch, with Rex sleeping on her chest? Cats understood. They made loneliness into high art. She thought of what the little boy had said. Five minutes is all it'd take. The heart would stop, he'd said with authority, as if he knew about things like hearts stopping.

She looked around the cabin. Across the way a man was sprawled over two seats, sleeping. He wore an old bulky sweater and a sports coat shiny in spots from wear. A bum, Margaret decided. He slept deeply, his mouth wide open, as if he were giving a testimonial for the comfort of some mattress. The old woman, the one with the beret, was sitting a few seats down from him. She was talking to an Asian man in a blue ski parka. Now and then she'd nod and toss her head back to blow smoke into the air. Nearby, some kids were trying to walk a straight line down the aisle. They pretended they were drunk, rolling their eyes, crashing into each other as the ship heaved one way and then the other.

Margaret spotted the little boy with the green blazer. He was by himself, near a window. His heavy oxfords barely reached the floor. He was reading, too. But unlike Margaret he was absorbed in what he was reading, not just using it as a shield. He didn't even look up when the ship seemed to tremble with a kind of palsy. She wondered what sort of parents would allow a child out here, alone. She'd never have allowed Kate or Bea out here by themselves.

After a while Margaret felt her stomach turn, she burped, then tasted the sour taste of bile in her mouth. Could she be hungry? Maybe the talk in the book about eating, the greasy smell of hot dogs and french fries had coaxed her appetite into making an unwanted cameo appearance. She hadn't had anything except for a cup of coffee, and here it was almost two o'clock. Maybe, to settle her stomach, she'd better get something. And then she wouldn't be starved by the time she got to Bea's.

She stood up, thought about leaving her bag as a sign of ownership, but decided against it. She headed toward the concession. She found the going much tougher though than she'd imagined. Somehow she'd assumed the other people walking in that comical weave surely must've been exaggerating the difficulty. But negotiating the room was really quite tricky. For balance she had to keep her legs spread apart and her rear end stuck out slightly, and then, as the ship paused between poundings, take quick, flat-footed steps—like learning some new kind of dance. When the ship listed sharply, she had to grab hold of one of the supports that ran from floor to ceiling. She clung to it, wondering if this were such a good idea after all. She wasn't *that* hungry. Holding onto the pole, for a moment she even considered turning back. But then she decided to continue on toward the lunch counter. She leapfrogged from the safety of one pole to the next, until she finally arrived at the food concession.

Everything looked uniformly unappetizing—rubbery hot dogs sunning themselves under a solar lamp, salads that wilted behind steamy glass doors, anemic sandwiches in clear plastic coffins. So she settled for a coffee and a package of peanut butter crackers. When she went to pay she had to juggle her pocketbook and bag, and try to keep her balance at the same time. She fumbled with her purse. There was a line of people behind her. Finally she managed to extract a ten-dollar bill and pay the cashier, a young, puffy-lipped girl who had a thick romance novel beside the register. The heroine on the cover had her eyes half-closed in moronic ecstasy as a bare-chested man kissed her neck. Margaret was staring at the book and had almost stuffed her change back in her wallet when she realized the girl had given her change for a five.

"Excuse me," Margaret said, holding out her change, hoping the girl would realize her mistake and voluntarily hand over the rest.

"Yeah?"

"I gave you a ten."

"A ten?" repeated the girl, crinkling her nose as if Margaret's statement carried with it a foul odor.

"Yes, I gave you a ten."

"You sure? I could've swore you gave me a five."

A moment ago she was sure. But now, her word challenged, a line of impatient people behind her, her own stomach grumbling, her confidence began to ebb. The girl stared hard at her. Her eyes looked lifeless, like the dark stuff inside a steak bone. Margaret searched her pocketbook, counting her money. She looked in the hidden compartment behind the credit cards where she squirreled away her larger bills. She tried to recall how much she'd taken out of the bank for the trip, but she could no longer be sure. So much was going on. Her ears throbbed. And the hard thing in her stomach she now felt wasn't hunger at all. She might've been seasick, she wasn't sure. She wasn't sure of anything. She turned to the man behind her in line, hoping he might have seen her hand the girl a ten—a witness. But he glanced at his watch and returned a look of mild impatience. She certainly couldn't count on him.

"I thought I gave you a ten," she said to the girl. Margaret had her credit cards and lipstick, her pills and hearing aid batteries spread out over the counter like a child with a fistful of coins. "I was sure of it."

Finally though, the girl conceded. "Well, all right then."

She summarily dismissed Margaret with a crumpled five-dollar bill and stared past her to the man next in line. The girl looked dreamily at the man, as if she half expected him to peel off his shirt and kiss her on the neck, take her away from all these tedious old fools who couldn't keep track of their money. When Margaret was only a few feet away she thought she heard the girl whisper something to him and they both giggled. Margaret didn't turn around.

She started to make her way back to her seat but saw it was now occupied by a college-age kid with a backpack. Scanning the room she found that, in fact, most of the seats were taken, as if the ship had somehow picked up more passengers in the middle of the ocean. She shouldn't have left, should've stayed put. In fact, she should've stayed home, shouldn't have listened to her daughters in the first place—let them bully her into coming out here, where she had to fight just to keep her balance?

At last, she spotted a seat over near where a sign said LIFE JACKETS and made straight for it. She'd taken only a few steps when the ship lunged suddenly one way and then the other. Margaret felt the hot coffee streaming onto her hand.

"Oh, God," she cried as the pain brought fully formed tears to her eyes. Then she dropped the cup completely. It exploded on the floor, splashing over her pant legs and sending a spray of coffee everywhere. The room became very still. It seemed as if everyone were staring at her. She didn't know what to do next. She felt like sobbing, like running and hiding somewhere. But just then a hand was at her elbow, steadying her, leading her toward a nearby seat.

"Here we go," a man said, pulling a seat out for her. He was short and more than solidly built, with a large raw-looking nose. Margaret thought she smelled booze on his breath.

"Thank you. It's just that I . . . " but she didn't know what to say.

"It's a rough one today," he said, his voice scratchy. "Do you come over often?"

"No," she said, then confessed, "this is my first time actually."

"Oh, well. Don't let today stop you. It's not always this rough. It can be a very pleasant ride actually. Especially at sunset. Here," he said, offering her a handkerchief.

"Thank you," she said again. "I'm such a clutz."

"It's not easy walking when it's this choppy out. They should warn people about that. Have you burnt your hand bad?"

"No, I don't think so."

"Can I get you another cup of coffee?"

"No, thank you. I didn't really want this one."

"Do you always buy things you don't want?" he asked, but not critically, not the way Bea would have.

She thought of the pantsuit and said, "I changed my mind."

Her ears still throbbed, and her stomach continued to turn on her. She got out the Dramamine from her purse, pushed a tablet through the foil back, and was about to swallow it dry when the man said, "Wait."

He got up and headed across the room, moving his thick body cleverly over the hurdles the ship threw in front of him. He returned shortly with a paper cone filled with water. "You'll get an ulcer taking pills without water. I guess I know my way around ulcers," he said putting a thumb to his swelling paunch.

"Thanks." She placed the pill in her mouth, then washed it down with the water.

"For what it's worth, I'm Dennis," he said, offering her a hand that was hot and moist and smooth as a baby's. For some strange reason it made her think of a warm internal organ, not a hand. Though Margaret didn't like the prospect of having to carry on a conversation with a complete stranger, she couldn't be rude, not after he'd helped her. "Nice to meet you, Dennis," she said. "I'm Margaret. Margaret the Clutz."

"Well, hello, Margaret the Clutz. I'm what you'd call a regular on this trip."

"Yes. Everybody seems to be a regular but me."

"Nonsense. It's just a matter of time. Till you get your sea legs under you."

"I doubt I'll get anything but these," she said, looking down at her pants legs, which had big splotches of dark coffee on them. Though she hated the outfit, out of habit she thought that as soon as she got to Bea's she'd better take them off and soak them. Put some seltzer water on the stains.

"Oh, you'd be surprised," Dennis went on. "A few times over and you'll be an old hand at it. It's like riding a bicycle."

He smiled at her. Margaret realized then he hadn't let go of her hand. It was as if he were trying to warm her own cool hand, or at least trying to get rid of some of the heat in his own.

"This was my daughter's idea," Margaret explained, withdrawing her hand. "She likes me to *experience* things."

"Nothing wrong with that. You got to be ready for whatever comes down the pike."

"I guess that's one way of looking at it," Margaret said, though she wasn't sure what he meant. "You visiting for the holidays?"

"I have a business over on the Island. I import rugs."

"My, that sounds interesting."

"Not so interesting really. But it's what I do."

"Like oriental rugs?" she asked.

"No, mostly from Eastern Europe. Poland, Yugoslavia. Finland, too. Nobody knows it but the Finns make a damn good rug."

"Is that so?"

"Absolutely. And because they don't have the name you can get them for a song."

"I didn't know that." Margaret had to admit she didn't know much about rugs period. She said, "Rugs can certainly make a room."

"A house, too. You invest in a good rug it'll last you a lifetime. That's if you take care of it. You know what most people do?"

"No," Margaret said. "What?"

"Most people want to vacuum the hell out of them. It ruins the nap. The trick is to beat 'em with a broom." He reached into his shirt pocket and pulled out a business card. He handed it to Margaret. The card had a picture of a small naked girl lying on a rug. Above it was written, "Henley's Imported Rugs."

"That's me. Not the girl. I'm Henley. She's my daughter," he said. "We didn't have one of those pictures so this photographer superimposed her baby picture on one of my rugs. She gets ticked when I use it as a business card."

"I can see why." Margaret didn't know what to say so she said, "I'm going to visit my daughter and her husband. They live over on the Island."

"Yeah? That's nice. Families should be together for the holidays. Do you have other children?"

"Another daughter. She dropped me off. One's dropping me and the other's picking me up. I feel like a football."

"I got just the one," he said, pointing at his card which Margaret still held. "But she's all grown. A lawyer with some hotsy-totsy firm down in Philly. Listen, I'm going to get a coffee. Sure I can't interest you in one?"

"Well . . . if it's no problem."

"No problem. How do you take it?"

"Black's fine," she said.

As Dennis went over to the lunch counter, Margaret wondered why she asked for black. Normally she took her coffee light with a sweetener. Don had always taken his coffee black. Lately she'd begun to notice she had started to pick up some of her dead husband's habits. Sleeping on his side of the bed, on her stomach. Leaving her clothes wherever she took them off. Even using some of his expressions, like the *whole kit and caboodle,* something she'd never used before. Jeananne called the other day to say she had some tools of Don's to return, and Margaret had said, "You can keep the whole kit and caboodle." It was as if by acting like him she didn't quite have to let him go. In a minute Dennis came back with two coffees.

"Here we go," he said. "How's your stomach?"

"Better, I think. I used to get carsick. Every time we'd go on a long car ride I'd get this queasy feeling in my stomach."

"To tell you the truth I feel more comfortable on this than I do in a car. Least here you can get up and stretch your legs."

"That's true."

"So, what do you do, Margaret the Clutz?"

"Do?" she repeated. It was odd that several people, strangers, had asked her that lately. Or maybe they'd always asked and she was just now feeling odd about it. Before she wouldn't hesitate to simply answer that she was a housewife. She didn't have to *do* anything. Now that didn't seem quite enough.

"Well, I don't have a job or anything, if that's what you mean. But I keep busy."

"That's the name of the game. If you slow down you're done for. Like with sharks."

"Sharks?"

"Yeah. They got to keep moving or they suffocate. Something about their gills."

"How do they sleep?"

"Got me. Sometimes I wish I wasn't so busy."

He talked for a while about his business. How he had to go on buying trips to Europe, China, the Middle East. He told Margaret how he'd thought of selling his business and retiring, but he didn't know what he'd do with himself.

"I'm not the Florida type. Not a big golfer or anything. Christ, I'd melt down there. They'd have to peel me off the sidewalk like a piece of gum."

He laughed as he said that. Margaret sipped her coffee, nodded, smiled occasionally. The pain in her stomach was ebbing and she was beginning to feel herself relax, to actually enjoy talking to this Dennis. Then he asked, "And your husband?"

"My husband?" she repeated, the word catching in her throat, the same odd, tender place that she'd become aware of earlier.

She followed his eyes down to her ring. For a moment she stared at it, too. The smoothly worn gold seemed unfamiliar to her, like a toy from childhood, something from another life. It was suddenly a mystery to her. She and Don had had all those years together, two children, a *life*—and now it was reduced to a ring and a few memories that she had to spruce up to make them seem more meaningful. She was about to say something when Dennis asked, "How long's it been?"

She didn't know how he knew but there was no mistaking that he did.

"Four months. It was four a week ago Saturday."

"Oh, you're still new at it, I see. I'm sorry."

"Thank you," she said, feeling, as she always did, stupid for accepting sympathy.

"Me, it's been two years. I'm an old pro. The first couple months are the roughest, believe me."

"Were they? I mean, for you?

"Me? No. I kept pretty busy. Traveled a lot. Went over to Europe on a buying trip. I muddled through. That's my MO. I'm a good muddle-through kind of guy. People would ask me how I was doing and I'd say I was doing just fine. At least I thought so. The worst part for me came later, when I slowed down. Like I was saying about the sharks. Then I felt it—*wham*. Like somebody hit me with a right hook. I said screw it. Started hitting the sauce like there was no tomorrow. I did things to my insides you wouldn't do to a garbage disposal." He leaned way back and laughed, so she could see the plate for his dentures on the roof of his mouth. "You want to know what hit me the hardest, Margaret?"

"What?"

"This is funny. Least I think it is," he said, leaning toward her confidentially. "I found a pair of Bertie's—that was her name, Roberta—a pair of her panties in the dryer. Who knows how long they were there. Months maybe. I never did the goddamn wash. I picked them up. They were just a pair of her undies. Nothing fancy or sexy or anything like that. Here I thought I was beyond all that. The grieving. That I'd gotten over it, you know. But Christ when I picked up those panties, I felt I was going to die. I mean, *die.* Can you imagine?"

He stared vacantly out at the water for several seconds. His eyes got shiny and his stare far-off and inward. Margaret noticed for the first time that one of his eyelids had no lashes—none at all. In their place was a smooth pink line. She wondered if he'd been born like that or if it were some sort of accident.

"Goddamned panties—pardon my French. That's a good one, huh?" Margaret leaned toward him and put her hand on his. It was hot. She felt she had to offer him something in return.

"You know what gets me?"

"What's that?"

"When I smell something that reminds me of him."

"Oh, you're right. You're exactly right. Smells can be bad. Smells can be downright terrible."

"A wood smell makes me want to jump right out of my skin. I don't know why wood. Don wasn't a carpenter or anything. It's just one of those things that you can't explain. But I tell you, if I smell like pine or something. *Whew.* Forget it."

"Wood, huh?"

"Yeah."

"That's funny."

"Any kind of wood. It doesn't matter."

"How about oak?"

"Yes, oak is bad."

"Hickory?"

"That too, I suppose."

He smiled playfully at her. The one eye without lashes made her think of something not completely finished, say, the eyes of a fetus—naked and pink and completely without guile. "I got one for you," Dennis said. "How about baobab?"

*"Baobab?"* she repeated. "What on earth's a baobab?"

"It's a tree they got over in Africa."

She hesitated for a moment, then realized he was pulling her leg. "Oh, I don't know about that. I draw the line there," she said, going along with the bit.

They both smiled. She couldn't believe she was joking with a complete stranger, telling him things she didn't even share with her daughters. But her daughters were always trying to tell her how to handle her pain, how to get rid of it, how to go on without it. And the thing was, she didn't really *want* to get rid of the pain, at least not yet. There would come a time perhaps, but not yet. Sometimes it seemed the only thing that was real and solid and with her from day to day, her only companion and friend, the only thing that gave her life any meaning right now, was pain. Her daughters wanted to take that away but with this man it was different. He understood the importance of it.

"Tell me something," Margaret asked. "How'd you know? I mean about my husband?"

"Easy. You get to know that look."

"Is it that noticeable?"

"To the trained eye. Plus, I saw you reading that book."

"Oh, that silly thing. My daughter sent me that. She means well."

"They all do. Christ, I had well-meaning up to here," he said, lifting a hand to eye level. "Don't listen to 'em. You do what you feel like, Margaret. Whatever that is. And tell the rest of them birds to go spit in the wind."

They sat in silence for a while. She was going to say something but then she realized that the silence was enough. In the last four months she'd become good friends with silence. The way her cat Rex seemed to surround himself with it, luxuriate in it. She could feel the ship slowing, hear the shuddering sound as it tried to overcome its own momentum. The noise was of some large and momentous journey coming to a close. At last Dennis said, "Well, I guess I should be heading down to my car. We'll be pulling into port in a minute. Need a lift anywhere?"

"Oh, no thank you. My daughter's meeting me."

"That's right." He stood up. "Well, it was nice meeting you, Margaret the Clutz," he said, shaking her hand.

"It was nice meeting you, too."

"We'll have to do this again some time."

"Yes," she replied. She knew, though, she wouldn't take the ferry again. It was just something she wouldn't do again, something that happened once and that was it. "Good-bye," she said.

"Don't forget," he said, smiling. "Baobab." Then he turned and walked toward the doors at the back and was soon out of sight.

Margaret got her things together, stood up, and decided to go out on deck and wait till they arrived. Outside, the wind was still quite fierce, and she had to hold her collar up around her throat. She imagined for a moment she were in the open cockpit of one of those old planes, Amelia Earhart, having survived and now returning, coming in for a landing. It was noisy, too, with the wind and the ship's engines groaning, the propellers reversing direction, the sound was almost frightening. They were still a ways out, but the land was growing more distinct. She could make out objects—buildings, a crane, some cars. She looked for Bea, yet the dock was too far off yet to pick out people. She could just imagine her daughter saying, "See, Ma. It wasn't so bad." The funny thing she was right, though not in the way Bea had meant it. Margaret wondered how she'd tell her about the man she'd met, their odd conversation. But she knew already she wouldn't try to explain it, for she knew she wouldn't tell her at all. It was something, like her loss, that was hers alone. Something private that couldn't be shared unless you'd experienced it yourself.

Below, the water appeared just as menacing as it had when she began: cold and dark and treacherous. That hadn't changed. As she gazed at it, she thought of the sharks swimming somewhere down below. Always having to be on the move, day and night, from birth until death—swimming to keep water passing over their gills, to keep on living. Constantly moving. Never at peace. Never at rest. Day in, day out. Endlessly. What an existence! The mere thought of it wearied Margaret. She angled her head slightly to look over the side. As she did, the wind caught her ear just right and her hearing aid popped out and fell into the dark water. *"Oh,"* she cried, watching it drop and then hit the surface, making barely a ripple. Everything became suddenly much quieter. Still and almost motionless, too, as if sound had kept everything moving. Staring down into the water, Margaret imagined a shark shooting up from the depths to swallow her hearing aid.

# The Smell of Life

The old man sits in the corner, his thin arms outstretched, pleading for Ira to lift him. Ira is reminded, as always, of a fetus in a glass jar: skin so colorless it's nearly transparent, a membrane barely containing that sudden upsurge of bone beneath, a too-large head suspended on a frail stalk of neck, rheumy, exaggerated eyes. If he tries to move him, Ira's certain the old man will fall apart in his arms, that the fragile skin will tear and he'll be left with a pile of bones he'll have to pick up one by one. Having heard the familiar throaty rattle, Ira's come down the stairs and now stands in front of the old man. A foul odor, of old dressings and flesh gone bad, pervades the air. The old man, his palms upward, his long white fingers clutching at empty air, asks to be brought to the bathroom. I have to go, he says to him. Ira doesn't move, though. The thought of helping his father to the bathroom, getting his pants down, being part of such a terribly intimate process—this makes him dizzy with revulsion. Yet before he can say anything, even no, he feels the old man's cold fleshless hand, like the claw of some crustacean, locked on his wrist. With a muted cry, Ira pulls violently backward and tumbles headlong out of the dream.

He wakes to a rasping sound, like a stick being scraped over a metal screen—*cccrrr.* His mouth is dry, and his chest feels as if a small hungry rodent is gnawing on his lungs. The rasping sound vibrates inside his skull. The baby, he thinks. Yes, it's his son. Its cry outraged and plaintive at once. The thing's hoarse from crying. Ira looks over at Susan and thinks of waking her. The dream, still too close, too real, makes the thought of getting out of bed in the dark more than unpleasant. He has to admit that he's actually afraid.

His wife, though, is already exhausted from the dual demands of a three-month-old and her recent return to work at the hospital. The baby doesn't yet sleep through the night but wakes hungry or wet, or for no apparent reason other than out of simple loneliness, howling insistently into the night for attention. And while they're supposed to take turns getting up to feed him, the duty falls more often to Susan than to him. A pediatrician as well as mother, she seems more attuned to those cries for help, her ear trained for such needs.

Let her sleep, he thinks. He untangles the hot, clingy covers and sits up on the side of the bed. The night is a dense, palpable mass, reduced to stillness by an oppressive August heat. Just inside the window, a patch of moonlight is spread over the floor like margarine. In this, the only light, he gets up and makes his way down the stairs and into the kitchen.

He sets about preparing a bottle, his movements as precise and impersonal as those of a chemist performing an experiment. He opens a can of formula, getting a whiff of the thick yeasty odor trapped inside. He stretches a plastic bag over the mouth of a bottle, then pours formula in and pulls the nipple on. He sets the bottle in a pot of water on the stove, turns the burner on high, and waits in the dark. He watches the burner element grow slowly red, its spiraling coil casting an eerie, resonating light, like the eye of a madman. *The dream,* he thinks once more. Despite the night's heat, his calves feel suddenly cold and stringy, as if he were standing knee-deep in a frigid mountain stream.

He heads back up the stairs and into the baby's room. He hovers silently over the crib for a moment. The baby stops its wailing and stares with wide-eyed curiosity at the night figure above it. Ira looks down at his son, whose legs and arms still contract into a ball, imitating the protective shell of the place he had called home for three-quarters of his short life. He whispers *Jacob* and then *Jake* several times, trying by this to place the child, establish a chain, with himself at the center. A chain extending both backward into the past and forward into the future. But the name seems as inappropriate as the baseball cap Susan insists on putting on his small, soft head when she takes him for a walk in their new subdivision. Jake was—is—someone else. A mistake to have used that name, he now feels. Just what was he trying to do? Did he think it could be *that* easy?

The baby starts crying again, his needs overlooked in Ira's reverie. He lifts him out of the crib, careful to support the wobbly neck, and carries him over to the changing table. On removing the diaper, he's struck by the sour smell of baby excrement. He wonders how a newborn could create something this foul. He has to breathe through his mouth as he cleans between the crooked grasshopper legs. Three months and Ira's still not used to the smell. Susan, who's so acquainted with those smells because of her job, kiddingly tells him he'd better *get* used to it.

"There's plenty more where that came from," she says with an experienced chuckle. She tells him it's the smell of life, as if life was defined by odors, given dimension in direct proportion to its foulness.

He buries the smell under a snowstorm of powder. He finishes the changing, puts another T-shirt on his son, then carries him over to the cane rocker, and in the dark begins feeding him. The baby frantically roots for the nipple, latches on to it, then falls into a steady rhythm of sucking. Its legs and arms jerk with a meaning Ira can't quite grasp. His son locks onto Ira's forefinger tenaciously.

When the baby's finished and fallen asleep in his arms, Ira gets up carefully and carries the child over to the crib. Before lowering his son in, he kisses the moist forehead. He can feel the skull pliable as warm wax under the pressure of his lips. Susan's told him that later the fontanels will harden, the soft spots will turn to bone, locking in his son's thoughts once and for all.

He then heads back to his own bedroom and climbs in beside his wife. He hopes for sleep but senses that such easy oblivion won't come to him tonight. He lies on his back, hands locked behind his head, looking into the flat, slate-colored darkness just above him. Again he thinks: *the dream.* As he listens to the spiraling, metallic hum of insects outside, he realizes how foolish he was to let himself believe it was over—that it could *ever* be over. His father—though now he only thinks of him as that old man in the chair—would stay away for months, sometimes even for a year or more. He'd let Ira think he was rid of him, free of him. He'd let him think he'd been forgiven. But as soon as Ira let his defenses down, dreamed other dreams, he'd show up in the middle of the night, arriving without warning, bag and baggage.

He can see him even now, sitting in that corner chair, the recliner they'd bought from Sears because the old man could no longer sleep lying down. He was slowly choking on the fluid in his lungs and sitting up he could at least doze off for periods of time. They'd put the chair in the den of the house Ira had grown up in and that's where his father would die. Slowly, stubbornly, bitterly, he died a little each day in that chair. In those last few months, he sat there night and day, his eyes hollow with fear and anger, his breathing sounding like no human sound Ira had ever heard. He could hear that terrible sound in the evening when he tried to study, at night when he tried to sleep. In the morning he'd have to pass through the den on his way to school and his father would be there like a sentry, staring at him with those wild, doomed eyes. Sometimes he'd ask Ira for something, a glass of water, his medicine, a pan of hot water for his feet. Or he'd ask for help to get to the bathroom, and Ira would have to hold him up as he undid his pants, help him onto the pot, and later help him wipe himself. Ira had all he could do not to gag. He couldn't wait for it to be over with. On the day his father would finally die, Ira had left the house early to take a test, a final exam in economics at the college he commuted to. He couldn't remember if they'd said anything to each other as he passed by the old man sitting in the corner.

Ira now turns toward Susan and thinks once again of waking her. He could tell her there's something the matter with the baby, minor but needing her more expert hand. Yet he knows she'd see through that excuse and realize exactly why he really woke her. "For heaven's sakes, Ira. He's dead. It's just a dream!" She'd say that he should go see somebody, that he'd let this "dream business," as she calls it, get out of hand. As he watches her he tries to picture her dreams—

bright affairs, alive with the hunger of living, of planning, of this child she's given birth to and all those others she cares for in her practice. That's her life now. Looking ahead, into an expansive future. He decides not to wake her. Instead he gets out of bed again and goes back downstairs.

From the refrigerator he gets the jug of white wine and pours himself a glass. He drinks that straight down. It's so hot out the liquid slides down into him without a hitch. He pours himself another and puts the bottle back. From the cold pastel light that spills out of the refrigerator, he's able to make out the clock on the wall. Ten after one. Four more hours till daylight. Four more hours of darkness to get through. Maybe he could do some work on the article he's been writing. An economics professor at a large university, he's been gathering research for the article for most of the summer. A forecasting model for business, one that would predict cycles of growth and stagnation.

He walks into the small room at the back of the house he uses as a study and picks up his data, a pile of green and white computer printouts, some notes, a couple of books. Then he heads out to the sun porch where, on nights he can't sleep, he reads or works under a lamp.

He sits on the couch, an old one they've had since his grad school days. Cycles of growth and stagnation, he thinks. Cycles of stagnation. That's it. In the dark he gulps the wine, feeling it fan out inside him once it hits bottom. He doesn't turn on the lamp but sits very still in the dark, as if waiting for something. Around the streetlight out at the road, he can see a swirl of bugs churning and diving like sparks from a grindstone. In the distance he hears the faraway but growing roar of a car with loud mufflers. Kids out for fun, trying to shatter the dreary stillness of a night so self-absorbed in rest, in complacency. The roar peaks as the car passes by a couple of streets over, then slowly recedes, finally merging into the anonymous insect racket. Though it's slightly cooler on the porch, he can still feel drops of sweat crawling like spiders down his chest, into his shorts. He can smell his own stale body odor.

How long had he been gone this time, he wonders? Six months? A year? Sometimes the old man would leave him alone for long, quiet stretches, during which Ira didn't seem to dream at all. He would almost forget about his father, the past, his guilt. He'd let himself think he'd been forgiven, that it was only a bad dream, as Susan had said, and now maybe he'd finally be able to put it behind him. Then, out of the blue, he'd show up and all the old wounds Ira thought healed were reopened.

He thinks it's funny how Susan calls it just a dream. Even funnier that she says he should go to somebody to have it explained to him. As if someone else could possibly tell him anything he doesn't already know, as if he himself hasn't analyzed it a hundred, a thousand times since his father died fifteen years ago and started these nightly visits. Long ago he'd ceased to analyze it, because it's very clear to him, because, in fact, it isn't a dream at all. That's the oddest part. The old man is very real and his visits are also real—as real as pain, as elemental as an odor. It's as simple, as irrefutable as that.

He heads back inside to the kitchen, opens the refrigerator, pours himself another glass of wine. He goes back out to the porch, lies down, and closes his eyes. After a while, the insect clatter recedes into a middle distance, the noise like the dull hum of an electric generator. Then, even that fades away.

Before he hears the voice, Ira can detect that familiar odor: like that of meat which has been left unrefrigerated on a hot day.

So. How's the smart boy? whispers a voice, close enough so Ira can feel the stale breath on him.

Though he's expected it all along, the voice nonetheless startles him.

How'd you do on the test, smart boy?

All right, Ira answers, his eyes still closed.

Just all right? You study all the time and all's you do is "all right"? What'd I raise, a moron?

An "A." I got an "A" on it.

A regular genius, says the voice. Hurray. He got an A on his goddamn test.

Listen, you asked and I told you. What do you want from me?

As soon as he says this, he wishes he'd waited. Maybe, goes the frail hope each time the old man shows up at his house, things could change between them.

Ira sits up, opens his eyes. The porch is altered, oddly unfamiliar. The darkness is different too, not a nighttime darkness but similar to that of a thunderstorm in the middle of the day, tinged with yellow and purple like a bruise. Also, the smell is stronger. For a moment there's a thin silence, broken then by a low groan rising up from the belly. Without turning his head toward the noise, Ira says, Can I get you something?

Jesus on a fucking crutch, cries the old man, his voice distorted by pain. You weren't thinking about me when you had your test, were you?

Let me get you some hot water to soak your feet. You'll feel better.

Feel better! That's good. That's rich. Look at me.

Ira wants to turn toward the voice, but he can't quite bring himself to.

You're a doctor. You know what's what, his father says. You know the score.

I'm not that kind of doctor.

Oh, I forgot. You don't help bodies. It's numbers you work with.

Yeah, says Ira, sick already of this endless ritual they always act out.

That's why you couldn't be there when it was my time. You had your numbers to think about, your test to take.

What do you want from me? Were you thinking about my future? Were you ever thinking about anybody but yourself?

Was it asking too much to be there when your old man was breathing his last? Was that too damn much?

A dry-throated rattle, like the sound of wind blowing through dry leaves in fall. Then his father slips into a coughing fit that Ira knows rakes bits of lung tissue and bright globs of blood from his chest. He can remember emptying his father's sputum cup. He can remember lying on his bed upstairs, studying for school, and hearing that cough, that terrible cough. Sometimes he'd study with the radio on to drown out that sound.

When the coughing subsides, the voice says, You only die once, you know.

What did you expect? You never acted like a father to me. You were drunk half the time. What did I owe you?

Owe me! You owed me, all right. A son owes his father that much. Hell, when I was your age I was already running the farm, supporting my old man as well as you birds. So don't talk to me about owing.

Oh, Christ!

Oh "Christ" nothing. You never want to hear that, do you? That I acted like a son to my old man.

I've heard your damn hero stories a thousand times.

It's the truth. My old man gave me nothing. A lot less than you birds had. You had a roof over your head, three meals a day.

What about love?

Piss on love. I gave you more than he gave me, that's for sure. We weren't close, my old man and me. You think I was tough on you? Let me tell you, my old man was one hard-nosed son of a bitch. But least I respected him enough and had the decency to be there when he was dying. *Decency.* Christ, you don't know what the word means.

I suppose you're the expert on decency.

That's right. You sure as hell don't know anything about it.

They both fall silent. Ira chances looking over at his father, whose eyes are closed, whose fingers nervously pick at his loose clothing. So frail, he thinks. His father had once been a large, imposing man, one of great physical strength. Now he was as delicate as a piece of bone china. Ira closes his own eyes. It's quiet for a while. But then the voice begins again.

I remember the day my old man died. He'd been bad for a week. He didn't even know who we were when we went in the room to see him. We knew it wouldn't be long. I was out in the fields plowing. It was my sister Mae who came running out to let me know he was slipping, that he didn't have long. I remember not even shutting the John Deere off, just leaving it and running like hell across the field. All the time thinking, No, don't die yet. Don't you dare go and die on me yet, you bastard. I could picture him doing it just for spite, and I didn't want that hanging around my neck. I wanted us even when he checked out, everything paid up and squared away. I remember I had mud all over my boots when I went in the room. It's funny the things you remember at a time like that. I didn't say a thing, didn't have to. I just sat on the bed and held his hand. Helped him through it. We weren't close, me and my old man, but I owed him that much. So don't talk to me about decency.

Ira wants to tell him he'd tried to get there in time, that he'd called home and Mrs. Rodalesky, a neighbor woman who'd been helping the family out, had told him they'd had to rush his father to the hospital. And how he'd driven straight to the hospital from school, but by then it was too late. He found only an empty room. He could remember asking the nurse, a heavy girl with big freckles like pennies, where his father was. She said to him that she was sorry. That was all she'd said. Sorry. He wants to tell his father he'd tried to get there but what good would it do? He would only try to twist it.

I was young, Ira offers.

What does being young have to do with it? If you had it to do all over again, say if it was happening again right now, would you do anything different?

Yes.

Just to get rid of me?

No.

Why? And don't go handing me any bullshit about love. Just the truth. The simple lousy truth for once.

Ira's about to reply when his father begins to cough again. Now, though, the noise is remote, muted, fainter.

Dad? he says. But there's no response. Then louder, I named him after you.

What's that supposed to mean?

Nothing. I just did.

Is that supposed to make us even?

No! For God's sakes, no! Stop it, would you?

Bring me in the house. I think it's time, says the voice, now formal with pain.

I . . .

Pick me up, quick. I feel it coming. Jesus Christ. My legs are gone. I can't fell a goddamn thing down there.

Dad . . . I . . . please. Dad.

Hurry, for crissakes!

Ira tries to lift his arms but he can't. They feel detached, lifeless. No matter how hard he concentrates on lifting them he can't.

*Ohhh.* It's too late, cries the voice, now fading to a whisper.

Dad, wait. Please don't die. Don't die on me.

*Ohhhhhhh.*

Please!

But the voice falters and then falls silent. Ira jerks awake. He feels as if he's crashing through something, a plate glass window, with shards of glass raining over him, exploding on the ground around him. He opens his eyes and sits up on the edge of the couch, looking out at the first salmon-colored rays of sunlight slashing through the trees to the east. He knows that his father will never be gone for good, that he'll always make these visits. Ira pictures living to be an old man himself, someday even on his own deathbed, and his father there taunting him, tossing his guilt in his face. There'll be endless meetings in which nothing will ever be settled, no forgiveness ever obtained.

He becomes aware of another noise. The baby again, crying. Getting up, he goes into the house and up the stairs. He can hear Susan in the shower getting ready to make her rounds at the hospital before heading to her office. He walks into the baby's room. His son is a bluish-red from crying, and there's a line of curdled milk running down the side of his mouth. Ira lifts his son out of the crib, cooing and rocking him to try to quiet him. He whispers his son's name, whispers into the hot ear that he's sorry, sorry for everything. He whispers this as if the baby might actually understand and what's more, have the power to forgive. His son continues to cry, though, to shout urgently for life's immediate needs.

Ira undresses the baby, then gets undressed himself. He can feel the tiny raging heartbeat against his own chest as he heads into the bathroom and joins Susan in the steamy shower.

"Ira? What on earth?" his wife says, alarmed at first. Then, realizing nothing is the matter, she says, "Isn't this nice." They embrace each other and their son. With the warm water the baby ceases to cry, staring up at Ira.

## Fugitives

Week after week that fall after his brother Gordy had the nervous breakdown, Tom would go to visit him in the hospital. Driving up on the interstate in his BMW, Tom found himself dreading the visits. He hoped an excuse would rescue him: that he'd get a call on his car phone, an important client, something that couldn't wait, and that he'd have to call his brother, say something had come up and he couldn't make it. He felt guilty for these thoughts, but it wasn't easy to see his older brother like that. Gordy, small and fidgety as a sparrow normally, would lie perfectly still on top of the covers of his narrow bed. Whatever they had him on, entire visits sometimes passed with him just lying there staring at the ceiling, his hands locked behind his head, fully dressed, right down to his shiny black work shoes. He smelled funny, too, like a pool with too much chlorine in it, and his hair always looked as if he'd just come in from a wild ride in a convertible. To tell the truth, it didn't even look like his brother. The man in the bed had different eyes, hollow and still as seashells, the blue shading into a milky gray. It was as if they'd replaced Gordy with some guy that only vaguely resembled him. But Tom told himself it was only because of the way things stood. Somewhere in there was the same old Gordy, at least he would be once he got through this mess.

Tom would bring his brother things, stuff you brought to people in hospitals: magazines and gum and cards that had dumb upbeat jokes written on them which Gordy never even bothered to read. And things to eat, like O Henry bars and butterscotch candies and fruit. His brother had lost so much weight his pants were bunched in front like those of a little kid who came from a poor family—in fact, like the family the brothers had grown up in. Once or twice Tom even sneaked his brother in a can of nonalcoholic beer, though Gordy was a recovering alcoholic and wasn't supposed to have any, even the sort without any kick. One beer wasn't going hurt anything, he thought. Besides, Tom felt Gordy had to tackle one problem at a time. But his brother didn't have much of an appetite, even for beer. Most of the things Tom brought him sat in his drawer or were given—stolen, Tom sometimes suspected—to his roommate, a heavy, balding, loquacious fellow named Barber, who was wheezing all the time as if he had allergies. Tom would see the candy wrappers in the roommate's garbage can, and even some of the get-well cards were on Barber's side of the room. Evidently, Barber had no visitors.

"How do you feel?" Tom asked his brother each visit.

And each visit Gordy would say the same thing: "Not bad," as he stared up at the ceiling.

"You feel any better?"

"Mostly I'm tired. I don't get it. All I do is flop all day and I'm still wiped out."

"Maybe he could use some zinc," offered Barber. The roommate was sitting on the side of the other twin bed polishing a pair of dress shoes. Barber, who usually monopolized Tom and Gordy's conversation, said he was in some kind of sales. He said in like it was a place, a shelter, somewhere you went to be out of the cold.

"What the Christ do I want with zinc?" Gordy said, shifting his gaze to the window. Tom followed his brother's eyes out at a small courtyard where leaves spun in sudden funnels, crashing against the windows like a swarm of excited bugs.

"For stress. Your body's under stress. That camel driver's only worried about your noddle. He could give two shits about the rest of you."

The camel driver was Dr. Nahim, their psychiatrist, a thin, dark man with a boy's awkward shoulders. From time to time he'd come in, look at Gordy's chart the way you would a magazine in a checkout line at the supermarket, and say, "Ah, yes. Very good. OK, see you tomorrow, Mr. Blakesley?" and leave.

"Well, I'm open for suggestions," Gordy said, yawning. Tom, standing at the foot of the bed, watched his brother make a circle with his thumb and forefinger, the way you would to say everything was A-OK, but instead he stared at Tom through the hole. That was another habit that bugged Tom. Gordy would close one eye and stare at him with the other like that, as if his fingers were a telescope and Tom some remote object floating in space. Tom smiled at him, like they both knew it was just a joke, but his brother didn't smile back, continued to gaze intently at him. *Jesus Fucking Christ,* he thought.

At first, Tom liked to think Gordy just needed some time, a sort of regimented vacation. He didn't have to be there. He'd signed himself in and could walk any time he wanted, though technically the door at the end of the hall remained locked. It was a locked ward, Tom sometimes said to himself on the ride up. Yet, he also said Gordy couldn't be too bad if he knew he had a problem. To tell the truth, Tom was pretty skeptical about the whole idea of mental illness, which he considered more a lack of will power than anything real. Except, of course, for the real crazies, the ones who kept body parts in the fridge or thought they were Napoleon. Gordy just seemed worn out, like he said, as if he'd been working too much and could use some R&R. A service manager for a car dealership in Springfield, Massachusetts, his brother needed some time to put things back together, the way he used to put an engine back together out in their barn, piece by careful piece. Tom, five years younger, could remember holding the drop-light as his brother arranged the seemingly random metal pieces into an order that resulted in this sudden catlike motion. Unlike his brother, Tom had never quite got the hang of how the parts came together. He was always more interested in the way cars looked, or in the way people looked at him when he was in an expensive one. His brother had ended up working on them, while Tom ended up behind the wheel of one expensive car or another.

Despite his skepticism, Tom had to admit his brother had gone through some pretty rough times. He was just getting a handle on his drinking when his wife, Terri, left him, took the two youngest kids, and moved down to Florida where her mother lived. And only the year before, his oldest son, Greg, drunk out of his mind, had plowed into a tree going ninety. Gordy had been too upset so it was Tom who had to go and identify the body at the morgue—the absolute worst thing he'd ever had to do. But Tom sucked it up and did it. Everyone considered Greg a royal screw-up, including even Gordy. Like father, like son, thought Tom. Still, it was his son, his first-born. Tom had two kids of his own and couldn't imagine losing them. It was no wonder Gordy needed time to sort things out, to put the pieces of his mind back together.

His brother's room resembled a budget motel room, functional and efficient, complete with framed prints of horses and snow-capped mountains, a bolted-down TV, and blood-colored, basement-quality carpeting that was easily cleaned. The room looked out on a courtyard of slender white birches, staked and held fast with bicycle tubes. It was a good room to rest, quiet, at the end of the corridor, away from the jabber of the nurses' station. When Tom came, usually on Sundays, they'd watch, without much interest, some football game or stockcar race from somewhere down South. Or, if Gordy was feeling a little better, they might head down to the rec room and shoot some pool. Gordy, recovering something of his old self, in the hall once even put a headlock on Tom, the way he often used to when they were kids, playfully yet with intent, squeezing until Tom cried out that he gave. "My kid brother," Gordy said to one of the nurses. "He makes like a hundred grand a year, but I can still kick his ass. And he *knows* it." Then he punched Tom hard in the arm, harder than was necessary, as if it was meant to show that he was indeed the older brother and could still kick his ass if need be. Gordy would laugh a thin, dry rattle. Tom felt a little embarrassed by this, two middle-aged men acting like kids, but at least it seemed to say his brother was getting better, that he wasn't in so deep that he couldn't be pulled out with a little help. At those moments especially, the whole thing didn't strike Tom as anything serious, which he associated with straitjackets and swan dives off of bridges. His brother wasn't in that league, wasn't like some of the characters Tom passed in the hallways. Some of those people made him actually shiver—that nearly transparent skin criss-crossed by haunting blue veins, hands that buzzed around like flies circling decaying meat. Lost souls trapped forever here. No, his brother was just tired, resting before he started on wherever he was headed now. Like a pit stop in a long race.

As the weeks passed, however, and Gordy didn't seem to get any better, if anything, seemed to slip further away—grow more distant, his eyes more milky, less able to focus on nearby things—Tom wasn't so sure. Once when he arrived, his brother was sleeping, so Tom stood quietly near the window. He didn't mind watching over his brother. In fact, he was almost grateful for the peace it afforded. Sleeping, his brother even seemed normal again, the old Gordy. They could've been kids sharing the same room again. Some Sunday morning and Gordy was sleeping late after a big night out. Soon though Gordy woke up, blinked several times, his bleary eyes raw in their sockets. "Who are you?" his brother asked. Tom tried to shrug the comment off but his brother wouldn't let it go.

"I'm talking to you, asshole. Who the *hell* are you, anyway?"

"Cut it out. It's me," Tom said. "Your brother."

"My brother?" He continued to stare at Tom for a moment, as if searching for familiar territory, a crevice for his memory to take hold in. "What're you trying to pull? My brother's fuckin' dead. He was killed in a car accident," he said. No sooner had he said this than his eyes fluttered, closed like a door being slammed, and he was sound asleep again. Tom never mentioned it to Gordy and chalked it up to the medications they had him on. Yet he wondered why he'd confused him with his own son, wondered what it could mean.

There were other clues that his brother was worse off than Tom had first thought: odd little gestures, like the circle he made with his thumb and forefinger, or a mouth frozen in an expression Tom associated with old people on park benches.

And Gordy's eyes would mist over as he told stories about their childhood, their dead parents. He sobbed openly once as he told how their mother, who had died when Tom was only nine, had breast-fed Tom but not him, as if he could actually recall being denied his mother's milk, and as if that had made the slightest difference in their lives. Several times he told Tom he never held anything against him, had no hard feelings, not even over the time Tom had put a bumblebee in Gordy's piggy bank. Nor all the times Tom had purposely broken his model cars. And in turn he was sorry for things he'd done: the time he'd beaten Tom up in the snow in the field out back, or the time he'd handcuffed Tom to the bed with a pair of toy cuffs he'd gotten for Christmas and then had left him there alone in the house all day, when he was supposed to be babysitting his younger brother. He laughed as he began the story, of Tom handcuffed to the bed, but then he started crying over that, too. "I was a stupid fuck," he admitted, sobbing. He said all this the way someone would who was trying to tie up loose ends, settle old scores while he still had the chance. Tom wasn't sure whether to be mad at the jerk for blaming things on him, or feel sorry for him for accepting his own blame over ancient childhood grudges he himself had long since forgotten, or to be afraid that such an accounting spoke of a mind at the very edge of the abyss.

Sometimes Gordy actually scared Tom, he seemed so utterly and irrevocably lost, so far away from what he'd once been. Would his brother become one of those people he saw wandering the halls? Would he, Tom, be making these trips for years? Some of the other patients' visitors had regular patterns, little rituals they practiced each week. They knew the first names of the nurses and other patients, where the clean johnnys and linens were kept, who was home on a weekend pass—as if they'd been coming for years, as if this had become an accepted and routine part of their lives. Tom would feel a tightness in his gut as soon as he got out of his car, a tightness that turned to a smooth, cool stone when he saw Gordy's sunken frame stretched out fully clothed on the bed, as if he hadn't budged an inch from the last visit. The tightness would relax only when he heard the end of visiting hours announced over the intercom.

"Well, I got to be shoving off," Tom would say, relieved. "You hang in there, OK?"

"What the fuck else am I gonna do?" Gordy said, but without a hint of anger. Just complacency. He smiled so his upper lip got stuck on his front plate and his face was a mask of scary yellow teeth.

"I'll watch out for Flash Gordon," said Barber, who was polishing a pair of shoes. Gordy's roommate was always polishing shoes though he never wore anything but the paper hospital-issue slippers. It seemed like he wanted to be ready to leave when the time came. That he had big places to go and important people to see. He even spit-shined Gordy's, as if the two of them had plans to go out on the town some night.

"Can I bring you anything next week. Some smokes?" Tom asked his brother.

"No, I think I'm all set," his brother said.

"What else could a man want?" Barber joked, waving a shoe-covered hand around the room. "Three squares. Color tube. Good friends. We could do a little better in the broad department."

"Listen to him," Gordy said.

"I get all lathered up for anything in white pantyhose," the roommate said, chewing on an O Henry bar Tom had brought for his brother. You could see the muscles working his thick jaws. Barber's face reminded Tom of one of those pictures at his health spa, the ones that peel away the skin and show all the muscle groups in different colors. "That Trish ain't half bad. Though she's all meat and no potatoes. She wants my ass."

"Big ladies man," Gordy laughed.

"I'm just waiting for the right moment. It's timing," Barber said. "Just like when you're selling. Any jerk can get his foot in the door. It's knowing how to close that counts." He winked at them, his teeth covered with chocolate and peanuts.

The roommate was a real character. A bullshit artist, Tom pegged him as right away. He told Tom he owned a 500 SL, a condo in St. Croix, had all his suits custom-made at Stackpole and Moore at a thousand a pop. He'd flirt shamelessly with the nurses, particularly this one named Trish, say she had the hots for him. He'd talk Tom's ear off, but sometimes, Tom had to admit, it made a welcome contrast to the awkward silence of his brother.

"I could tell you some things, Tom. Hell, I dropped five grand—*on one night out.* One lousy night. Like that," Barber said, snapping his thick fingers to make the money disappear. "I didn't care cause there was plenty more where that came from. Easy come, easy go. That's me."

"Mr. Big Timer," Gordy said. "What the hell you doing in this joint then?"

"Just biding my time," Barber said. "When I'm good and ready, I'll blow this place in a minute."

"Yeah, sure," replied Gordy.

"You watch me. Maybe I'll bring you along, too, Gordo. Fugitives from justice, the both of us," he said, laughing.

"Yeah, some fugitives."

"You fellows don't do anything I wouldn't do," Tom said, putting on his coat and hoping to ease out while the two of them were still talking. On leaving, he always felt vaguely guilty, as if he were abandoning his brother.

"What wouldn't you do?" Gordy tried to kid, but it came out flat, like a question. He finally got up from the bed and shook hands with Tom.

"Take care, Tom," Barber said. "Thanks for coming. And don't worry about us. We're OK," he said, winking at Tom and wrapping his arm protectively around the much smaller Gordy. His brother looked annoyed but didn't try to shrug the arm off.

His brother would lead Tom to the exit, all the while Tom noticing the shiny steel-toed work shoes, the small, shuffling steps his brother took. At the exit an aide named Javier unlocked the psych-ward door from a stringer of keys. Javier, a young kid of twenty, would take his sweet time, like a real guard in a real prison, seeming to enjoy his status as the giver of freedom. The controller of fates. Just before Tom left, he and Gordy would shake hands one last time, awkwardly and formally, as if they'd just arrived at some business agreement. It was the closest gesture they ever came to a show of affection. The Blakesleys had never been a touchy family. That's the way their father, after their mother's death, had been with them, cold and distant and hard—except sometimes when he was drunk, when he might turn maudlin and begin crying over their mother—and that's the way the brothers were with each other, too. Stiff and distant. When his nephew died, Tom stood in front of his brother, gave him a formal pat on his shoulder, and said, "What can I say, Gordon?" He felt he should've done more, but he didn't know what. Now, as he walked down the hospital corridor, Tom might look back once to see Gordy watching him through the small reinforced windows. If he did, he'd give him the thumbs-up sign, or, as a joke, he'd make a face at him like he was some crazy who'd managed to escape, and pretend he was slinking off toward the outside world. Sometimes, he'd see Barber there waving, too, his big grinning face taking up the entire window, as if pushing Gordy aside.

As the visits dragged on, though, Tom stopped looking back. He'd look straight ahead and hurry out into the sharp autumn air where he could breathe again. Once, he even had this crazy thought: what if someone had seen his mock escape routine and thought perhaps he was a real patient? What if they were coming after him right now, intending to haul him back inside? It was just one of those crazy thoughts, but still it sent a shiver down his back. He'd quickly get in his car, lock the door, and fly away from the hospital. On the interstate, driving back to his family and his normal life, he'd get the BMW up to eighty and hit the buttons that turned down the windows. He hoped to drive that chlorine and shoe polish smell from his nose—the odor he came to associate with sickness, with his brother. Then he did an odd thing: he'd close his eyes and let go of the wheel for a moment. Just a moment. This is what it must feel like, he'd think. A blind loss of control going at high speed. Insanity, that is. But he never completely closed his eyes, just sort of squinted so he could grab the wheel before anything happened. The car's thick leather seats made him feel protected, Vivaldi assured him the rest of the world was still healthy and vibrant and in tune, while the honey-smooth drone of the German motor promised a quick return to his solid life.

Tom's dread of the visits grew. He found himself putting them off, leaving later and later on Sunday so he wouldn't have to spend much time at the hospital, or coming up with excuses for not going at all. The owner of a successful apartment maintenance service, Tom didn't have to look hard for problems to keep him tied up. People who worked for him were always calling in sick, landlords complaining about lawns or snow removal or fixing a leaky pipe. When he called to tell Gordy he wouldn't be able to make it, that he had a ton of work, his brother said he understood. "I'm not going anywhere," Gordy said. "I'm here." He said *here* like it was somewhere permanent, a fixed point on Tom's horizon. A lighthouse perhaps. And the next time Tom did show up, full of excuses and plagued by guilt, his brother didn't seem as if he'd missed him all that much. Sometimes whole visits would pass and they wouldn't say more than a few sentences: about one of the other patients or something Barber brought up. They didn't have much to talk about, didn't have that much in common. They'd grown up in the same house, had shared the same room, the same parents, but that was all. Their lives now were worlds apart—the only bridge the one made of shared guilt. That's what attached them: guilt. Tom stopped just short of feeling a certain smugness about his success, while his brother seemed to stumble along from one defeat to the next, getting better at failure the older he got. It was probably why their father had always liked Gordy better. The two had had that in common: both were losers, both drunks, both liked to blame the world for their own failures.

Tom found himself beginning to dislike, even hate, his brother for getting into this mess, for making him feel so guilty. There wasn't really anything wrong with him. It wasn't as if he had cancer or anything like that—a real sickness, something tangible and blameless and out of his control. As Gordy had done before with his drinking or his wife leaving him, he was giving up, letting his life just drift. And it was Tom, the younger brother, who'd have to step in and give of his time or his money or both. More than a few times he'd lent Gordy money, which, Tom's wife Sharon said, was as good as burning it, and once he'd had to go and bail him out of jail when he'd been arrested for DWI. And now this. What could you do for someone like that, someone who just didn't want to help himself, didn't want to get better, who actually reveled in his own misery? Tom wanted to take Gordy by the shoulders and shake him until he woke up and snapped out of it.

Yet as he sat at home and thought of his brother, Tom had this strong sense that things, inevitably almost, were going to turn out badly. He didn't know why he thought this, and he didn't let himself picture *how* things would turn out for the worse, but he definitely had that feeling. A premonition almost. And he knew if anything terrible did happen, there'd be this ponderous guilt he'd have to shoulder for the rest of his life, and for that, too, he felt a bitterness toward his brother.

Then one night in early December, he got a call from the hospital. He hadn't been to see his brother in several weeks but right away he sensed the call was about Gordy.

"Thomas Blakesley?"

"Yes?"

"This is Dr. Nahim, from the hospital. There's been an accident."

Tom felt that stone-hardness in his gut as he waited to hear the worst. His mind rushed ahead: he pictured having to drive up and make arrangements, call Terri and try to convince her to come back for the funeral. He saw his brother's skinny white ankles jutting out from under a sheet, like that time with his nephew. He shuddered at the prospect of having to do that again. No, he thought. Christ, not again.

"An accident?" he asked weakly.

"I'm afraid so, yes. Your brother hit one of the aides."

"He hit somebody?"

"Yes."

"How's Gordy?"

"Your brother is under sedation. The aide might have a concussion, though. Very bad business, I'm afraid. As you can understand, this complicates your brother's situation. We have put him under a seventy-two-hour hold."

"What happens now?"

"If charges are brought, he'll have to be transferred to a state facility until his trial. It would be a good idea if you came." His tone was that of an accusation.

"Of course, I'll come," Tom said. "I'll be right up."

The cold, starless night smelled of diesel and dead fish as he drove up along the Sound. He kept thinking, *The stupid fuckin' bastard.* Now he'd really screwed things up. Now he couldn't just leave whenever he wanted. From here on in he really was a prisoner, his fate out of his hands. Tom thought how Nahim had called it an accident, like it was something no one was to blame for, something beyond anyone's control. A hurricane or a tornado.

His brother was sleeping when he entered his room, a different one this time, one that no longer looked like a motel room. He was in a different bed, too, a regular hospital thing with rails on the sides and controls, and Gordy lay in the middle of it like something framed. His hands were tied with canvas restraints to the metal rails, and he was wearing a hospital johnny. It was the first time Tom had seen him in anything but his civilian clothes. Now he looked like he belonged here, looked like a permanent resident. A radical change had come over his brother. He appeared suddenly very old and depleted, as if something had gone out of him that was never coming back—the way their father had looked in the last stages of his cancer. His nose was prominent, and his eyes looked as if someone had pushed them way back into his head.

*God,* thought Tom. For the first time the word *sick* came into his head as he looked at his brother.

"You missed all the fireworks," said Barber, who'd just come into the room behind him.

"How is he?"

"All right. He busted up that Puerto Rican kid pretty good. They're talking fractured skull. But you know how they all feed on drama around here."

Barber stood on one side of the bed, Tom on the other.

"What happened?" he asked, though Nahim had told him all about it in the hall only moments before. How his brother was playing pool when the aide said it was time to go back to his room. There were some words, the kid put his hand on Gordy. The next thing Gordy had slugged the kid with a pool cue, laid him right out so they feared he was dead at first. It took a half-dozen aides and security guards to "get him under control"—the doctor's words. Tom saw a forest fire raging, people with axes and shovels struggling to get it under control. That was Gordy now—not his brother anymore but something raging out of control.

"I wasn't there," Barber said. "But you ask me that kid was asking for it. He thought he was King Tut around here until your brother wised him up. Good for him, I say."

"Good for him?" Tom said, incredulous.

"Yeah. Old Gordo. Didn't think he had it in him. That's a good sign."

"What the hell you talking about, he almost killed somebody!"

"Least he's getting it out."

Tom stood there struggling to make out his brother's chest going up and down. He was deeply sedated. Tom wasn't sure how to feel, whether to feel relieved that it hadn't been worse or to wonder if this meant his brother's sickness had taken a decided turn for the worse, had reached some critical mass. It sure as hell wasn't a good sign. He knew that much.

"Your brother plays his cards pretty close to the vest," Barber said.

"What do you mean?" Tom asked.

"We've been roomies for all this time and I hardly know the guy. I do all the talking."

"He's pretty quiet, I guess."

"He keeps it all here," Barber said, poking himself in his large T-shirted gut. "Your brother's got a lot of steam in him."

"Who doesn't?" Tom said.

"No, I mean it. I'm pretty good at reading people. His wife taking off on him and the thing with his kid. He's pissed. The camel driver probably has some name for it, but when you come right down to it he's just plain pissed off. And you can't blame him either."

Tom sucked some air in and let it out slowly. *Steam,* he thought. The goddamn guy thought it was just a matter of steam.

"I've been this route before," Barber said. With his fingers he was tapping out a tune on the bed rail. "Not here. But I was laid up before. It was right after my old lady went AWOL on me. Talk about being pissed. I couldn't see straight. If I could've got my hands on an Uzi, I would've inflicted some damage. This sounds nuts now, I know, but I actually pictured going into some place, a supermarket or a restaurant, like one of those post office guys, and just letting it all fly out. All that anger. Same with your brother. He wants to do some damage, that's where he's at right now."

"I don't know about that," Tom said. He knew his brother better than this guy did, and he'd never do anything *really* crazy. Not hurt anybody intentionally. It was one thing to hit somebody with a pool cue in an argument. Anybody was capable of that. But it was something else again to get a gun and start shooting.

"Don't get me wrong," said Barber. "I'm not saying your brother would actually *do* anything like that. I'm just saying it's not out of the question. All this stuff is building up inside him. It can only build up so much and then it's got to come out. Like—" But Barber paused suddenly, as if a gear in his brain had gotten stuck. He stared absently out the window for several seconds before saying, "Gordy's lucky he's got you."

"Me?" Tom said.

"He's lucky you two are tight. Some brothers aren't. I can tell you two are pretty tight."

"I don't know about that."

"He doesn't say too much, but he speaks well of you. My kid brother this, my kid brother that. You should hear him. He's real proud of you. It's good he can count on you. That's what he needs now."

"I guess I do what I can," he said, not so much a lie as just to get Barber to shut up.

"Sure you do. Like tonight—he needed you and here you are. That's what I'm talking about. Loyalty."

Loyalty, Tom thought. He wished Barber would just go away, wished he could wait quietly there until it was late and he could go home. Maybe his brother wouldn't even wake up before he left, but the nurses would tell him he'd been there, watching over him. Doing what a brother was supposed to do. So his visit would count even though he didn't have to deal with Gordy.

"If he asked you, I bet you'd give him the shirt off your back," Barber said.

"I'm no hero. I do what I can."

"Sure you do. If Gordy needed you you'd be there. Damn right you would. I can tell that about you. Now you take my brother. Jesus. I could be in this joint until hell freezes over and you think he'd ever come visit me? Take me out for a drive? Lay out seventy-five cents for a lousy call? That'd be the goddamn day. Don't even get me going."

Tom knew Barber was itching to get going, but he wasn't about to give him the chance. He went over and looked out the window at the courtyard. It was dark and windy and very cold. He couldn't see beyond the small lit area that had spotlights shining down on it from the roof, like a small stage. Beyond the roof the night was blacker than he'd ever seen it, a sticky black like carbon paper. On the drive up he'd heard it was supposed to snow tonight.

"Robert," Barber said.

"Who?" Tom asked, half-turning. He thought Barber had forgotten his name or something and was calling him Robert.

"My no-good shit for a brother. Robert. But everybody called him Buddy. Buddy—that's rich. Some fucking buddy. I used to have this bladder problem, you see."

"Bladder problem?" Tom repeated, wondering what intimate problem Barber was going to share with him.

"Yeah. When I was a little kid. You know, bed-wetting. Sometimes I couldn't hold it. I'd have accidents. Buddy used to tease me. He'd threaten to tell everybody if I didn't do what he said. Can you imagine that? What sort of brother does that?"

"Kids do rotten things to each other," Tom offered.

"You don't have to tell me that. But brothers?"

"Even brothers. Sometimes *especially* brothers."

"But there's limits. There's a difference between doing something dumb and something that's cruel. I'm sure you and Gordy never did anything cruel to each other. Maybe something you regretted, something you wished you hadn't done. But not cruel."

Tom tried to think if he'd ever done anything actually cruel to Gordy. He'd been unfair and thoughtless and selfish often, sometimes vindictive. What kid hadn't? But had he ever done anything that he could say was downright cruel? Maybe.

"We had our differences," Tom said, looking over his shoulder at his brother. Gordy's eyes were open slightly, and for a moment Tom thought he was looking at him, listening. But he was sound asleep. He wondered where his brother was now, at that moment. What were his dreams like? Did he dream about his dead son? His ex-wife? About their mother not breast-feeding him? About the time he'd handcuffed Tom to the bed?

"That's normal," Barber said. "All brothers have their differences."

"I did my share of rotten things. My brother really liked to build model cars. That was his big thing. I used to break them, on purpose. He was bigger than me and used to beat me up sometimes, so I paid him back like that."

"Huh," Barber said haughtily. "That's nothing."

"Once I put a bee in his piggybank."

"A bee?"

"Yeah. I caught it outside on the lilac bush and put it in his piggybank. A joke, I guess. Or maybe to pay him back for something. I forget. Anyways, he got stung on the eye and had to go to the hospital."

In the reflection in the window, he saw Barber dismiss that with a wave of his hand, like it didn't count. Tom found himself annoyed. He suddenly didn't like this Barber discounting the small cruelties he'd committed against his brother. It was strange but those cruelties seemed suddenly important somehow. They were now something that helped to define the brothers, helped to clarify his love for Gordy.

"He almost lost his damn eye. For a week he had this yellow pus coming out. And it was my fault. It was a lousy thing to do. There's probably others, too. Plenty. Why go on though?"

Barber didn't say anything for a while. Tom could hear his fingers tapping on the metal railing. Outside he could see the first snowflake, then another, and another—seeming to slip down through the net of darkness. Finally Barber spoke. "Tom, you're right. What you did *was* lousy. But you're here, ain't you. When the chips were down you showed up. That's what being brothers is all about."

Tom was silent, watching the snow fall.

"My brother! Christ, I could be on my deathbed and he wouldn't give two shits. Listen to this. A couple years back I'd had my first MI. I was going in for a triple by-pass. Not exactly a hernia repair. So I decided to bury the hatchet and give Buddy a call. I wasn't asking for a favor or money or anything. Not even sympathy. Just thought it might be nice to say a few things, you know, brother to fuckin' brother—just in case. Square things in case I never made it off the table. And you know what the sonovabitch says?"

"No," Tom replied.

"He says, 'What the fuck do you want from me. After what you did to your heart I'm supposed to feel sorry for you?' That's exactly what he said. The guy didn't care whether I lived or died. Now you'd never be like that. I can tell. No matter what happened in the past between you two, Gordy could book on you."

When Barber finished he just stared at the back of Tom's head, waiting. When Tom didn't say anything Barber said, "That's the only goddamn family I got in the world. You don't know how lucky you guys are you're close."

"I should be going," was all Tom said.

"You and me both," Barber said. "I'm breaking one of their rules by even being here."

A nurse came in then, a new one. She was around forty, with short brown hair and the don't-give-me-a-hard-time expression of someone who'd worked her share of evenings. She went over to his brother and checked his pulse, his blood pressure. She lifted up one eyelid, as you might a rock to see what squirmy thing was under it, and shined a narrow flashlight in his dark eye. Her movements were efficient, even brusque. She inspected the restraints to make sure they were snug. When she was done she made a couple of notes on his chart. Then to Barber she said, "*You* need to get back to your own room."

"Yeah, yeah. In a minute."

"No, now. Mr. Blakesley needs his rest."

"Personality plus, this one," Barber said in an undertone to Tom. "We'll be seeing you later. Have a safe ride home."

After Barber left, Tom took a seat near the window. He felt exhausted, his muscles aching way up in his shoulders. Maybe he was coming down with something. Maybe he was going to be sick and have to stay in bed for a while. He looked over at his brother. His hands tied, all in white. Ghostly. Gordy reminded him of someone being readied for a sacrifice. He pictured them wheeling him out in the morning, strapping him down on a stone slab, performing some irrevocable operation on him that would change his brother forever. Or maybe they'd send him to some terrible prison where real criminals resided, where small, pathetic Gordy would be eaten alive.

He thought, "I should be going." But he slumped farther down in his chair. Outside, he saw snow coming down hard now, dropping out of great big rips in the darkness above the lights. The flakes swirled wildly before landing, hesitant almost to touch down. Worn out, feeling that hard stone pressing down on his stomach, Tom allowed himself to close his eyes for just a moment—a brief rest before getting up to drive the two hours home. Images floated through his mind. He saw old times when he was just a child. In one image, which took place in the broad field that stretched to the highway behind their house, Gordy and he engaged in combat. It was winter, and the snow was deep with a thick crust on it like glass. His brother was on top of him, pressing down on his stomach, his knees pinning his shoulders. He was mashing the jagged snow into his face. Tom couldn't recall much of what had happened, why they were fighting, the details. But he could recall the metallic taste of blood in his mouth and the fact that he couldn't scream, could hardly breathe. Then somehow he was up, free, and running away from his tormentor, toward the safety of the house. But the snow sucked at his feet and he could hardly raise them, while from behind him he could hear Gordy laughing, gaining ground as the snow crunched under his boots. But just when Gordy was up to him, he flew on past Tom, toward home. Then Tom found himself behind, struggling as it had always seemed during childhood to catch up to his older brother, pumping his legs and crying, "Wait up, Gordy. Wait up, you dumb jerk." And the fear that he'd had of his brother catching him now changed to that of his leaving him behind, abandoning him out there in the cold white snowfield. The two of them running, his heart pounding, Gordy up ahead, crashing through the snow with Tom behind, trying to step in his brother's footsteps to make the running easier. Trying to catch up. Trying to be big like Gordy.

The plan—if you could call it that—was sitting fully formed in his mind when he opened his eyes and saw he was no longer in the snowfield, though his heart was still chugging with fear and with the effort to catch his brother. He got up from the chair and went over to Gordy's bed. His brother was still sleeping. Tom checked the door first, then loosened the restraints tying Gordy's hands to the bed. His brother stirred, opened his eyes.

"What? What's going on?" he asked.

"We're leaving," Tom whispered.

"Leaving? Where the hell we going?" Yet oddly enough, his brother didn't seem confused, seemed actually to be more with it than he'd been in a long, long time.

"I don't know. Just somewhere. We'll figure it out. Trust me, all right?"

"Trust you?" his brother said, smiling conspiratorially.

Tom wasn't so sure they would figure it out though. There were so many obstacles to overcome. Too many. Doors and locks and guards and rules. All against his plan. Then, if they were lucky enough, everything that remained once they got outside this place. No, the chances were against them. He wasn't sure at all about any of this, but he didn't want Gordy to see that he was afraid. That the chances of success were really quite slim. He was only sure of one thing: that they had to try.

# Three Whacks a Buck

It was 1962: the autumn of the phony missiles, a time of threat and counter-threat, of Kennedy and Khrushchev taking over our Philco. I was in sixth grade, and, as if we were practicing for a school play, it was a time of rehearsing for our own annihilation. Intoxicated by the prospect of sanctioned anarchy, we followed Miss Robleski's puffy brown ankles down into the grammar school's basement. There, facing the wall to protect against flying glass, we hoped something, *anything,* would happen, that the entire business was more than just another pointless fire drill. Could doom *really* be a possibility? Would the brick walls crumble, books and rulers landing in a fiery heap? Secretly you wished the adults would quit their blustering, their phony posturing, and really go through with it, just once. But it was only talk, you grew to realize. Just more talk. What adults said and what they did were two different things. The siren would fade to a ringing in your ear, and you'd head sullenly back up to your classroom, and to the growing conviction it was all just a complex game played by a surly Russian with a broad fat head, a man angry over the cocky good looks of our American president. Like two boys bluffing each other on the playground. Even Miss Robleski, a grim failure of an ex-nun, seemed disappointed and irritable. She terrorized us afterwards, whacking her ruler on desks, shaking Auggie Fournier silly for launching paper ICBMs across the room. The autumn of 1962.

But it was also the autumn of falling in love, and of recognizing that my parents had managed to fall out of it. Tony Falcone, a new boy in school, would stand next to me as we waited in the basement for the bombs. Tony, whose mother we'd heard was divorced, would pass me notes that said, "Want some gum" or "I heard Robleski fart," and I felt the first real tremors of passion rumbling, not in my chest but in my stomach, a feeling similar to what you felt going fifty over the bump on Mullen Road. And at home that fall, I came to understand that my parents were two very unhappy people, the way America and Russia were unhappy, and like them committed to harassing the other. I can't think of the missile crisis without picturing them: my mother with her sick headaches, my father at the kitchen table with a green bottle of Tangueray. I can't watch old clips of that comic Russian bear taking off his shoe and pounding it on the UN desk without seeing my father swinging that sledgehammer, or thinking of my mother's defeated face as she watched him.

Every year my parents took us girls—Peg, Wendy, and me—to the Eastern States Expo, a huge sprawling fair held each September in western Massachusetts. On a Saturday as broad and seamless as only childhood Saturdays can be, we'd spill out of the newly waxed Vista Cruiser, and my father would hand us each a single crisp dollar bill, its edge a razor-sharp metaphor of financial caution.

"Now try not to spend this on junk, ladies," he'd advise with that air of absurd formality he'd sometimes put on in front of our friends, to embarrass us we thought. It was the sort of gentlemanly condescension I both hated and secretly came to expect from the opposite sex.

"Oh, Daddy," I'd say. After all, it was *exactly* our intention to trade in our perfect buck for some of the fair's high-priced junk. As we passed through the gate, quickly getting beyond the dopey farm equipment and snowblowers, we greedily inhaled the aroma of cheap delights that canopied the fair-grounds. But after this bit of advice from my father, he'd leave us "ladies" alone and wander around by himself, looking at livestock and tractors and hay-bailing machines and God knows what else. He was a city boy now living in the suburbs, but somehow farm items struck a chord in him. He'd dole out a five to my mother, and they'd arrange to "rendezvous"—a movie-star word my mother loved to utter—at the bandstand green. "What say we rendezvous at the bandstand," she'd say, winking at my father, almost as if the plan were something illicit. Like good soldiers on a mission, they even set their watches.

Before getting a chance to fritter away our dollar, though, my mother would have her crack at trying to ruin the day. She'd drag us to free exhibits in the states' pavilions: a slide show, say, on the safe method of canning beans, or to a demo by a heavily jowled man who looked like Ed Sullivan, showing a new kitchen utensil that chopped potatoes ten different ways and saved valuable time for the happy homemaker.

"Pay attention, girls," my mother would say. "This is *your* future the nice man's talking about." As if our future was a vegetable we had to prepare carefully and skillfully, or risk a case of botulism or worse, a disappointed spouse. To my mother, a sound marriage was based in no small measure on kitchen success. Things like Tupperware containers and egg dicers, food blenders and Teflon pans helped ensure marital bliss.

*"Bor—ing,"* Peg groaned as an attractive blonde woman petted a futuristic side-by-side Amana that spit out cupfuls of ice at the push of a button. "Can we *go* now, Ma?"

"Just a minute, young lady," she'd say, gazing at the fridge the way she would her wedding album or Tyrone Power in an old movie. She'd stand there fondling an earlobe, a habit that showed a variety of emotions: anxiety if my father were late from work, nostalgia at weddings, a vague longing when she listened to Perry Como in the den and sipped a glass of Man O' Manoshevitz. It was longing now.

"Is it frost-free?" she might ask the woman.

"Of course," the blonde woman replied, offering a secretive woman-to-woman smile. "No more chiseling ice," she said in an undertone, as if she'd just passed on a tip to a younger sister about a padded bra.

"That would certainly be nice," said my mother, already picturing it in place of the slump-shouldered, whirring Norge at home, whose ice compartment my mother had to hack at with an uncharacteristic anger every few months. "Frost free."

Finally, we might be able to pry her away from an upright Electrolux with a power nozzle and drag her off to the glittering midway. The tattooed hawkers and carnie men made us think of escaped convicts: dark, wild-eyed, scary-looking creatures. More unfathomable even than those Russians, with their itchy trigger-fingers. Once, Peg and I let a man with a livid red scar over his cheek try to guess our weight for a prize. My mother and Wendy were getting something to eat, and as he eyeballed Peg's scrawny frame, he whispered to her that she had nice tits! Horrified, but also vaguely thrilled, we ran back to my mother but didn't dare tell her as she wouldn't have let us out of her sight. She'd warned of such men, men whose black and unknown desires were closer to those of wild boars than they were, say, to my father's.

At around noon we'd meet for lunch. We'd spread an army blanket on the grass near the bandstand, where they gave free concerts. The bands were never any good, just old men in Salvation Army-looking uniforms, who played the sort of frumpy wedding music that made my mother rub her earlobe and look retarded. But she made wonderful chicken salad sandwiches, and we liked to take off our new school shoes and rub our toes in the grass. She'd be handing out food, scolding Wendy for spilling her Kool-Aid, and generally praising the day for its thoughtfulness.

"We always have such nice weather for the fair," she said to no one in particular.

She used that word, *nice,* a lot. There were nice days, meals, trips, Christmases. There were nice girls, too. Things that moved her to comment were nice, unless of course they were not nice, like swearing and bad manners and those carnie men. And, of course, there were women who were not nice. Like Tony Falcone's mother, who had several "men friends," I'd heard my mother say to my father. My mother was a woman of no visible ambitions or daring passions, other than to make sure days like this were nice and ran without a hitch.

My father, who took a sort of distant and mostly financial interest in the family's affairs, was by all standards nice: a nice provider, a nice husband, a nice neighbor, one who mowed his lawn twice a week in summer and helped people jump-start their cars in winter, who belonged to the Rotary and the American Legion, who showed up for his girls' school plays, though he fell asleep halfway through, and who shaved every morning except Saturday, his rebellious day. A large, fleshy man, he'd sprawl out on the blanket after eating, his big belly straining the shirt buttons my mother was forever sewing back on, as if his bulk was constantly being corseted by her, held in check. He'd look up at the yellowing leaves overhead with an appraising eye, the way a botanist or a philosopher might.

"The jerks in personnel said I had only seven vacation days left," he offered.

"Well, you should call them, dear," my mother said without looking at him. "Lord knows, you deserve it. Wendy, get over your plate, please."

"Of course, I deserve it. That's not the point, Evelyn," he replied, still looking up at the leaves. "It's *their* job. They're supposed to know. That's what they get paid for."

"Everybody makes mistakes, dear."

"What's that supposed to mean?"

"Just that everybody makes mistakes. You want some more potato salad?"

"No, I *don't* want more potato salad," he replied crossly.

"Well, you don't have to get in a snit, for Pete's sake. All's I said was nobody's perfect. Let's not let it spoil such a nice day."

My father might snort. Then he'd proclaim, "What do you say? Let's get this show on the road." He often said that. After dinner out or at the end of vacation, he'd say, "Well, let's get this show on the road," as if we were a traveling road show ready to pack up and move out to our next venue.

After lunch, we'd wander around some more, this time with my father accompanying us, the comptroller of our funds the way he was for the machine tool company he worked for. We'd make a couple of quick passes through the horrid-smelling livestock buildings, to appease my father. When we'd complain, my mother would defend him (defending her husband was as much a part of her wifely duties as ironing his shirts or, say, providing him with "other" unmentionable services). "Your father would *like* to see them, girls. After the nice day he's treated us to, that's the least we can do."

"It's free, too," my father would add. "And you might learn something."

What he hoped the animals might teach us was never explained. They always looked stupid and somehow guilty of an offense, their heads bowed in mute shame as they waited for their sentence to be carried out. All except the pigs, whose jaunty ignorance was beyond shame. They'd stare out at us through remorseless eyes, slop dribbling from their blunt snouts, thoroughly enjoying what might be their last meal.

Later, we'd spend whatever money we had left (usually only Peg, the miser, had any) on trinkets or souvenirs. As evening collapsed like a dark tent, my parents would herd us slowly toward the gates. Before reaching them, though, we'd beg my father for just one more ride. One last fling before returning to our dull, normal lives. He'd give us a brief lecture on how money didn't grow on trees, how he had to haul his carcass out of bed each and every morning, rain or shine, to put food on the table. Then, feeling benevolent and generous, he'd finally hand us over enough for one last ride. We'd pick something memorable, something we'd still feel in the car on the way home: the double Ferris wheel or the Tilt-A-Whirl. Below, my parents gazed up into the sky—we could never be sure they saw us even though my mother waved. As I looked down at the two, I thought of them as a kind of safety net, that they'd be there to catch us if anything were to happen way up here. From where I sat, they appeared solid and steadfastly rooted to the ground.

Finally, our bellies full and our legs still jiggly from the ride, we'd pile into the Vista Cruiser, climbing into the way-back seat so you could face backward. Watching the fair vanish into the night, we'd head toward our nice, snug ranch house, arrogantly confident in our happiness as only puppies and children can be.

There were of course clues that everything wasn't quite so nice. My father sitting at the kitchen table, long after supper, staring at the ice cubes in his Scotch as if, in melting, they translated into some important message. Or my mother's "sick headaches," which didn't let her get out of bed all day—sometimes not even for days. We'd have to tiptoe around the house and speak in sign language. She'd come shuffling out of her room, pale, her eyes narrow cuts, red and painful looking as fish gills. And then there were the tight-lipped, guttural whisperings late at night in their bedroom. There were never really full-blown fights in our house. My parents didn't usually swear in front of us, and if they did it came out sounding more like a cough than a curse. They weren't pan-throwers or door-slammers or breakers-of-things. In fact, they said or did little in front of us to make us question their happiness. And we didn't. Not even when I heard things late at night, after Peg and Wendy were asleep in their room.

My father, who often worked late, would bang around the house as if my mother had secretly rearranged the furniture after he'd left for work. He drank, but except for Christmas parties and summer barbecues, he never got drunk, never grew loud and obnoxious or lost control the way Trudy Borrup's father did. When my father was drunk his eyes would focus on your Adam's apple. His breath smelling like lighter fluid, his eyes locked on my Adam's apple, he might tell me, "Bev, just remember one thing: you can always talk to the old man. All right?" I would nod, though we seldom talked.

One night I heard him come home. My mother, I knew, was sitting in the kitchen cutting out coupons from a magazine and arranging them by supermarket aisle in a metal box she had. For a long time neither spoke. Then my mother said, "What do you take me for?"

"What's that supposed to mean?"

"Do you think I'm a fool? How long?"

"What!"

"You heard me. How long?"

"Jesus Christ," he cried, louder than I'd ever heard him swear before.

Right after that I heard something break, pieces scurrying across the floor. Then silence. Later, I could hear my mother quietly sweeping up the fragments with the broom. The next day she drove into Hartford and went to G. Fox, a large department store, to replace the cup. It was part of a set she'd got for her wedding.

At school that year of the phony missiles, Tony Falcone joined our sixth-grade class. He was stunted and cute in the way a bulldog puppy is, which means he would've made a fairly homely man, with sad, droopy eyes, a bluish shadow of beard already across his cheek—and trouble tattooed on his forehead. Tony, or "The Falcon," as the other kids called him, had a special talent for getting into trouble. At least once a day Miss Robleski banished him to the corner, a place previously occupied by Auggie Fournier, or she packed him off to the principal's office. When we practiced our air-raid drills, Tony often stood next to me and, for my sole benefit it seemed, wrote funny, obscene things in chalk on the brick walls. "Robleski has a fat ass," he wrote once. She caught him, screamed at him, "Do you think this is a *joke,* young man? This could be the *end* of the world. Are you ready to meet your Maker?" Miss Robleski liked the thought of apocalypse, of one last shot at sainthood. The rumor was she'd fallen for a priest and had been drummed out of the nun corps.

Tony lived with his mother, a *divorcée,* a word which, in my mother's mouth, seemed to suggest something both distasteful and well deserved, like cirrhosis. As rumor had it, his father was either in prison, about to enter it, or just escaped from it. Despite all this, or possibly because of it, he was the first boy I allowed myself to grow silly over. He passed me love notes during lunch and wanted to go to the movies together. But when I asked my mother if I could, she cried, "Absolutely not, young lady! His father's a jailbird and his mother's . . . well . . . she's a *divorcée.*"

We went to the fair as always that year. This day Peg and Wendy went with my mother while I decided to follow my father. At twelve, I was at the age where I wanted to separate myself from my younger sisters, from their childish and uncomplicated fun. I held back, aloof, at once cynical and a little confused by that cynicism. Peg said it was because I was in love with Tony the Hood, another name they'd hung on him. But for whatever reason, this day I didn't want to tag along with them, so I went with my father, whose silent distance appealed to my own sudden need for privacy.

He and I wandered aimlessly around. We walked into exhibits neither of us cared to see. We listened vaguely to a Martian woman in an aluminum foil suit say what the clothes of the future would be like. We spent a quarter to take a look at Hitler's car, a sinister, gleaming black roadster that had a silly uniformed mannequin in the back seat. You were supposed to know it was Hitler because of the mustache. As we looked at it my father said, "That's not Hitler's car. Who're they trying to bullshit?"

"It's not? How can you tell?" I asked, but he didn't answer, just left the trailer where the car was and moved on.

We sat at a picnic table under a big yellow tent and ate hot dogs for lunch.

"How's the hot dog?" my father asked and I told him it was good. He asked me if I wanted another and I told him no. After that we didn't have much to say.

Later we made our way over to the buildings where the livestock was kept. Though I didn't want to go in, I went anyway. We walked from one squalid pen to another, staring in at blue-ribboned pigs and cows whose defeated eyes looked like those of death row inmates we'd seen in movies. As we looked in at a bloated Hereford steer, my father said, "Next week the stupid bastard'll be hamburg." Then he smiled at me, his eyes as sad and guilty-looking as those of the steer. "It's all a goddamned game, Bev. The whole business." I nodded, as though I understood, yet I felt terribly uncomfortable around him suddenly, as uncomfortable as if he'd begun to tell me about sex, as he had on one occasion. I wanted to get back to the others, to have things be like they were.

It was later than usual when we rendezvoused with them. My mother said she had one of her headaches and wanted to head home a little early. Wendy threw a tizzy-fit, but my mother stood her ground. I didn't care.

After eating, we moved in the general direction of the gates. My mother in front, followed by a grumbling Peg and Wendy, then me, with my father bringing up the rear. As always, before we actually got to the gates, my sisters pleaded for one more ride.

"No, girls. My head is splitting," my mother said.

"Please. Pretty please," my sisters begged.

My father, however, was already taking out some money and handing it to Peg.

"Richard," she said sternly. "I *want* to go."

"One more ride's not going to break us. I'm the one who has to bust his tail to make it." Then he turned to me and asked, "What about you, Bev?"

I hesitated for a moment, then quickly decided to go along. I didn't want to be left on the ground with them. We got on and shot way up to the top, where we stopped to let other people on. Peg made our seat teeter so it scared Wendy.

"Cut it out, you jerk," Wendy said.

"Baby," teased Peg.

"Look," I said. "There they are."

"They don't see us," Wendy said.

"They're not even looking up. Up here," Peg yelled.

My parents were standing off by themselves and they weren't looking at us. They were doing something in place of talking. My father, red-faced, was waving his arms up and down, flapping them like a thick-bodied, flightless bird. My mother gestured with one hand very close to his face, as if she were trying to hypnotize him.

"What's the matter with them?" Wendy asked, still innocent.

"They're both acting retardo," Peg said. "I betcha it's about Dad's job."

"How do you know?" Wendy asked.

"I heard them talking. How he might have to go somewhere else."

"Will we have Christmas presents?" Wendy said.

I didn't say anything. I looked off toward the west and could see the sun, a fat blood blister about to rupture. I thought about how the sky would look from up here if one of those bombs hit, the mushroom rising white, then red, then black into the sky. I thought of Tony, too. His pretty yet sad eyes. How he never seemed to care that he got in trouble, how he'd probably end up like one of those carnie men, or worse, like his father. And I thought, too, dangling up there in that fragile seat, about the nature of love. I already knew enough about its unpredictableness to realize things didn't always turn out right despite its presence, in fact, how things often went wrong exactly because of it. Not for Miss Robleski. Not for my mother and father. Not for Mrs. Falcone and her husband. I pictured myself married to Tony Falcone and waiting for him to get out of prison, sending him love letters, knitting him sweaters, baking him things and going to visit him. A martyr, I would be, savoring as young girls do the sweetness of doomed love. At the top of that Ferris wheel it was as if I could suddenly see all of my life, all that was waiting out there for me, and I would only have to step into that life, put it on like a coat and button it up.

Then the Ferris wheel started up again and spun us in a frantic circle. I felt my stomach drop out of me, and I couldn't decide whether it was from the ride or from thinking of Tony. For long moments we couldn't even see our parents down below, just a blur of movement and color. I closed my eyes, felt dizzy and nearly sick.

By the time we got off, my parents had stopped whatever it was they'd been talking about. My mother was pale and had the frustrated look of someone who has to sneeze and can't, while my father's face was flushed, like he'd just bent over to lace his shoes. We knew something was up. Without a word we continued toward the parking lot. When Wendy asked for some popcorn, I shot her a look and she quickly got the message too.

Near the gates was an open lot, trampled bare, dusty as the cattle drives in *Rawhide.* It was empty except for a single car. But it wasn't a regular car. It looked like a bomb had fallen on it. Or actually, it looked like it'd been used as a bomb, as if it had been dropped from the sky. All the windows were shattered, the shards of glass strewn over the bare ground like green ice. The roof and hood and all the doors had been viciously caved in. You couldn't even tell what make it was anymore.

The oddest thing, though, was the small misshapen man who stood beside the car. He wasn't quite a dwarf, but he was very small with a large head and something terribly wrong with his back. Another carnie man, like the hawkers on the midway, only this one was ancient. He held a sledgehammer, and a sign nearby said, "Three Whacks a Buck."

We were passing the shattered car when my mother stopped and waited for my father to catch up.

"Why?" she asked when he got close. "I deserve that much at least."

"Not here, Evelyn. For Christ's sakes," my father replied.

"Yes, here. Right now."

"You're a fool. You know that?"

"A fool!" she cried. "For marrying a bastard like you, I am."

We stood and stared at them, amazed. It was the sort of quiet like after you've thrown a firecracker and you're waiting for it to go off, half-thinking it's only a dud but afraid to go near it. And then . . . *bam!* As they stood there it occurred to me exactly what was wrong, what had been wrong all along: they hated each other. Bitterly, passionately. It was as simple as that. I could only wonder why I hadn't noticed it before.

After a few seconds, my mother regained her composure. Turning to us she said, "All right, girls. Let's go. It's been a long day."

"What's the matter with you guys?" Peg asked.

"Nothing's the matter," my mother replied, lightly, her voice fluttering as she gathered us together under her protective wing.

"Why's Daddy mad then?"

"Nobody's mad. We're all just a little tired. How about hamburgers and scalloped potatoes, for a special treat tonight?"

I'm sure my mother still wanted to believe we were all just a little tired. That a nice meal would fix everything. Then, incredibly, she turned to my father and, without a trace of anger or sarcasm, said, "Dear, we're ready." Even I could see how preposterous her attempt was.

My father glared at her for a moment, seemed about to go along with the game. But right then the little man with the crooked back called to him.

"Hey, buddy. Three whacks. Only a buck." The man winked and smiled lewdly at my father, conspiratorially, as if he were offering some unmentionable vice. It was in some way the same sort of shared-understanding smile the fridge woman had once given my mother.

"Richard," my mother said, "we're going now."

But my father was walking toward the car, fishing in his pocket for one of those crisp, hard-earned bucks. He paid the man, picked up the sledgehammer, and headed over to the car.

*"Richard!"* she called again, her voice full of fear, of desperation. "For heaven's sakes. What are you doing?"

He didn't seem to hear her. He carefully looked the car over for an unblemished spot, one meant for him. He even touched the car with his hand, feeling for the right spot.

"Give 'er hell, buddy," the man goaded him on. "Get good and mad. Put your weight behind it." He was making fun of my father but my father didn't seem to care.

He set his jaw and raised the hammer over his head. He was a large, heavy, red-faced man wearing a white dress shirt. He looked odd and out of place. He paused for a second—or at least it would always *seem* that he paused, as if still contemplating not going through with it, still weighing the consequences. It'd be years before we learned, in bits and pieces, of his affair with a woman at the tool company, and years more before he actually left my mother, though not for the other woman. But it was in that brief moment of hesitation that he knew, and we knew, and certainly my mother knew, despite her pretense to the contrary, that all was lost, that nothing would ever be the same again. Some time later, as I stood in the school basement waiting for a violence that would never happen, I'd remember the moment just before he swung, and not the crash of the hammer hitting metal, the shattering of glass, the terrible, funny look on my father's face as he raised the hammer again and again, until the little old man told him he only got three whacks for a buck.

A little before Christmas that year, Tony Falcone and his mother moved out of town. The story was they were moving back to live with his father, who, it turned out, wasn't in prison at all, but worked on an oil rig outside of a place called Pig Root, Wyoming. I remember the address because of the letters I sent there. Pig Root. Tony kissed me finally during an air-raid drill, and before he left he promised he would write. I wrote every week. I waited. I watched the mailbox. He never wrote, but then again I can't say I was really surprised. I had already known that about love anyway.

# Instincts

They haven't mentioned her all day, not once. Not on the drive down and not here at the zoo. I wonder if that's a good sign. I'm to the point where I read into every little thing: always trying to second-guess what they're thinking, play the shrink. Take a few days ago, for instance. Robin, my older daughter, had one of those mother-daughter lunches at school. The kids made all the food, decorated the cafeteria with a banner that said "Welcome, Moms." I was the only father. I stuck out like a sore thumb. Robin didn't say a word all during lunch and I wasn't so sure she even wanted me there. I wondered if she was embarrassed. When I was out in the hall I looked back to see Robin giggling with her friends.

"How come their butts are like that?" asks my younger daughter, Crystal, seven.

"Like what?" I say, though, of course, I know exactly what she means.

"All mushy and pink."

We're sitting on a bench near the chimp enclosure and eating baloney sandwiches so dry they hurt going down. (Robin reminded me: "Next time, Dad, don't forget the mayo?") It's one of those temperamental days in March. Aimless clouds, like bored children, stir up trouble: they wander into the sun's path, turning it downright chilly. An occasional gust of late-winter wind sends our potato chips flying to the ground where a pair of obese mallards wait to pounce on them. Across a moat from us, a pair of chimps huddle together against the cold, their hairy arms encircling each other. Though I'm no Marlin Perkins, I think one of them—a female, by the looks of it—must be in estrus since her behind is, as my daughter noted, pink and swollen.

"Mushy?" Robin laughs, staring at me with a nine-year-old's look of patronizing disbelief. "They're girls. That's their girl parts."

If Jennifer were here, she'd insist Robin use the right term. She'd give me hell if I said things like *girl-parts, boobies, bum-bum, pee-pee.* She used to say kids were tougher and smarter than adults ever gave them credit for. It was just a matter of finding the best way of saying it, the right words. She hated the way the people were always patronizing kids. When she'd go into the hospital, I'd be the one to explain to the girls she was just going in for a little rest, that she needed some peace and quiet. But Jennifer would give it to them straight, which I thought was crazy. What's the right way of explaining depression to a seven-year-old?

"Is it, Dad?" Crystal asks. "Is that really their privates?"

"Yes, sweetie. They're girl chimps. Some anyway."

"See," Robin taunts.

"They're in heat," I explain, frowning at Robin. "I think they are anyway." All I know about animals is what I pick up on the Discovery channel late at night when I can't sleep. Which is most nights. The other night, for instance, I learned that swans mate for life. That if one dies the other will often pine away and die of a broken heart. Or that scientists think that pilot whales run themselves aground because of a malfunction in their ears, and not because they are bent on self-destruction.

"But it's cold out," Crystal reasons.

"Not that kind of heat."

I wonder how to explain this without making it into a complex biology lesson. There'll be plenty of time for that later, when they're older. I picture a moment somewhere down the line. I'll take them aside and explain whatever they want to know, calmly and thoroughly. I'll explain the facts of life. I'll tell them about nature. About life and sex. And about death, too. In the meantime, I make a mental note to pick up a book on teaching kids about reproduction. One with lots of pictures.

"Heat for making babies," I explain.

"Something to do with keeping the eggs warm. Right, Dad?" offers Robin.

"That's pretty close," I say.

"They lay eggs?" Crystal asks, her sandwich poised in front of her gaping mouth. "You mean like ducks?"

"Not *regular* eggs," Robin lectures. "Inside eggs. And the boy chimps have little fishies swimming around. And when two chimps love each other very, very much, the boy chimp . . . "

"Let's finish up," I say, hoping to cut this short. Crystal, however, screws up her small face and won't be put off so easily. She's hunting for some answers. "They have eggs inside them?"

"You do too, silly," Robin says.

Crystal turns to me. "Do I, Dad? Do I have *eggs?"*

"Well . . . yes. Sort of."

"And you'll have periods when you get bigger," Robin throws in.

"What's a period?" she asks me.

*Jesus,* I think. Not today.

"It's when girls . . . " I begin and then pause, hoping the right word will just appear. When it doesn't I say, "It's when they begin to . . . mature."

"You mean get wrinkles?"

"No, not wrinkles," I say. "You know . . . to develop. To start having to wear a bra. You remember we talked about that. We *did* talk about that."

"So having a period is when you start wearing a bra?"

Robin laughs out loud and I shoot her a look. "No. It's when you begin to menstruate."

"Men what?"

"Menstruate. To . . . bleed." And as soon as I say this I know I'm in up to my elbows. I quickly add, "But not till you're older. So don't worry about it now."

"Bleed?" she asks. "Where?"

"From . . ."

"From your vagina, dodobrain," Robin interrupts. "Boy, don't you know *anything?"*

Crystal stares from her sister to me in disbelief. "Get out. Who told you that?"

Robin is about to say, which of course would spoil everything, would bring the day crashing down on our heads.

Because, of course, it was Jennifer who told her. But smart girl that she is, she senses this, too, glances at me and says only, "I just know, is all."

"You're lying," Crystal says. But she suspects this secret is too odd, too intricate and mysterious, to be anything but the truth. And she also suspects just who gave this secret to her sister.

"It's true."

"Liar," Crystal yells, as if by sheer force of will she can keep adult mysteries at bay—at least for the time being.

"You don't know anything," taunts Robin.

The two go back and forth like this until Crystal's voice cracks and tears literally jump from her light-blue eyes. It amazes me how much and how quickly she can turn them on, as if something actually ruptured inside, like a water pipe. And lately she cries over every little thing. If her shoestring breaks in the morning as she's getting ready for Mrs. Kleckner, the woman who gets her on the bus in the morning, she cries. At night she cries because of rats under her bed—the sort she saw in *Lady and the Tramp*. Sometimes she crawls into Jennifer's side and falls asleep. In the morning, I feel this odd heat emanating from over there. I put my hand out and touch warm skin. It throws me for a loop. It takes me a moment to remember how things stand. In two days, it'll be eleven months ago that on a bright spring day just after she'd planted bulbs in the front yard, Jennifer went out into the garage, started up the Buick, put Vivaldi's *Four Seasons* on, and, without moving an inch, left us forever. Since then Crystal, previously an independent kid, has turned into a needy and whining crybaby; on the other hand, Robin, who used to be a protective big sister, has become a taunting bully. The two of them, so close before, are always at each other. Always vying for my attention.

"Robin, apologize to your sister," I say.

"She started it, the little brat."

"I did not," Crystal counters. "You fat pig."

"Geek."

"Knock it off. Both of you. Or we'll go home. This was supposed to be fun."

An old guy in a zoo uniform approaches, hooking garbage with this long clawlike thing. He looks over at me and winks. He has gray eyebrows puffy as dandelions. Blow on them and they'd scatter.

"It gets worse," he says.

"That's good to know," I say, wishing he'd stick to picking up garbage.

"I got four. These are the easy years."

"The easy years?" I ask.

"Sure. Before the hormones kick in. Then watch out. You'll be flying without a rudder then." I feel rudderless now, drifting, floating without direction. The old guy hooks a napkin that got away from us, sticks it in a bag attached to his waist. "By the time things level out again," he adds, "they'll have flown the coop and you'll thank your lucky stars for it. So enjoy 'em while you can."

The easy years, I think. Enjoy 'em while I can.

"I wish she was dead!" Crystal spits at her sister.

"Don't say something you don't mean," I say.

"I *do.* I mean it."

"No you don't. Now stop it this minute, young lady."

I glance over at her, knitting my brows. But she can be stubborn as a mule when she wants to.

"I do," she says. "I wish she was dead. D-E-A-D. Dead."

"So," Robin retaliates. "I wish you were dead."

"Ladies," I say, trying to intervene. "I'm warning both of you."

"I wish it was *her,"* Crystal says. She doesn't have to say anymore, doesn't have to add *instead of.* We all know what she means.

The guy picking up garbage smiles at me, shoots me a look that says, "Good luck, pal. You'll need it." Even some of the chimps across the moat seem to be watching me, their black eyes gleaming. They look sober and formal, like judges.

I guess I'd counted on this day a little too much. I banked on it making something click in our lives. I kept them out of school, told Mrs. Kleckner I wouldn't be bringing Crystal, and took a day off from work. I own my own company, a landscaping business, so I can do that. Besides, March isn't that busy. Just putting down some lime and fertilizer, raking up oak leaves that had dropped since the fall. I packed us a lunch, bought boxes of fruit juice, chips, cupcakes, apples, and we drove down into the city. I wanted things to be perfect. A change of scenery, I thought, would do us all a world of good. Despite Mrs. Kleckner's occasional help and that of a cleaning lady who comes in once a week, the house is always chaotic, depressing because it hints at incompleteness, at lives that have been put on hold far too long. Our lives have that suspended feel of people who are about to move, who have their things packed in boxes and are between homes, who act tentatively, just getting through to the next day because this is not their *real* life, just a temporary one they happen to find themselves in. Tomorrow, next week, next month—that's when we'll be in our real home and we can start to live once again. For the longest time we've been eating on paper plates to simplify things, many times right out of the greasy wrappers of fast-food places. We try not to dirty dishes, try to remain light and mobile for the big change that's surely about to come. We feel packed and ready. Yet nothing changes and each day finds us in the same place as the day before.

The trip, I'd hoped, would make that sort of click in our lives, when things fell in place and everything that was once so cluttered and confusing became clear. You know the sort of click I'm talking about: when you can see the hidden fish in the tree, or when the name of a song you'd been humming to yourself for days just pops into your mind. And for a while today things did go smoothly. On the drive down we played the silly song game. Jennifer had made it up. Someone says a word, any word, the sillier the better, like *orangutan,* and somebody else has to make up a song about it. We stopped for doughnuts and hot chocolate. When we got here we found the zoo almost deserted. It was ours, the animals like our own personal pets. No long lines, no fighting for a bench or a spot from which to view the tigers. We saw the polar bears and the big cats and a giraffe that Robin thought looked like my Uncle Danny, who has a long neck and large, dull-looking eyes. In the tropical rain forest we saw a black leopard sitting motionless on a tree limb just inches away on the other side of the glass partition. The girls stared at it, didn't want to leave. They spoke to it, waved at it, made faces at the animal, trying to get it to move. They even gave it a name: Marv. Marvelous Marv the Leopard. The thing finally condescended to yawn at them, sleepy-eyed and content. A big, dumb kitty. It was so warm and cozy in there, the moist air smelling like fertilizer or peat moss, rich with potential. The day was turning out good, exactly the way I had hoped for.

But then came the chimps. That's when things turned sour. They made me think of grim old judges sitting in their enclosure, black-coated, reserved, with their stern yet comical expressions. I could feel the rich potential of the day slipping away, could feel myself losing control of it. I can remember Jennifer explaining—trying to anyway—how that would happen to her sometimes: how things would just suddenly start to slip away from her and she'd feel this panicky loss of control; how everything—the mailman being late, a run in her stocking, a gray hair—would begin to overwhelm her and she would feel very small and at their mercy. A leaf, Jack, she would say to me. A goddamn leaf being blown all around.

To make up for the fight, Robin crams the rest of her dry sandwich into her mouth and tries not to gag. Then she gathers up the rest of her things and stuffs them all into the backpack. She looks at me and says, "You done, Dad?" I nod, and she says, "It wasn't so bad. Just a little dry." Her look is sweet and patronizing, and my heart just aches for loving her. She picks up the remains of my sandwich, walks a few feet away, and begins throwing crumbs to the ducks.

Crystal sits at the far end of the bench, her knees pulled up to her chest, her arms wrapped around them and her head buried. Curled tight as a woolly bear on a cold day. Once she peeks out from under an arm, but she sees me looking at her and stubbornly won't return my gaze. She's filled with anger. All of her fifty-one pounds, from her lemony-blonde hair down to her black high-top sneakers—all of it is angry. With her mother, for leaving her and not telling her secrets she'll need to know. With her sister for knowing things she doesn't. With the chimps for having pink behinds and starting all of this. And of course, with me, too, for not being straight with her about how sick Jennifer was. I didn't know myself though. I don't think anybody did, not her doctors, not her friends. Maybe not even Jennifer herself, not until she washed the dirt off her hands, got in the car, and turned the ignition on. Probably not till that moment. Otherwise, why would she have planted those bulbs if she knew she wasn't going to be around to see them flower?

For weeks afterwards neither Robin nor Crystal said a word about their mother's death. When I'd try to talk to them they'd glance at each other and one of them would say, "OK, Dad. OK." They didn't want to talk about it. So I thought, fine. They needed time to digest it. It was just too overwhelming for them. Then one night I was tucking Crystal in bed. Out of the blue she asked, "Why did she do it?"

"She was depressed. Unhappy."

"Why?"

"I'm not sure, sweetie."

"Was it on account of us?"

"No, it wasn't us. I'm sure of that. She loved you and your sister very much. It was just something . . . I don't know. Something she had wrong in her head."

"Couldn't the doctors fix it? "

"They tried. It didn't work."

She sucked on her thumb, thinking for a moment. Then she took her thumb out of her mouth and said something that shocked me. "I hate her."

"What?"

"For leaving us. I hate her."

"Don't say that."

"I do. I hate her. If she loved us she wouldn't have left."

"She couldn't help it, sweetie."

"But she did it herself."

"She couldn't help it," I repeated.

"Yes, she could. She could have."

"What would you like to do now?" I ask Crystal.

She touches her shoulders to her ears, sits there huddled against the sudden chill of the March day. She has on only a light jacket. I should have made her wear something warmer. I ask if she's cold, could use the extra sweater I stuffed in the backpack.

"I don't want anything—*from you,"* she hisses at me.

"Lookit, Dad," Robin calls. She's standing by the fence near the chimp enclosure, leaning way over.

"Don't get too close," I caution.

"Don't worry. Look!"

I get up and walk over. Down below, a female chimp sits in the long grass. In her big hairy paw is a doll. The doll is almost bald, just a few frizzy clumps of dull yellow hair remain on its shiny plastic skull. The chimp cradles the doll against her chest, almost as if she's nursing it.

"What's she doing?" Robin asks.

"I don't know. Playing, I guess."

"Like a person," she says.

I nod.

"Would she hurt you, Dad? If you fell in?"

"I don't know. Maybe. She's a wild animal."

"She doesn't look wild."

The chimp shifts the doll from one arm to the other. Occasionally, she'll look down at it, a profoundly human expression on her ancient wizened face. Somehow the expression reminds me of the way Jennifer used to look at the girls, after a late-night feeding. From bed, watching them in the rocker, I felt myself at the periphery of a great secret the two of them shared. Something I might be allowed momentary glimpses of, even to share in second-hand, but whose essence would remain forever out of my reach. A mystery from which

I was excluded. Watching the chimp and doll together, I feel the cold wind cut painfully across my eyes.

Robin's hand slides into my coat pocket. *"Brrr."*

"You cold?"

"A little. Dad?" she asks, looking up at me.

"Yes?"

"Do animals ever do that?"

"Do what?"

"Kill themselves?"

The question, like many of the things she says lately, takes me by surprise. One late night about a week ago, she came into the kitchen. I had a glass of Dewar's in front of me. She stood there silently in the doorway for a moment. Then she said, "Can somebody die if they drink too much?"

Robin stares up at me, waiting for an answer.

"No, I don't think so. Not on purpose anyway."

"But if we're smarter than they are, how come people do?"

"It's not a matter of being smart, Robin. It's about the way people feel. You can't control that. Animals go more by instinct."

"Like ducks flying south?"

"Yes. Animals have an instinct to survive."

"And people don't?"

"No. Usually they do. It's just that sometimes something gets screwed up. And instead of wanting to live they want to die."

"Like with Mom?"

"Yes."

"I'll never do that. No matter what."

"Of course not."

"I'll never leave you and Crystal."

"Thanks," I say.

"Dad. I'm sorry about before. About making Crystal cry."

"I know." I glance over my shoulder at Crystal, who peeks out at me from beneath her arm and then ducks back inside her fortress of anger.

"She misses her," Robin says.

"We all miss her."

"Will it ever be regular again?"

"Regular?"

"You know. Like it was. Before."

"Sure," I say, but too quickly, too flippantly, the patent answer an adult will dismiss a child with.

"No, I mean *really*. I'm a big girl now. Tell me the truth."

Just then a young male chimp comes up and grabs the doll away from the female and runs away. She takes off after the thief, howling and baring her teeth. Suddenly she looks terrifying, a pygmy King Kong after Faye Wray. Seeing she means business, the male finally drops the doll and the female picks it up and goes over to the corner of the enclosure. She huddles protectively around the doll.

"I hope so, hon," I say. "I sure hope so."

"We'll do the best we can, right Dad?" Robin says.

"Right."

I go back over to the bench and pick up our stuff. "You ready, Crystal?"

She gets up without a word and starts walking ahead of us.

The afternoon has made up its mind finally to stay cloudy. It gets cold enough that snowflakes wouldn't come as a surprise. The big cats, which had earlier been sunning themselves outside on the concrete of their enclosure, have all gone inside. The musk oxen, however, stand with their sheepdog faces into the wind, enjoying this last bit of cold. As we head toward the gates I think about Robin's question: *Will it ever be regular again?* Regular for me meant getting up every morning and not having to think twice about each move. Just letting the momentum carry you along. But it's hard even to picture that life anymore. It's like trying to picture what that ape was thinking about back there, the one holding the doll. Or what Jennifer had in mind when she sat in the garage with the engine running. A mystery.

Robin clutches my hand, while Crystal shuffles along ahead. Her neck is scrunched down into her shoulders against the cold but she'll tough it out rather than ask for her sweater. And that toughness will have to serve her well.

We're passing a concession stand, the last before the exit. The smell of grease and coffee suddenly warms me. Crystal, ten yards ahead, stops in her tracks and turns. She stands there waiting for us, looking as menacing as a wolverine, and I can only wonder what's up. I imagine another confrontation.

"What's the matter, Crystal?" I ask.

She has her hands planted squarely on her narrow hips. Her head's level so her eyes are tipped way back in the sockets, almost lost under the brows. She looks pretty formidable, almost scary. God help the guy she marries.

"I'm still hungry," she says.

"You're hungry? Is that all?"

"*Very* hungry."

"I think we can handle that. How about a hot dog?"

"Yeah. And french fries," she bargains.

"Me, too, Dad," says Robin. "I'm still a little hungry."

"What's the matter, you guys didn't like my sandwiches?"

"They were good," Robin offers. "Just next time, remember the mayo, Dad."

"They were kinda dry," Crystal says.

"Kinda dry, huh?"

"Very dry." Then, gaining confidence, she screws up her face and adds, "If you want the truth, Dad, they were gross."

"You're saying my sandwiches were gross?"

"Wicked gross, Dad," Robin chimes in.

"Barf city," Crystal says, breaking a smile.

"All right. I get the point."

While we're waiting for our order, Robin says she has to go to the bathroom. I ask her to bring her sister, but Crystal says she doesn't have to.

As soon as Robin's gone, Crystal looks at me. "How come she didn't tell me . . . you know . . . about the eggs?"

"She probably thought you weren't ready yet, honey. She would have, believe me. She would have told you everything you needed to know."

Crystal sucks on the collar of her jacket, mulling this over. Then she asks, "Who's going to tell me all that stuff now?"

"I will."

"Everything? Even the gross parts?"

"Everything. I promise," I say. "OK?"

She chews on that one for a moment, then nods.

Robin comes back out and we take our food over and sit at a table. The girls are hungry and tear into their food, and I can't honestly say anything has ever tasted much better. The girls exchange looks and start giggling.

"What?" I ask.

But Robin says, "Don't be so nosy, Dad," and smiles conspiratorially at her sister.

I picture them years from now, as teenagers, sharing secrets about dates and boyfriends. Private things. Excluding me, or maybe telling me just a little, things they might have shared with Jennifer. And I'll look back and recall a moment like this: a cold day at the zoo eating hot dogs. Or maybe in the mall feeling silly as I help them look for their first training bra. Or making sandwiches and not forgetting the mayo. Some small insignificant thing. Though I probably won't have recognized it at the time for what it was. The moment when we hungrily, desperately tore into our new life.

# The Cardiologist's House

The past two nights Frank Pierce has been parking his car in Ginger's garage. Even in the dark, I know it's his. A patent-leather-black Porsché Carerra (he got it used but you're still talking a second mortgage). One of those lacy garters dangling from the rearview mirror, and, though it's too far to make out, a license plate I know which says "Coach." I'd seen the car enough times in the high school parking lot. I don't know if Pierce has his own garage door opener or if they've worked out some sort of signal. Perhaps he calls from the Dairy Mart down the street, or maybe he drives by once and blinks his lights to let her know he's arrived. But on cue the door lifts to receive his car and then quickly closes behind it like something out of *The Arabian Nights*. You'd have to be watching to catch it, the whole business is that slick. Later, sometimes midnight or one in the morning, I'll hear the garage door open, the car ease stealthily out, the powerful engine uncharacteristically restrained. Pierce, a married man with kids, on whose coach's salary he couldn't possibly afford both the sports car and child support, doesn't turn the headlights on until he's safely away.

Ginger's house is directly across the street, the old Schaub place, a family I delivered newspapers to half a century ago. I can still remember Charlie Schaub, the old German in his sleeveless T-shirt and suspenders, the day I handed him the paper that said, "Germany Invades Poland." He just stared at it for a while, then wagged his large head and said, "Gott im Himmel—those gottdamn Polacks, Vaslee." That's what he called me—Vaslee. He couldn't say Wesley. Up until a year ago when I retired, I'd pull into Ginger's driveway in the morning to pick her up, and we'd ride to school together. I used to be the chair of the social science department at the high school, where Ginger teaches French and Spanish.

Sometimes in the morning I'd brush up on my French with her. *"Tu* is the familiar, not *vous,* Wes," she'd correct, as if I were one of her sleepy-eyed sophomores. I marveled at the way her mouth would turn pouty as she said *"tu."*

I'm witness to my neighbor's private life because I have time on my hands, and like all people with time on their hands I make other people's business my own. You look at most of the great travesties in history and nine times out of ten it's some guy with an army and nothing to do. Most nights I'm up late anyway. The den window looks right out onto the street. Ours is not a busy neighborhood and what cars do go by at one in the morning, especially those with their lights out, you tend to notice. What I do when I can't sleep is work on my houses. I build dollhouses, a diversion that has turned into a direction. It started as a hobby while I was getting back on my feet after my first MI a few years back but has, inexplicably and ironically, turned profitable. My wife Mel has suggested I take out an ad in *The Reminder,* go to the craft fairs, think bigger, come up with a catchy name for my "business." She's not so much concerned about the money as she is with seeing that I stay busy, which she's big on. But even without advertising, people are always calling to order houses for their daughters. Dentists, opthamologists, lawyers, real estate agents wanting them for their offices. They're willing to pay several hundred dollars for my work. Right now I'm building a house for one of the doctors in my cardiologist's group. It's a fourteen-room Queen Anne he picked out of a catalogue I showed him. A thousand bucks! A product of the Depression, I find my head swimming by such sums—for a dollhouse. I'm behind schedule and the heart fellow calls me almost daily asking if it's going to be ready for his daughter's birthday party, now less than a week away.

I often have three or four houses in various stages of completion—Tudors, salt boxes, colonials, though Victs, as we call them in the biz, are by far the most popular. People like harboring the illusion that life was once that ornate and formal, that leisurely. The houses are spread out all over the place, in the living room, the den, the dining room. Mel, who is neat to a fault, still hasn't gotten used to the chaos: the small cans of paint, the slivers of wood and fish scales of glue that lie everywhere. The disorder of children, even though we are childless and never had to put up with toys underfoot. But while the mess upsets her, she allows me this one vice. It keeps me—and I can just picture her saying this to the people in the tax collector's office where she works—out of mischief, as if I were one of my bored ex-students who needs to be kept from the frightening abyss of his own idle brain. She is, of course, right, probably more so than she can even imagine. I'm sure she secretly feared the early retirement my health had forced upon me—my ending up the cardiac cripple that Dr. Rivera spoke of. Or worse. I think she envisioned coming home one afternoon and calling out, like she always does, "Home from the tax wars," only to find me already stiff in the Barca Lounger, a copy of Dr. Johnson's *Lives* spread over my still chest.

Before I tell you anything else, I guess I ought to give you the scoop on one Wesley Alexander McNulty: Mac to most people, Wes to a few close friends, Vaslee to old man Schaub when he was alive. I've lived in this small New England town of Wessex (Wessex and Wesley—I've always liked the connection between the two) for all but two of my sixty-one-years, those two being spent as a radioman in Korea. I'm an ex-high school history teacher with a house full of unfinished houses, a backyard full of moles, and a heart that refuses to feed itself blood anymore. A little more than a year ago as I was pulling lunchroom duty at school, I had my second MI. My first, a year before that, though it scared the hell out of me, was barely enough to get a rise out of my doctor, a pretty tough cookie. This one, on the other hand, had eternity written all over it. It was as dramatic as one of those small crop-duster planes dragging a message behind it, but instead of "Get a Good Deal at Balch Pontiac" the message said, "Adios, Wes." I was breaking up a fight between two football players when I felt this bolt running through my sternum. It seemed as if some joker from shop class was behind me tightening the bolt with a ratchet, torquing the thing down so I couldn't suck in any air. I ended up sitting on the cafeteria floor with the two kids who'd been fighting looking down at me, confused, the way a pair of boxers would be if the ref went down. It was Frank Pierce, "Coach," who bent over me. "Jesus, Mac," he said. "You ain't going to make me do mouth-to-mouth, are you? Not here?" He was only partly joking. He didn't want to put his lips to mine, not in front of all his players. What I considered then to be my last mortal thought was this man who smelled like a pair of old sneakers blowing his beer breath into my lungs. That was enough to engender in me the ole fighting spirit, enough at least to send the Grim Reaper packing yet once more.

I was in intensive care for a week and at least once, I was later told, my heart had stopped and it looked as if my ticket had been punched yet again. (The closest I came to one of those out-of-body experiences was a dream of my father trying to get a homemade plane to fly.) My cardiologist, Dr. Rivera, isn't putting even money on me to pull it out a third time, however. Rivera, who has the unblinking eyes of a pigeon looking for food, instructed me on how the heart works—or in my case, doesn't.

"Think of it as a sump pump, Mr. McNulty," he explained as if I had no more than a wet basement problem. To help me understand he used a plastic toy model he keeps on his desk. The heart opened up like a lover's locket so you could see all the small, secret chambers and tubes inside. The sweeping yellows and reds and purples looked like the variegated empires on a map of fifth-century Europe. "See this. Coronary artery. And these five little ones. They're the problem." They branched off like the invasion routes of the Huns, Ostrogoths, and Lombards. He went through their names—right coronary, left anterior descending, circumflex artery. He didn't expect me to remember, of course, even though I did and surprised him next visit by reciting all five. What, after all, is history but names in motion, flowing like the blood in an artery or clogged up in battles and sieges? The Berlin Wall was little more than a blood clot; the Bolshevik Revolution, a major hemorrhage. He told me I had three that were nearly fifty percent occluded, but said in my shape I wasn't a good candidate for by-pass. Rivera, not one to mince words, said he doubted if he'd get me off the table and he hated what that would do to his batting average. He told me I could get a second opinion if I wanted. Said I could probably find somebody that was, as he put it, "quick with the knife."

"But you walk the straight and narrow, Mr. McNulty," he said, "and I think we can buy you some time. Some *quality* time."

So I walked the straight and narrow. He had me cut out the booze and the butts, and put me on an ascetic diet that would've shamed Gandhi. He gave me medication to thin the blood, and prescribed Nitro for my angina. He also said I should retire. I had plenty of sick leave coming so they hired a long-term substitute and I stayed home. At my official retirement dinner at the Ramada Inn last June, they lauded my thirty-four years of service. They spoke of my enthusiasm for my students. They talked about the minds I helped to shape (I thought of my best student, a brilliantly erratic kid named Kevin Spires, who was serving time in a federal prison for sending threatening letters to Reagan). After being roasted by Bill Van Outen, the vice principal, they gave me a bunch of gag gifts, including a fifty-dollar gift certificate for Frederick's of Hollywood, which made Mel blush (it's still sitting on top of the fridge). Publicly, they called me a "trooper" and knew that I'd "bounce back." Then they turned me loose into retirement as if I were a horse and my future a green expanse of clover. Yet in the men's room I overheard Al Mitchell, a math teacher, say to someone, "Christ, Mac looks lousy. I give him a year at the outside."

The first few months home were the hardest. It's not an easy thing awaiting one's own demise. Don't listen to what they tell you. It's tedious and uneventful, punctuated only now and then by the faintest tremors of oblivion: a tightening in the chest, breath that fails to bring relief, the faintest whiff of, as Lear says, mortality. While Mel was at work, I caught up on my reading, mostly biographies of other defeated men—Chinese Gordon, Custer, Scott, Huey Long, even Nixon (funny, but I found myself actually gaining a new appreciation of the old scoundrel, even wincing when I read the part about him saying they wouldn't have him to kick around anymore). In their cases, however, it was glorious defeat: defeat that would make them more memorable than any victory ever could have.

Shortly after my first heart attack I'd started fooling around with this dollhouse idea, to keep me busy. I'd always liked to build things as a kid, used to play around with my father's tools, loved building model cars. I'd come across an ad in the back of one of Mel's home magazines. It was a kit you could send away for from a place called Blue Isle Reproductions, Blue Isle, Maine. Everything was included, all the wood and paint, the glue, even the accessories—the miniature antique furniture and gas-lamp fixtures, the stained glass for the entryway and tiny beveled mirrors for the bathrooms. It turned out to be hard work, something that takes both monkish discipline and an accountant's attention to detail: cutting out the ornate balusters, making sure the glue doesn't show, carefully stenciling the intricate cornices on one of my Victs. Authenticity is important, though it takes more time. I do research in the library, look up old photos of original houses to get it right. Sometimes I'll go up and knock on someone's door, just to see what the moldings and wainscotting inside look like. Funny how most people don't mind, will even let me in though I could just as well be a rapist with a creative MO. While few of my customers will ever see the tiny corbels supporting the cornice of the interior rooms, or care about the glass doorknobs or the exactness of a bevel, I still take the time to make sure they are correct. A striving after not perfection, but precision.

I get this trait from my father, who taught me the importance of precision. An early aeronautics engineer, he worked with none other than Igor Sikorsky on the first helicopters back in the forties. One of the original pioneers. He used to have all these balsa models at home. He'd be up to two o'clock in the morning sometimes working in his study. "Damn flying pigs," he used to scoff, because the contraptions were so fat and clumsy-looking then, and because I think he worried that if they never figured out the mysteries of vertical flight his life would have been a failure. But they did and it wasn't. They even named a rotor blade after him: The McNulty 9–17 Corrugated Rotor. There was a picture in his study of him standing with several other helicopter pioneers behind Igor himself as the little Russian shakes hands with none other than Truman. Men who'd defied gravity. Men of genius and vision and courage who'd be remembered after their deaths.

Yet my houses, precise and charming and wonderful as they are, will have no such lasting effect on the grand scheme of things. There will be no McNulty Doll House, no inscription on my tomb that says, "Here lieth Wesley Alexander McNulty, Maker of Quality Doll Houses." But it's what I do, what, as Mel likes to say, keeps me out of trouble.

I often work on my houses until I see Ginger's bedroom light come on in the morning. As I stand with a cup of decaf in my hands, looking out the window, I'll imagine her sitting on the side of the bed getting ready for school—sprinkling that lilac-scented powder on her tiny feet, pulling on her nylons. As I put a pot of real coffee on for Mel, I can picture Ginger trying to bend her unruly hair into that single long braid that dangles down along her bony spine. I see her fighting to subdue the thick, dark mass that wants to throw off the hair band and spill recklessly over her white shoulders, shoulders with small, bird-like bumps and soft recesses where shower-water remains even now, long after she's dried off. Then I feel that ratchet going off, tightening my chest, and I have to slip a Nitrostat under my tongue.

You see, before Pierce began parking his car in her garage, Ginger and I were lovers. Our affair began not long after my first heart attack. In fact, it started when I was still home recuperating. Since she lived nearby, she would drop off my students' homework. I would make her some tea and as we sat at the kitchen table and talked about school, I would find myself staring at her braided hair. My mind played over the notion of what it would feel like to rub it over my face, to feel it in my mouth. I'm not even sure how it began, who did what first—one never is in these situations. A lingering glance, skin "accidentally" brushing skin, a double-entendre that turns out not to be double at all—the romantic-novel stereotypes of illicit love. No better or worse. In any event, one afternoon we found ourselves rolling around on the kitchen floor Mel waxes faithfully every Saturday morning, clawing at each other like a couple of ferrets in heat.

Ginger is not unbecoming. She has beautiful hair and perfect white teeth her parents had invested a lot of money in. A lovely voice, especially when saying, *"Comment vas tu?"* However, while she is not unattractive, she is hardly an object on which one would normally squander one's desires, and certainly not one's final desires. In her early thirties when she came to Wessex High a dozen years ago, she is now rapidly approaching that point of no return for women who live alone in small New England towns and teach at the high school, the ones who join as many altruistic organizations as they can to keep their dance cards full: the Naturalists Club, the book club, Greenpeace, the Wessex Historical Society, the Save-This-Group and Protect-That-Club. Women with hard, furrowed mouths and bodies that hint at dry rot. We'd driven to school together for years and I can honestly say I'd never thought of her in *that* way. If I had been looking around for pleasure I certainly would have looked elsewhere. Yet I wasn't really looking for pleasure—that's just it. What was it then? I'm still not quite sure. I don't want to put too fine a point on this. A falling man isn't choosy about what might break his descent—and I was certainly a falling man. Captain Scott, only days before he himself froze to death coming back from the Pole, wrote in his diary that the recent suicide of a colleague, though terrible, might be a blessing in disguise. It would mean more food for the rest. I've read of inmates at

Buchenwald making love to total strangers moments before they were ushered into the gas chambers. Or what of those men on death row who get married, who kiss for the television cameras, yet are within sight of the waiting electric chair? What is it other than the desperate hunger of those of us who have gotten a whiff of our own smelly mortality and are willing to grasp at anything?

Anyway, after that first time we felt my kitchen floor was a little too risky—for both our hearts. Mel might come home early some afternoon and then what? I could just picture the look on her face. Or actually, I couldn't. So we used to meet at a place called Pandora's Box, a blunt cinder-block motel a couple of towns away, where you could rent a room by the hour. Both teachers, we couldn't afford much in the way of extravagant pleasures or elaborate deceptions. You would see these people coming out of the rooms, men whose ties were crooked, women with their slips showing and their lipstick smeared—all of them with the look of a child who'd gotten into the cookie jar. Some of the rooms had water beds and whirlpool tubs, and all had this shiny aluminum-foil wallpaper, so you could see your distorted, slightly comical reflection as you made the beast with two backs. After school, while Mel was sending out delinquent bills, Ginger and I would be splashing around in the whirlpool and doing things which even now make my heart go into arrhythmia.

We carried on like this for about a year. Then I had my second heart attack. Ginger thought we should slow down for a while, consider my health. No doubt, too, she had poor Nelson Rockefeller in mind and didn't like the idea of having to explain to a school board considering cutbacks what exactly she'd been doing with a bare-assed dead man holed up in Pandora's Box. But by then, the affair had pretty much run its course anyway. We began to argue over things that spouses do: whose turn it was to pay for the room, who had the worse headache, who was slighting whom by not calling. She'd be upset if I was a few minutes late and I'd be jealous if she had a regular date and couldn't meet me. So we stopped meeting at Pandora's Box. And it was right around then that she'd started seeing Pierce.

He's a former college wrestler, an honorable-mention Division II All-American, says the framed newspaper article on his office wall. In it he stands in a half crouch, his hands ready to grab you by the knees and break your femur. He's now in his early forties, impressive in the way new major appliances can be considered impressive. He has short, powerful legs that must have helped his center of gravity, and the smug half-smile of someone in possession of a secret which makes you vulnerable: the look he must've given opponents in whom he spotted a weakness and would soon pin to the mat. Even before he took my place in Ginger's affections, he was not someone I liked. He'd sit in the faculty lounge in his sweat pants, telling moronic jokes and bringing that genital-after-shave odor with him from the gym.

The first time I noticed his car pulling into Ginger's garage was about a month after I came home from the hospital. Though I was exhausted all the time, I couldn't sleep at night. I'd get up and wander around the house. I'd watch TV or read, or putter around with one of my houses. I happened to look out the window one night and see this dark car slide into Ginger's garage. I turned the lights off in the den and waited in the dark. A couple of hours later the car pulled out and took off down the street. I could tell it was Pierce's car. There aren't that many black Porsché Carreras in town, and fewer still with a garter dangling from the mirror. She'd given me up for Pierce, I thought. Even though I knew that wasn't quite true, knew that our affair had foundered on its own, that's the way it stood in my mind. I'd been beaten by a man like Pierce.

Like I said, the one thing I have plenty of is time on my hands. After seeing Pierce leave Ginger's on that occasion, I took to sitting in my car in the parking lot of the diner across the street from the high school. I'd wait till school was over and follow his car. It was crazy, I knew. Insanely juvenile. But I just had to see if it was headed for Pandora's Box.

Fortunately they never went there, though they did go to other motels, even the Ramada Inn where I'd had my retirement dinner and where the cheapest rooms are eighty bucks a night. I would feel this ribbon of pain in my shoulder when Ginger, out getting the mail, might wave to me as if she were totally innocent or I a total idiot. Watching from the den with the lights out, I started to see Pierce's car pulling into Ginger's garage on a regular basis. I'd have this image of the two of them eating fig newtons in bed (as we used to do), and I'd feel this golf ball lodged in my chest.

Melvina and I have been what I prefer to think of as well-mated partners for forty-one years. Like a mixed doubles team complementing the strengths, hiding the weaknesses of the others, one having a good serve, the other a solid net game. I like nice clothes but hate to shop, while she loves shopping; I abhor getting up in the morning, while she wakes chatty and has single-handedly carried a conversation through many a dull morning. We've shared history together, too: Truman was in the White House when we said our "I do's"; we were living with my parents on Prospect, just one street over from where we live now, when the Russians exploded the H-bomb; we were part of the crowd that paid their last respects to JFK in the Rotunda; and once, in New York, Mel and I shared a taxi and an interesting conversation with an old man who turned out to be none other than Douglas MacArthur. That's more than a lot of couples can say.

And there is the question of loyalty, too. I have no doubt Mel has been faithful to me all this time, and I'm sure she feels the same confidence in my fidelity—and she'd have every reason to, if it were not for Ginger, and one other time with a Korean girl in Pusan during the war (but when speaking of fidelity, wars don't count). You could say we are happy, at least as happy as two aging people living at the tail-end of a very unhappy century can be. We still have things to talk about at the dinner table, and when we go out I still hold the door for her and she still thanks me sincerely. We may not have known ecstacy—that thing saints and women in certain perfume commercials know of—but we have managed to live peacefully together under the same roof, pay off a mortgage, commit no heinous crimes.

Before the heart attacks, before Ginger, too, I had coveted a certain image of old age. I had liked to think that in our quiet retirement, Mel and I would do some traveling: bathe in the pure light of the Greek Islands, maybe see Fiji once, walk Heathcliff's moors. That we would spend our "declining years," as they say, reading the letters of Keats and Suetonius' *Lives* in bed, warming each other through the cooling nights of our late autumn. We would be content with our choices, and, if given the chance to start over, we would have made no major changes—this was the best of all possible worlds. I had this image of graceful old age, of wisdom and serenity and acceptance keeping the growing darkness at bay. And when death finally came knocking, even if I didn't have my bags packed and ready, even if I dragged my feet a little and asked for just five minutes more, I would have gone. Yes. I wouldn't have put up a big fuss, embarrassed myself. But when He, the Great Humbler, did arrive, I was just as frightened, just as pathetically hungry for more as the next guy. Ready to claw and kick and sell my soul for just a few moments more. It always comes as a shock, I suppose, when people learn they're not who they pretended to be. That in the small, stuffy closet spaces of their souls, they are really scared, primitive creatures, chased by fears, chasing after fantasies. And so it was with me.

A few days ago I was in the drugstore getting my Nitrostat prescription refilled when I ran into Pierce. He was a couple of aisles over.

"Mac," he called to me. "How's retirement treating you?"

"I keep busy," I replied.

He tries to maintain this front that neither knows of the other's relationship with Ginger. I have to work very hard at avoiding the thought that the two of them, in bed, discuss me.

The things I used to drop into her ear in our most intimate moments, the silly, absurd oaths and promises and superlatives.

"And the ticker?" He placed his hand on his chest and patted it, the way a young girl would to say she was in love for the first time.

"The ticker's ticking. No problems there."

"I saw you out in your garage the other day. You had something or other on a table. It looked like a goddamn dog house."

"Yes," I said. "Dogs need a place to live, too." I wasn't about to say it was a dollhouse. Not with Coach, I wasn't. I knew, too, that the only way he could've seen me was from Ginger's house. It's the only one in the neighborhood that has a direct view into my garage. There's a privacy fence on one side of our property and on the other a windbreak of white pines I planted when we first moved in.

"That mutt of ours needs a new house," he said. "Maybe I'll stop over some time and check out your work."

"Stop over anytime."

I said good-bye to Pierce and left the drugstore. Out in the car I put a pill under my tongue and sat there until the pain dissolved in my chest. When I finally pulled out of the parking lot I had to fight a temptation: the thought of running the bumper of my beat-up old Rabbit against the fender of his shiny black Porsché was as sweet as honey. I came within inches of doing it before cutting the wheel and saving my dignity.

Dr. Bonnard, the cardiologist whose house I'm working on, called from his car phone today. In the background I could hear Beethoven's *Eroica.* He wanted to know where his daughter's house was. Her birthday is just a few days away, and he's worried about it being ready. I'd met him in Dr. Rivera's office. He's the hot-shot of the group, the glamour boy who does the heart transplants. Makes money by the wheelbarrow-full, so I'm told, and is always flying here and there playing Cupid, matching up hearts. A tall man with a high forehead that always looks sweaty, though I suppose I'd be sweaty, too, if I were in his shoes.

"Alexis' birthday party is Saturday," he said to me. "The house *is* going to be ready, right?"

I told him these things take time. I told him I was working on the library, that I was waiting on the miniature books I get from a distributor in Racine, Wisconsin. It's the only place I know of that actually makes miniature books for dollhouses. The books have real writing in them. They are abridged versions of classics, of course, but you can actually read them with a magnifying glass, though I don't know anybody who actually would. He said he didn't give a damn about the books. He said he'd do without the library altogether. I told him people in those days had libraries, people read books.

"You said it'd be ready."

"And it will. You have my word."

"Imagine what would happen if I was late," he informed me.

"That's different. You deal with perishable goods," I tried to joke. He didn't laugh. Then he offered me a two-hundred-dollar bonus if I finished it on time. I told him not to worry, that he'd get a heart attack. He didn't think that was funny either, so I assured him I'd have it by Saturday.

I went to a hobby store and bought some leather and paper and paint, and decided to fashion my own library. I worked on it all day, all evening, too. Mel called me for supper but I told her I'd eat later. Before she went up to bed she came in the den with a low-cal cheese sandwich and a cup of herbal tea.

"You're working too hard," she said. "Come to bed."

"No," I said. "I have to get this done. He wants it by Saturday."

Mel came over and paused behind me for a moment, before hugging me.

I could smell that reassuring odor of cigarette smoke in her hair. Since Rivera has made smoking *verboten,* as old Schaub used to say, she does me the courtesy of smoking out behind the garage. I sucked in her aroma, delirious with nicotine. She kissed me on the neck. "Come to bed, Wes. Please. I don't like sleeping alone."

For a moment I almost gave in. But as with my father working on his flying pigs, I felt the pull of duty. I'd made a promise. A little girl was counting on me. "I'll be up later," I said.

"Anything wrong?" she asked.

"I'm having some problems with the library," I replied, though I knew that was not what she meant. Mel looked disappointed but she's a trooper; she turned and headed up to bed, glancing back once before she closed the door. Sometimes I suspect she knows something. She is more tentative now in our relationship. A certain hesitancy creeps into her gestures of affection. Other times though, I just chalk it up to my heart. Perhaps she is trying to prepare herself for the day—not so far distant—when she'll be sleeping alone for good.

I cut paper into little squares and made these tiny, leather-bound books. With gold paint and a single-hair paintbrush I even wrote the titles on the spines: *Macbeth, Leviathan, Tom Jones, Rassellas, Don Quixote.* I tried to pick short titles to fit. At the beginning of *Moby Dick,* a book my father used to read to me in bed, I wrote, "Call me Wesley," though I knew no one, least of all Dr. Bonnard, would ever notice.

Late tonight. I put my work aside, throw a windbreaker on against the cool October night, and leave the house. I go out to the garage where I keep hidden a bottle of Jack Daniels. I take a short swig, then figure, what the hell and chase that with a good strong belt. I can feel the whiskey wrapping its warm fingers around my heart, kneading it. With bottle in hand, I walk the perimeter of my yard. I can feel the treacherous bumps of the mole runs as they give way underfoot. I haven't been keeping up with the yard work and the moles, ever the opportunists, are slowly taking over. Above me, the tops of the pines are swaying in the wind, and somewhere a branch groans like one of the souls trapped in Dante's wood. Leaves scurry here and there as if with a secret mission. My breath turns to steel wool as nearby a white streak cuts through the darkness toward the Sepowitzs' house next door. It takes me a moment to register it's only her cat after one of my moles, which he is more than welcome to. Funny how the night shapes itself around your own fears.

I walk out to the street in front and stand in the shadow of the rotting silver maple. I take another drink from the bottle. I'm dying for a smoke right now, too. Across the street the kitchen light is on in Ginger's house. The rest of the place though is dark. Pierce's car is still tucked away in the garage. It's almost two in the morning but he's still there. Is it becoming something serious? I can only wonder what his wife must think. Does she know and not really care? Several times it's occurred to me to call her, anonymously, and tell her where her husband is. Fortunately I haven't stooped to that, though it's as much out of self-interest as anything. People in glass houses and all that.

I wait in the shadow for a long while, looking up at Ginger's bedroom. I'm starting to feel the cold, and am about to head inside when I hear the garage door open. Then the car starts up. For a moment I fear getting caught in the accusatory beams of his headlights, a voyeur. But then I remember that he always drives into Ginger's garage, and besides he never turns the lights on until he's down the street. Pierce backs up but stops when he's halfway down the driveway. A ghostlike figure emerges from the garage.

I hug the tree and watch as Ginger, dressed only in her underwear, walks toward the car. When she gets there I hear them talking. Though I strain to make out what it is they're saying, I can only deduce that it's an argument. The one thing I do make out clearly is Ginger telling him to "go fuck off." With that Pierce puts the car in reverse, shines his bright lights so it is Ginger who is caught nearly naked in the sudden brightness. She folds her arms over her small breasts. Her skin is the translucent white of one of Botticelli's women, though Ginger is bone-thin, with girlish legs and slim, pointy hips. She stands there with a smirk on her face, while Pierce freezes her a moment longer in the headlights, before gunning the engine, making his tires squeal.

Ginger stands there for a second in the wake of darkness the headlights have made, watching him vanish in the night.

Her arms are still folded over her brassiere, sheltering those small pale breasts of hers. And it's in that moment that I feel something that makes me wince—it's as if a thorn has pricked my finger. I consider going over. To offer my support? To lend a shoulder? To say that life will . . . what? Get better? That she won't be a lonely old maid, relying on the occasional affections of horny married men bored with their wives, or those afraid of approaching age? But then I realize how foolish that would be, how it's none of my business, and, keeping in the shadow of the maple, I wait for her to go back inside before slinking into my house and heading upstairs to where Mel is dreaming of mil rates and property appraisals.

Friday afternoon. It's raining hard. The earth smells raw, of mud and wet leaves and age-old secrets. I'm in the den finishing up the cardiologist's house. It's all ready except for some stenciling on the gingerbread. With the completion of a house there comes the same sort of vague sadness that accompanies the end of a novel, the conclusion of a vacation, the consummation of the sex act. That's when I hear the knock at the sliders off the den. Thinking it might be one of those religious people and not wanting to get caught in a tedious lecture about sin, I peek out through the curtains that cover the doors. Yet it's Ginger. She's wearing a long overcoat and slippers that are soggy from the grass. Her hair is matted from the rain and wild-looking, the single braid is frayed and coming undone, like an old shoelace.

"What's the matter?" I ask, opening the door. "Ginger, didn't you go to school today?"

"I called in sick," she says, pulling the door shut and locking it behind.

"Sick?" I say, yet when she straightens up I see that her eyes are bloodshot. She's been crying.

She looks at me for a moment, then says, "Oh, Wes. I'm such a fool. I should've known better than . . . well, you know. With Frank. You do know about Frank and me?"

"Yes," I say. "I'd heard . . . something."

"The guy's a basket case. He belongs in an institution."

"What'd he do?"

"Jesus," she says, holding together the lapels of her coat and shuddering.

"Did the son of a bitch hit you?" I ask.

"If it *were* only that. He wants . . . Jesus, he wants to get married."

"Married! He's already married."

"He wants to leave his wife. The guy's flipped out. He's wacko."

"And you don't want to? Get married?"

"To him! You got to be kidding," she says, pushing back the hair from her face. As her hand drops away from her lapel, I see that she has nothing on underneath. The fine bones of her upper chest rise and fall with each breath. Water has collected in a depression near her clavicle.

"Where is he now?"

"He went down to the store to get some more beer. I sneaked out before he got back. I can't take it anymore. Wes, I hate to ask you, but could I stay here for a little while?"

I'm about to say, yes, of course, when I hear someone else pounding on the glass. It's Pierce. He's using his palm so the whole place shudders. The slate shingles on the Victorian, ones whose glue hasn't yet set, come raining down onto the tiny front yard.

"Go away, jerk," Ginger calls from behind me.

"I want to talk. I love you, Gin," he bellows. He's drunk, or near enough so he doesn't care how foolish he sounds. Through the curtain you can see his big shape swaying on his heels. "I want to be with you," he says.

"Shove it," she replies. "Go away. I mean it."

"Come on out, Gin. You know I love you."

"Leave me alone."

"I just want to talk, Gin. Just talk. What's that gonna hurt?"

"Go away."

"McNulty, you hear me," he calls. "Wes, this ain't none your business. It's between me and Gin. Stay out of it."

Ginger leans close to me, so I can smell her hair, baby shampoo and conditioner, and I want to put her dark hair into my mouth.

"I'm sorry," she whispers to me. "He's right. I shouldn't've involved you. He might be dangerous."

I say, "Don't back down now. You've made your decision and it's the right one. He's no good for you."

She looks at me, her hazel eyes inches away, as if to say, *Were you?*

Pierce yells at that moment, bangs on the door. "Fuckin' open up. I don't want to break the door in, McNulty. But I will. So help me God."

"Call the police," Ginger says. "No telling what he'll do when he's like this."

I consider calling the police but think over the problems that might raise for everyone—Ginny, Pierce, myself. Instead I go into the living room and pick up the poker from beside the fireplace. The one I use for noises in the middle of the night. For the prowlers I've never actually had to encounter and prove myself a coward before.

"Don't let him in," Ginger warns me. "He's wacko."

Through the curtains I can see Pierce has his face against the glass, his hands forming parentheses to deflect the glare. I push open the lock and slide the door back. Pierce has to duck slightly as he comes through the curtain. For just a moment he's disoriented in the relative darkness of the room. His eyes are narrow red arcs, like tomato wedges, and with the water in them he has difficulty focusing. For just a moment he's vulnerable. I can do with him what I please, crush his skull with one swing. I'd have every right, too. He'd threatened me and Ginger. I'd only be protecting myself—us. I'm still considering this when I feel Ginger's hand tugging at the poker. At first I think she's trying to stop me, that she doesn't want him hurt after all, that she really loves him and what they've had is simply a lover's quarrel. But then I realize she's actually trying to get the poker away from me to use it on him herself. When I turn to face her she spits out the words, "Hit the bastard. Hit him."

Once he's through the door, however, all bets are off. I now no longer have the advantage. Pierce straightens up. He's broad-shouldered, fleshier through the middle than he was in the photo of his honorable-mention days. Larger even than I remembered him in the faculty lounge. He takes one look at me, the poker I grip tightly, Ginger peering over my shoulder. We must seem comical to him. But it's the dollhouses in various states of completion that catch his attention most.

"Jesus Fucking Christ. Would you look at that?" he says, laughing. "Dollhouses. Is this what you fuckin' do, McNulty? Build *doll*houses?"

"You'd better get out, Frank," Ginger says behind me, but I can tell she's frightened. Suddenly I can feel her fear, too. In my house is a drunken, crazy man, a big ex-wrestler, a jilted lover whose lover is dumping him, and doing it in front of an ex-lover holding a poker. At best he'd be looking at second-degree manslaughter and he'd be out of Somers in four years. I feel that ratchet going off inside my chest, that *click, click, click* of something being tightened.

"And who's gonna make me? This old fart? Gimme a friggin' break."

"Get out. This is my house," I tell him, trying to sound unafraid.

"Your house? What's she doing here then?"

"She's welcome. You're not. You're trespassing."

"Am I now? Whyn't you just put me out then?"

He smiles that smug smile so his mouth is all stitched together on one side of his face like a wound. Waiting. Just hoping I'll be stupid enough to try something and he can use one of those moves that made him honorable-mention All-American. He reaches out and touches one of the chimneys of the Victorian. It's all tiny pieces of real fieldstone, and it took me nearly a day to chip the pieces and glue them into place.

"Fuckin' lookit this." He snaps off the chimney and crumples the thing in his hand, the way Gulliver might do to a house in Lilliput.

"Frank, don't be an asshole," Ginger pleads. "Leave him out of this."

"Fine with me. You're the one got him in. Let's go."

Ginger looks at me, tears bunching on her lids and ready to spill over. They turn her hazel eyes blackish. She says, "Thanks anyway, Wes." She makes a move to go with Pierce. He looks at me, not satisfied with getting what he came for, with winning the match, but needing to let me know the depth of my defeat, that I'm an old man with a small portion of a heart remaining, a silly old fool who builds dollhouses while he waits for death. He smiles at me again, the way I imagine he used to smile at defeated opponents. He's still got his hand on the roof of the Victorian, smugly resting it there as if he just might destroy the entire house, as if it's well within his power to do it. And that's where I hit him, right on the back of the knuckles, as hard as I can.

*"Goddamn!"* he howls, holding his shattered hand and dancing like a bear at a circus. "Goddamn crazy son of a fuckin' bitch." He recovers enough to think about coming after me but I strike the house again—strike it instead of him. I swing again and again, like a man possessed, like a man who's been waiting his whole life for just this very moment. Pieces of roof and clapboard and floor go flying everywhere, as if a miniature tornado has struck. I keep hitting the house until it's flattened, smashing it into splinters. I can just picture Dr. Bonnard. But what makes me sad, even as I strike, is his daughter's face when she doesn't get her house tomorrow.

"You want another one?" I ask him.

"You crazy old fucker you," he says. But he doesn't come nearer. His hand is bloody. Blood is dripping down onto Mel's oriental, which I'll have to explain. Then, after an indecisive moment or two, he says, "Go to hell, Gin. Fuck the both of you. You deserve each other." Then he turns and leaves.

After he's gone, Ginger helps me over to the couch. I'm short of breath, wheezing. My heart feels cold and hard, like an old drumstick stored in the freezer too long.

"Wes, are you all right?" Ginger asks.

"Get me a glass of water, please."

I put a nitro pill under my tongue. Ginger comes back over with the water and sits down next to me. She pats my forehead, holds my hand.

"Are you sure you're all right?"

"I think so."

"Should I call an ambulance or something?"

"I think I'll be all right in a minute. I just have to catch my breath."

"I'm sorry, Wes," Ginger says, beginning to cry. "I didn't mean to get you involved."

"That's all right."

"It was sweet what you did for me," she says. One of her tears falls and lands on my cheek. It is warm and I can almost taste the salt. My heart is on fire, consuming itself. I feel like I haven't felt in ages: heroic and content, and about as ready as I'll ever be to leave this life.

Of course I didn't—die that is. Otherwise, I wouldn't be telling you this part. It's taken me three weeks to rebuild the house. It was late for the little girl's birthday party but I told Dr. Bonnard that a vandal had broken in and busted things up. Incredibly he believed me and that seemed to calm him down. I haven't seen Ginger since that day, although I have seen Pierce, twice. Once was in the parking lot of Grossman's Lumber, where I buy some of my building materials. I was loading wood into my trunk when I noticed this black car behind me. When I turned around Pierce was already out of the car and moving solidly, committedly toward me. I thought he was going to hit me right there.

"Look," he said, holding up a bandaged hand. "Damn thing's busted. Thanks a lot."

"You're welcome," I managed to get out.

"Welcome! You goddamn old fart. Who the hell do you think you are?"

"I was just protecting myself. And Ginger."

"Protecting her? From what? She doesn't need protecting, that bitch. And sure as hell not by you."

"That's not how I figure it."

He stood there for a while, as if still considering hitting me. But he smiled and said, "You're not even worth it. Six months and you'll be history." He then turned and got back in his car and took off.

The other time was two nights ago. I was finishing up the trim around the eaves on the dollhouse, when I heard a car pull into Ginger's driveway. It was Pierce's. In some way I wasn't even surprised. He pulled it into the garage and the door shut behind him. I didn't notice when he left. I didn't bother to watch.

One other thing. When Ginger was on the couch with me that day, she leaned over and kissed away the tear that had fallen on my cheek. I put my arms around her and hugged her. I could feel her tiny vertebrae beneath the wet overcoat, her earlobe cool against my nose. Her hair smelled of ripe grapes. Then she opened her raincoat. She was wearing nothing underneath. Five more minutes, I thought. Just five and I'll be ready. You can have my worthless carcass then. Next thing I knew we were rolling around on the hardwood floor. I didn't even hear Mel's car pull into the driveway. Luckily Ginger did. She hurriedly threw me off, pulled on her overcoat, rushed to the sliding doors without looking back, and fled across the street just as Mel came in the back door. "Home from the tax wars," my wife of forty-one years cried out.

# Voices

As Lauralee paid for the cigarettes, she had a hard time looking at Hector's outstretched hand. Where the last two fingers should've been were these ugly stumps, the ends flattened into tiny pink mushrooms. She pictured the guy losing them in a sudden moment of violence, in a back room somewhere, over a gambling debt or a woman. He looked as if he'd lived that sort of life. Though she was curious, she never asked, because she knew she'd probably be disappointed to find out the truth—frostbite as a child, a baling accident, splitting wood. The U-Totem store where he worked was just around the corner from Lauralee's apartment. She'd stop there on her way to school to buy cigarettes or lipstick, or just to get out of the oppressive sun for a few moments.

The early morning rush for caffeine and nicotine and lotto tickets had passed, and now she was the only customer in the store. She stood over by the window near the L'Eggs display. Hector had the air conditioner turned so high Lauralee felt goose bumps popping on the backs of her thin bare arms.

She started to light up a cigarette but Hector said, "Jesus, not in here. Drew'll have my ass he sees you." Though she was underage, he still sold her cigarettes so long as the manager wasn't around.

Hector was all right, not like some of the asshole older men she knew, hitting on her or worse, acting like some kind of father figure to her.

Lauralee dropped the cigarette, crushing it under her sandal. She looked out the window. Her mother, she knew, would be in a flurry of last-minute camouflage preparation for work—pulling on dark pantyhose to cover her varicose veins, yanking out another gray hair. Occasionally she even wore this dumb wig, something her new boyfriend, Moe, liked. His name was actually Maurice, but people called him Moe, like one of the Three Stooges. He joked once, right in front of Lauralee, that with her mother wearing the wig it was like he had two women for the price of one. Lauralee thought it made her mother look silly, like a woman playing a secretary in a sit-com. Some mornings her mother would sit at the kitchen table with a warm tea bag against her eyes, trying to make them look less puffy. It didn't help. Getting to sleep at a normal hour might, instead of staying at Moe's all night and then trying to sneak into the apartment carrying her shoes so as not to make noise. Like she was fooling anybody.

"How come you ain't in school?" Hector called over to her.

"We're in mourning."

"Mourning? For what?"

"Some kid shot our principal yesterday," she replied.

"You shitting me? I ain't heard about it."

"It was on the news last night. Gunned him down in the parking lot. Three fifty-seven," she said, holding a finger to her forehead. "A major mess."

"They say why?"

"He suspended the kid for smoking in the lav."

"Son of a bitch," Hector said, shaking his large head. "It just goes to show you. If some joker comes in here he's fuckin' with the wrong hombre." Hector slapped his hip pocket where Lauralee knew he kept a silver-plated snubnose .32 caliber. He said he was just itching for the chance to use it, too.

Lauralee spotted her mother's tired Skylark, spitting a trail of blue smoke in its wake, her mother adjusting the rearview for one last reassuring glance that she couldn't really be pressing forty. Lauralee ducked behind the L'Eggs display and watched until her mother disappeared onto Evans. Then she told Hector to take it easy and left. She cut through a vacant lot where she once found a dead cat in the weeds before reaching the Arapaho Arms, her apartment building.

Though only eight-thirty, it was already hot. A dull high plains heat. Everything—the buildings downtown, the foothills west of Denver—wavered in broad bands, creeping upward as if the vertical hold was messed up. She walked around the pear-shaped pool in the courtyard, the cloudy water resembling Gatorade. On the day they'd moved in a year ago, her mother said, "Look, Laurie. You can keep up your swimming." Lauraleee had been on the swim team back in her hick Wyoming town. She wasn't bad in the back stroke, but individual medley was her best. She hadn't even bothered going out for the team here and hardly ever swam in the murky pool water of the Arapaho Arms. She'd gotten mostly D's, that is when she even bothered going to school. She climbed the outside stairs to her third-floor apartment.

Before she went in, she glanced around the courtyard to make sure no one was watching. She'd read how rapists would do that, spy on women, then follow them into their apartments. Across the way, looking up at her out of a first floor window was this narrow, bearded face that made her think of a marmot. Frank Bruso. The guy hardly ever left his place. The lone time Lauralee had seen him outside, he was sitting near the pool in his wheelchair. His skin was the color of a blister about to peel off, and even though it was eighty degrees he was dressed for a blizzard, a sweater and long slacks draped over those ropelike legs. He was with a loud, coarse-looking red-haired woman who was drinking a beer and dancing all by herself, without any music. The guy seemed to smile up at Lauralee, but she wasn't going to give the sicko a chance. She quickly went into her apartment and locked the door behind her.

Inside, it was quiet and stuffy, the apricot smell of her mother's perfume lingering in the air. She pictured Moe shoving his nose into her mother's neck and saying, "You smell real nice, baby." Lauralee lit up a cigarette to cover the smell. She saw a note held by a clothespin magnet on the refrigerator: "Spaghetti sauce in freezer. Don't wait for me. Love, Mom." On the bottom of the note was printed, "Be my Valentine," though it was September. Lauralee had bought the stationery for her mother as a Valentine's gift. It was now their usual means of communicating with each other. "It wouldn't hurt you to pick up a little," her mother might say.

Or "I went to the mall." Or, "Sorry if I was a little mad last night. That time of month. Ha ha!" Things like that.

Lauralee got undressed in the kitchen and stood in her underwear in front of the refrigerator, the freezer door wide open. The air conditioner had been broken for a week and the super was slow to fix things. He worked nights somewhere and this job was only to get a free place to live. She stuck her head way in the small freezer, savoring the gray, fishy-smelling air inside. She tried to imagine being one of those kids she'd read about, getting caught in a refrigerator, dying alone in the dark. She wondered if you'd talk to yourself in the dark and if it'd sound like your own voice—or maybe some other voice, the voice of God, say. Her stomach turned on itself. She wasn't sure if she were hungry or about to be sick. She looked in the refrigerator for something to eat. There was still a wedge of sagging birthday cake, but she decided she wasn't hungry after all, that her stomach felt funny. Maybe she was coming down with something.

She walked into her mother's room, sat on the side of the bed and started looking through her mother's bureau drawers. Hidden under a pile of sweaters she found a book called *Coping with Change.* Inside it she found an empty envelope, addressed to her mother in her father's handwriting. She looked in the bottom drawer, where her mother usually kept her wig. Sometimes Lauralee would try it on, look in the mirror and pretend she was someone else, the way her mother probably did. But it wasn't there. In the back of her underwear drawer, Lauralee came across a package of rubbers. On the box a woman tilted her head back in blurred ecstasy, like someone who had been possessed by the holy spirit. For a moment Lauralee had an image of her mother, her face scary with passion, the wig sliding half off, and Moe, all broad, hairy back, humping her like a shepherd. She just had time to make it to the bathroom before she was really sick.

Later, she lay curled up on her bed. She looked over at the phone and wondered if he'd call today. Her father usually called on her birthday, but that was two days ago and she hadn't had a word from him. No present, not even a lousy card. Last year on her birthday he'd called from a phone booth in some arcade near where he'd parked his rig. She could hear electronic noises going off in the background. *Wish you were with me, lollipop,* he'd said, boozy and sentimental. That's what he called her—lollipop. *Think about coming to stay with us,* he'd said, though he hadn't offered to come and get her, and never called back.

Lauralee decided to try calling him now. Maybe she'd tell him she wanted to come, that she couldn't take living with her mother anymore. She let it ring fifteen, twenty times. She saw it echoing through the run-down ranchhouse he shared with Georgia, his new wife. Lauralee had been there twice to visit. They lived outside of Pocatello. Georgia was her mother's age, but she looked older because she wouldn't dye her long witchy-black hair, and she didn't wear makeup. She was one of those all-natural types. An ex-hippie with hair under her arms and spaced-out eyes. While it rang, Lauralee practiced a voice, a meaty, Texan drawl. *Is this Georgia Sammons? Mizzus Sammons, this is Nurse Ramos from St. Luke's Hospital. I have some awful bad news. I'm afraid your husband's rig ran off the interstate. That's right. I'm very sorry. Please accept my condolences.* She let it ring some more, but no one on the other end answered so she finally hung up.

From the floor near her bed she picked up the Denver phone book and started flipping through it. She skimmed through the V's, the W's, then slowed going through the X's. She couldn't think of anyone in the small town she'd grown up in whose name began with an X. In fact, the only *word* she could think of was *x-ray. X-husband* she thought, but that was spelled *ex.* She selected one, *Peter Xavier,* and dialed. No answer. She tried another—*L. Xefos.* What sort of name was that? An old woman with a cold or sinuses answered.

"Hello."

"Mrs. Xefos." Lauralee pronounced it *Ex-e-fos.*

"It sounds like a *Z,*" the woman corrected. "It's Greek. My husband's side is anyway. What can I do for you?"

"Mrs. Xefos. I'm dying."

There was scratchy silence on the other end for a moment.

"You're what!" the woman said finally. Then, with a shrill laugh, she added, "In this heat, we're all dying, honey."

"No, I mean I'm *really* dying. They say I got two months. Maybe less."

"I don't know you, do I? Is this a joke?"

"It's no joke, Mrs. Xefos. I have terminal leukemia."

"You could get in trouble for doing this. This is a terrible thing you're doing, young lady."

"It's the truth."

"I'm going to hang up, you hear me. Don't you have any morals? Good heavens, you should be ashamed of yourself to joke about something like that."

"I wish I was joking. *God,* how I wish I was." Her voice was somber and yet relaxed, not straining at all. Her own voice, it occurred to her suddenly. And just like that Lauralee was crying, sobbing so her voice actually quivered and big hot tears pushed out the corners of her eyes. It was beautiful. Sometimes nothing came at all and she sounded phony even to herself. But today it was just amazing. She even surprised herself.

The woman didn't say anything for several seconds. Lauralee pulled her knees up to her chest to make the sick feeling in her stomach go away.

The woman said, "You aren't joking, are you, dear?"

"No ma'am. It's the God's truth."

"Why are you calling me though?"

"I was just laying here in bed and I wanted someone to talk to. I can't talk to my mother about it. She can't handle it. She can't even mention the word *death.* She's still in denial, you see. Besides, she's got her own problems."

"But why *me,* child?"

"Never mind. I'm sorry for bothering you. Good-bye." She made as if to hang up.

"No, no. Hold on," pleaded the old woman. "I didn't understand, that's all. What's your name, honey?"

"Patricia." Lauralee picked the tears off with her tongue as they slid down her face. They tasted like seawater. She looked out the window and could see a plane nosing slowly upwards from the airport. It reminded her of a trout rising to a fly. Her father took her fishing up on the Yellowstone River once, where the rainbows were as fat and stupid as goldfish.

"Listen, Patricia. I'm real sorry, honey. I thought you were kidding. Can't they do anything for it? Chemotherapy or something?"

"They tried everything. Chemo. Radiation. Even bone marrow transplants." She'd heard that on *ER*. "Now I have mets to the brain. Once it spread there, you might as well forget it. I mostly have all my marbles still."

"Oh," the woman sighed. "Oh, you poor, poor thing you. You shouldn't lose hope though. You're young. They're always coming up with new things. The way you need to look at it is each day they might find the cure. Right today somebody might come up with something. You never can tell."

"Oh, I'm ready for it. I'm in the fifth stage. You have to go through the first four to get where I am. The fifth stage is where you accept."

On a talk show she'd heard about the stages people go through when they're dying, like checkpoints. They had several fifth-stage people on. One an emaciated little boy who wore a baseball hat to cover his bald head. Another, a woman, who had to be hooked up to a machine to breathe, wore a flaming red wig. They all spoke with pride of their impending doom, as if it were a goal they'd worked hard to achieve and were looking forward to, like retirement. Somehow it sounded too neat to Lauralee. She was sure that whatever dying was it wasn't as neat as that.

"You poor thing," the woman said to her. "You poor brave thing. I'll pray for you. I promise. I know it's frail comfort—"

But Lauralee, already grown bored with the woman, placed the receiver in its cradle. She curled into a ball and tried to remember her father's voice, as he tucked her in at night. It was crisp, like toast, and sometimes he'd whisper in her ear, his breath smelling of stale beer and chewing tobacco, "You my, lollipop?" And Lauralee would say she was and then slip into dreams as easily as if she were dropping down a waterslide into cool water.

The phone woke her in the middle of the afternoon. She'd been dreaming about her father. They were in his big Kenworth, coasting along, only the truck didn't seem to touch the highway at all but to drift along above it on a cushion of air. He'd let her shift it, and each time she did the truck would lift higher off the ground. Pretty soon it felt like they were on a plane, taking off. The phone call brought her quickly down to earth.

"How come you're home, young lady?" her mother asked. The *young lady* business was her mother's attempt at asserting her authority, something Moe told her she needed to do more of. "They said you weren't there."

"I'm sick."

"What's the matter?" she asked, suspicious.

"I think I'm coming down with something. I feel lousy."

"You want to have a good year at school, don't you? Not like last year."

"I told you, I don't feel good."

"You got a fever or anything?"

"I think so. And I'm throwing up, too. If you don't believe me I won't flush next time and you can see it when you get home."

"Of course, I believe you, sweetie," she said, her voice softening. "You take anything?"

"No. When you going to be home?"

"I don't know. Something came up."

Lauralee knew what that meant. Moe came up. He wore anaconda skin boots and a string tie, though he was raised in Philadelphia. He owned a van conversion shop over on Colorado Boulevard and made a lot of money. Once when Lauralee's mother had him over for supper he'd called them—Lauralee and her mother—his "gals." Lauralee thought she'd puke. For her birthday he gave her a used Blaupunckt car stereo he'd gotten out of some van. He said when she was old enough for a license he'd see what he could do about getting her something to put the stereo in. Mr. Big-timer. Lauralee's stomach turned just looking at him.

"You'd better go ahead and eat without me," her mother said. "But don't push the food. Have some toast and tea. That's better for you if you don't feel good. I'll have Dr. Krauss write me out something for your stomach."

"Yeah."

"We'll talk later, OK. We need to talk."

Her mother always said that—they needed to talk—but they never did. Between her job as a receptionist in a doctor's office downtown and the snake-booted Moe, they hardly saw each other. A few days before, Lauralee had waited up for her mother. She'd watched a scary movie on TV and couldn't sleep. But as usual her mother was late. After midnight Lauralee happened to look out the front window. Down at the courtyard she saw a woman sitting on the edge of the pool, in a long print dress that was soaked. The woman's hair hung down in her face, and she held a pair of pumps by the straps. The woman sat there motionless, as if she'd been in an accident and was afraid to move. Lauralee stared for several seconds before she realized it was her mother. The next morning she found the dress hanging over the shower curtain, still wet.

If Lauralee let herself think Moe might become a permanent fixture in their lives, she felt something ripping open in her gut: this hot, bitter pain, similar to the feeling of the appendicitis she'd had. Moe had these yellow toadlike eyes and a way of looking at her mother that made Lauralee's skin crawl.

"Lauralee, honey? Is something else the matter?" her mother asked. "You sound funny."

"You're not going to marry the guy, are you?"

"Who?" she said, as if she didn't know.

*"Maurice,"* she said, her voice dripping with sarcasm.

"Where's this coming from?"

"Well are you?"

"That's my business, Lauralee. Moe is a nice man. A very nice man. He's successful. And he knows how to treat people, too. I could do a lot worse than him."

"But he's—"

"Just watch what you say, young lady."

"He looks like a lizard, Ma."

"You never mind. Looks aren't everything. Your father had looks and what'd it get me? Or you, for that matter? It just goes to show you can't tell a book by its cover."

Lauralee said, "If you do I'm leaving."

"Don't you dare threaten me, Lauralee Sammons."

"I swear, I will."

"And just where do you expect to go? You think he'd take you in?"

"He would. Like *that.* You're just afraid I'll go this time."

"We've been over this before. He couldn't take you even if he wanted to, which he doesn't."

"Bitch."

"Lauralee. Listen."

"I knew you'd say that. You always have to say something rotten about him. I can see why he left you."

"Wait a minute. Let's set the record straight. I was the one left him."

"Liar."

"I did. Just not soon enough is all."

"Bitch."

Her mother started to say something, but Lauralee had already hung up. The phone rang again, several times in fact, until Lauralee unplugged it from the wall. Then the apartment was quiet.

Somebody was playing a stereo loud. Lauralee felt the dry bass thump coming up through the back of her head, her skull going *doof, doof, doof,* as if someone were taking a staple gun to it. The room felt hot, the air almost unbreathable. She thought maybe she did have a temperature after all. She got up and went into the kitchen and grabbed a handful of ice cubes from the freezer. She returned to the bedroom and lay down. She rubbed ice over her neck and forehead. Water dribbled down over her ear, making her shiver.

It was a quarter after three. She thought about going out and taking a dip in the pool, even though she didn't like the murky, slightly greasy water against her skin. But she also didn't want somebody to see her and then tell her mother, when she was supposed to be sick. Like that Mrs. Sturgis, from the second floor. The old witch stared out the window all day, watching the courtyard as if it were a daytime soap opera.

Lauralee looked up Frank Bruso's number in the phone book. She plugged the phone back in and dialed.

"Hello," a man's voice replied. "At the beep please leave your name and number and I'll get back to you soon as I can." Lauralee knew, though, it wasn't an answering machine, that it was a real voice.

"What do you do with yourself all day?" she asked.

"Oh, it's you," said Frank Bruso. "Little Miss Ballbuster. I was wondering when you'd call." In the background, she heard the applause and shrieks of a game show. "Wouldn't you like to know how I keep busy?"

She'd called him the first time just for kicks, curious about what he did in his apartment all day. She hadn't seen the red-haired woman in a while. Now she called when she was bored or wanted somebody to talk to, but she never let on she lived in the same apartment building. The first time she called him she pretended to be a DJ from a radio station she'd been listening to. She told him if he could name the song playing then, he'd win a free membership to a health club. Instead of getting mad, Frank Bruso laughed as if it was the funniest thing he'd ever heard. He told her he was a gimp. Collected 100 percent from Uncle Sam.

"You like in a wheelchair or something?" Lauralee had asked, pretending she didn't know.

"Something like that."

He'd laughed, a smoker's laugh punctuated by dry coughs. "I bet you're going to tell me you were paralyzed in Nam. Right? Everybody was crippled in Nam."

"Nope. Car accident. I was drunk out of my everlovin' mind. Tried to tangle with a tree. I lost."

"Am I supposed to believe that?"

"You believe what you want," he'd told her.

Since that first time she'd probably spoken to him half a dozen times. Sometimes she'd peek out between the curtains at his apartment, to see if he was looking back. But he never was.

She put an ice cube in her navel and watched it melt, the pain running in a line down over her ugly appendicitis scar. After a while she asked, "Is it hot where you are?"

"Hot? It's downright chilly. I got me a sweater on it's so cold. The air conditioner was one of the few things my old lady left when she flew the coop. Took everything that wasn't bolted down."

"Man, you're so full of it it's coming out your ears."

Frank Bruso seemed distracted for a while. Then he said, "Tell me what state begins with the letter *d?"*

"What?"

"Come on, quick. For bonus points. What state?"

"I don't know. Depression."

He made a buzzing noise. *"Bzzzz.* Wrong. You blew it. You wouldn't win shit. The correct answer was Delaware."

"Maybe she had her reasons," Lauralee said.

"Who?"

"Your old lady. You ever thought of that?"

"Course she had her reasons. Everybody's got reasons."

"You got to admit, it can't be a picnic being married to a cripple."

"Watch it now. Physically challenged. I'll admit, it has its disadvantages. Especially for mountain climbing. And what about you?"

"What about me?"

"What's wrong with you?"

"Nothing," Lauralee said.

"A perfect lady. Now *that* I'd like to meet. Listen, I got me an idea. I got a quart of Cuervo and all's you need to do is some limes. You think you could handle the limes, Little Miss Ballbuster? There's nachos and bean dip here. And I think I could scrounge up some frozen pizzas. We could do some afternoon partying. There's a pool here. Or did you know that already?"

"Now how would I know that?"

"Never mind. From your voice I bet you're a pretty foxy gal. Am I wrong?"

"Up yours."

"I ain't bad once you get to know me. If all goes well we might do a little boogie-ing.

"I thought you're crippled."

"I'm a master at improvising. You wouldn't believe the things I'm capable of, Little Miss Ballbuster."

"Asshole."

When it was dark, Lauralee put on her swimsuit, the black and pink one-piece job she used to swim competitively in. Before she headed down to the pool, however, she glanced over at Frank Bruso's window, to be sure he wasn't looking. His drapes were closed, though the iridescent light of a TV shone behind them. She was the only one in the courtyard. She sat down on the edge of the pool, near the diving board. The underwater lights glowed eerily in the murky water: she didn't know why but they made her think of something that had been exposed to radiation, something she'd seen on TV. Though the night air had cooled off, the water was still warm, oily to the touch, or at least in her imagination. She could see a pile of sediment at the bottom, dirt and leaves and things, all lumped together like a wet dustball. The manager seldom vacuumed or cleaned the pool despite complaints from the tenants. Now and then he blasted it with chlorine so your eyes burned for days.

She slipped quietly into the pool, treaded water easily. Above her, she could hear TV sets, the whirring of air conditioners, muted voices. One, a woman's, said, "Send her whatever you want. She's your damn mother." Lauralee dipped under the water and tried to swim the length of the pool and back. She was—or at least had been—a good swimmer, though now her arms were trembling and her wind was gone. Yet even when her lungs began to hurt she didn't stop for air. She kept stroking, trying to keep her rhythm, keep her arms close to her sides. It was a game she sometimes played. If she could swim all the way underwater, a wish would come true. It was something she used to do as a little kid. One wish: her father would pull up in his rig, honk his horn for her. Her mother would drop Moe and stop being such a bitch. The bumpy scar on her stomach would fade and she could wear a bikini again. But she couldn't make it all the way this time. She had to stop short and gulp air, her lungs screaming and her mouth tasting of hot copper.

As she treaded water in the deep end, she happened to see something at the bottom, mixed in with the sediment there. As she looked down through the cloudy water she realized what it was. Some sort of small animal. A cat. *God,* she thought, shivering. How gross. She'd never heard of a cat drowning in a pool. Someone must've killed it and thrown it in. Though repulsed by the sight of it, Lauralee nonetheless took a breath and dove under. She swam down to take a closer look. When she was only an arm's length away she had a strange urge to touch it. She reached out with one finger, cautiously, as if the thing might come alive and bite her. But then she grew bolder, poked it one or twice. Finally, when it didn't move, she grabbed a handful of the tan fur. What startled her was that there was nothing to it, no body or bones, just hair. Like a pelt. It was then she realized it wasn't an animal after all—it was a wig. A blond wig sitting there amid the leaves and crud.

Lauralee yanked her hand back as if she had been bitten and swam quickly to the surface. She left the water and wrapped herself in a towel and climbed the stairs to her apartment. She was out of breath when she reached the top. She tried not to think about the wig, how it came to be there.

As soon as she opened the door she heard the phone ringing. She hesitated for a moment, then picked it up. She hoped it would be her father calling to say, *Sorry, about your birthday, lollipop.* She knew though it would probably be her mother, calling from Moe's to say *she* was sorry. Whenever they fought it was her mother who apologized. She told herself she'd let her say it, that she'd even forgive her. But it was a man's voice on the other end.

"How was your swim?" It took a few seconds before she recognized it as Frank Bruso. He sounded funny, like he was drunk or stoned.

"How'd you get my number?"

"Who you think you're dealing with here? Listen, what you said before."

"About what?"

"About it being no picnic married to a gimp."

"Yeah. I wouldn't know really. I was just talking."

"Well, it wasn't no picnic being married to her either. I'm not defending myself. I just want to set the record straight." Just like her mother, Lauralee thought. Setting the record straight. "She had things going on, if you know what I mean. I'm no saint. I might've done the same myself, who knows. But it was her."

"Yeah," Lauralee said.

"I would've walked on her but she had the good pair of wheels. You understand what I'm saying? I'm the aggrieved party in these proceedings."

Aggrieved, Lauralee thought. Aggrieved. She pictured the wig sitting at the bottom of the pool, collecting junk. At the end of the year the manager would pull it out, hold it in his hand and wonder what the hell it meant. And she pictured her father, alone, gearing down somewhere as he took on a steep grade, shifting neatly, with bursts of diesel, climbing higher, making the crest finally before plunging down the far side. Lauralee considered saying something to Frank Bruso but he'd already hung up.

# Heights

Eddie takes the call on the radio while I'm cleaning up after supper. Somebody trolling over in North Bay can't get his motor started. Gussy Moran, the fish and game agent, says he'd stopped to help but the guy said he knew his way around motors. Said it was just flooded, and he wanted to get in a little more fishing. Gussy, his voice popping over the CB like bacon grease, says he knew it was one of ours. Along the side of every rental boat Eddie'd painted the name of our place—Camp LeRoux—in bright red with fancy lettering that took him a couple of weeks.

Out of habit, I scrape meatloaf off our plates and into the can we used to save for Toby, and look out the kitchen window. Dark clouds, the color of smoke from green wood, come humping in over Mt. Kineo. Down at the dock the flag is snapping in the wind. Not a time you want to be five miles out with a motor that won't start.

It turns out it's one of those fellows in number 5. I know the one they mean. Just a kid, twenty-three, twenty-four. I'd seen him go out, tearing ass across the lake like he'd just been released from prison or a bad marriage. Him and the other one both downstaters, away from their wives or girlfriends for a week and feeling their oats. Thinking nothing and no one could stop them. Two nights ago I was cleaning out number 6 after a couple of pigs from New York—they're always the worst, I swear—and I was passing by their cabin. They were inside, and drunk, and laughing in that way drunk men laugh when they're alone but acting always like they got an audience, even if they're fifty miles out in the woods. A stage sort of laugh, put on. We get families and some newlyweds, and once in a blue moon a pair of nature girls in L.L. Bean outfits, but mostly it's men: they come up here so they can act the way they think men are supposed to act. These two had brought along a VCR and had picked up a couple of those girly movies, and were making throaty noises, like dogs in heat. It was still warm out, one of the last Indian summer nights we're lucky to get up here, and their windows were open. I thought the family in 4 would complain, but they didn't. And as I passed by I could see this one, Andy, the one who'd signed the register, sort of look out at me and catch my eye, and do something you might've taken for a wink, if you were in the right mood. I wasn't. I had work to do. As I walked up to the house I could hear him laugh to his friend and I could imagine the rest.

"Send Lyman out," Eddie calls from the den. Lyman's the kid works for us. He helps clean out the cabins, does some guide work, lends a hand when a guest messes up. At night plays cards with Eddie, too. A handyman is what we were looking for and what we got with Lyman.

"That's OK. I'll go." I was looking for an excuse to get out anyway. My father used have this expression when one of us kids started getting on his nerves. He'd say we needed to get out and blow the stink off. Funny how in the last few years I've gotten so cabin fever comes on me earlier and earlier. I used to be able to make it till April before I started feeling I was in a bubble that was running out of air. Now I start getting antsy by December.

"Well, take the Evinrude," Eddie orders. "I need to get at the Merc. The choke's all fucked up."

"Sure," I say, knowing that he'll get to it about next spring. Like with the motor that kid from number 5 has. I'd told him about it. Said we're going to have trouble some time. But he just said it wasn't on his priority list. His priority list. He's got this list he puts on the fridge. Like he's flat out with things to do. Most of them never get done. Or he does things that don't even need doing. He's got plenty of time to fool around with fancy lettering on the boats but not to fix the motors. I don't bring that up though. I hardly bring anything up anymore. I let things lie. I figure Eddie'll get to it when he's good and ready, not before. So what's the use.

I pass by the den and there's Eddie watching a movie on the satellite channel. Some kung-fu thing. He's big into those.

But he's got the sound off so he can listen to the CB. He'll look at whole shows with no sound, so I won't even sit and watch with him anymore, it drives me nuts not knowing what they're saying. He's propped himself up in the lounge chair. His wheelchair is waiting next to him like Toby used to before we had him put to sleep. I know that's where Eddie'll sleep tonight. He says he sleeps better sitting up. And besides, it's easier to get out of bed in the morning.

"Need anything?" I ask, as I put my coat on and get the keys for the gas pump.

He shakes his newly bearded face, reconsiders a moment, then says, "Yeah. Could you get a cold one, hon? So I won't have to get up."

From the fridge, I grab Eddie a couple of Miller Lites—he's trying to work on his spare tire. He's really not heavy, not much anyway. In fact, if you were to see Eddie, say you were both sitting at a stoplight, you'd say he was still a good-looking man. Better than most, especially for what he's been through.

He says, "Thanks, hon." Before I leave, I grab the afghan and throw it over his legs. He says "Thanks" again, but he doesn't know why I did it. Before the new beard I might have kissed him on the cheek, but I won't come near that thing. My face breaks out bad.

"Don't take any chances," he says as I put on my Miami Dolphins hat. I don't even like football but Judy Provost, a friend of mine, brought it back after she went down to Florida. She doesn't like football much either, but she does like Dan Marino's rear end when he bends over for a snap.

"I'll be fine," I say.

"Asshole should've known better," he throws after me as I head out. Funny but I have this picture in my head of Eddie. He's staring at me walk away, staring at me the way he used to, his eyes the hungry, nice sort they used to be. Course I don't know because I don't turn around to see.

It's twilight, and the used-up yellow light filters down like that in an old train station restroom. And while it's not exactly cold, the wind carries with it that first reminder of real cold. It says, Get ready, sucker. Out on the lake I can see jagged whitecaps, sharp as the teeth a raccoon shows you when you got him cornered in the barn. It's the sort of evening you don't want to get stuck out in North Bay with a motor that should've been worked on.

I walk down to the water, unlock the pump, and fill up the tank in the Merc. It starts harder than the Evinrude but after it gets going I like the feel of the seventy-five horses. It's got more spunk. When I get far enough away I'll open it up so the supper smell of our kitchen gets peeled away. Blowing the stink off. Eddie won't even know I took it and not the Evinrude, which is dependable but for old ladies. When I get back he'll probably be snoring anyway with the kung-fu guys silently kicking each other's brains out.

We bought the place eight years ago, with the insurance money from Eddie's accident. If you got to be stuck someplace, you could do a lot worse. The lake's pretty, especially early on summer mornings. I like waking up to the sound of loons. They have a cry that makes your throat catch, makes you think of a real beautiful poem on a get-well card. I'd love to try to raise one as a pet but Lyman, who was a forestry major at UMaine for two years, says they don't make good pets. Birds of prey aren't like ducks, he says. It's quiet around here, too. Except for a few busy weeks during ice-off and again during hunting season, you don't have to bust your tail. You're your own boss, and I like that. Before we bought the place, I used to work in a shop in Waterville that made screws—flathead and sheet metal, slotted and Phillips head, every kind of screw you could think of. There'd always be some jerk giving you a hard time. This one foreman name of Kyle Prendergast was always making jokes about screws. He'd come up to me and hand me a shiny brass-plated job they use in aircraft. He'd wait for about ten seconds, so everybody was watching, then he'd ask when was the last time I had a good screw. Like I really needed that. Least me and Eddie got nobody looking over our shoulders. That's one thing.

Eddie used to work in construction, mostly office buildings and big projects down around Portland. The money was good when the work was there, though it was either feast or famine. That's the way it is with construction. But with me working and no kids, we made ends meet. We owned our own place and we went away on vacation nearly every year: Lake Champlain one year, Niagara Falls another. Eddie used to like high work because the money was better and being way up never bothered him. In fact, he liked it. I guess the way some people like being on a ship or in an office all day. Then a scaffolding collapsed and Eddie fell fifty feet and broke his back. The doctors said how lucky he was. Said he could've died. Another guy he worked with wasn't so lucky. They said if his spine had been crushed just two inches higher he'd have lost his hands, and three, well, forget it. They made a big point of telling us that. Sometimes Eddie, when he's in one of his moods, will look across the supper table at me and hold his thumb and forefinger apart: the way you would to show how thick a real fine steak was. But that's only when he's in a bad frame of mind. Mostly he does OK. We both do.

Back then I knew what we were looking at was bad but I never let on because of Eddie. He was thirty-four, still a young man. He liked to go out dancing at the Iron Kettle and play softball in the summer and do some hunting in the fall. Sometimes he'd take me, even though I was never much on killing defenseless things. But I did like going through the woods with him, the smell of his jacket, coffee on cold mornings as we sat together waiting for a deer. Once we even made love in his sleeping bag and missed a twelve-point buck not ten feet away. The accident changed all that. To tell you the truth, back then I was pretty naive. I didn't know how things were going to turn out. Paraplegic. What did I know? Just a word. The only thing I had to go on was what I'd seen on TV. You know, those shows where somebody's paralyzed and then the rest of the story's about how they battle back and all that. Go on to win a wheelchair race and live "meaningful" lives. Have some supportive wife who keeps telling him he can do it. I could remember the movie *Coming Home* where Jon Voight plays this paralyzed vet who falls in love with Jane Fonda. In this one love scene he tells her he was just like other men except his legs didn't work. That's what I thought I was looking at. A little inconvenience. What did I know?

But you learn to make adjustments. That's what they used to tell us back in the PT sessions at the spinal cord place down in Atlanta. And it's true, though not the way they'd meant it. They used to say things like "Go for it" and "Handicapped is only a state of mind." Like cheerleaders. They'd say it so many times you even started to buy it. But after the haze following the accident wore off and what we were facing began to sink in, I think Eddie'd had enough. He was ready to get out of there. It was just about then we got the settlement. This place came up for sale and we grabbed for it. We thought we could make a life here. And some mornings when I wake up, I really think we can. Even after I realize Eddie's not there beside me in bed but out on the lounge chair sleeping off the six-pack, I make it a point to say things could've worked out a whole lot worse. It's just a state of mind.

The water's rough but nothing the big Merc can't handle. When I get out of the channel, out past the little spit of land no one's ever bothered to name, I open it up full throttle. It doesn't even hesitate, just pulls the front of the boat in the air and bangs over the top of the waves. It works just fine. My attitude has always been, if it ain't broke, don't fix it. But you watch, Eddie'll get his hands on it and then the thing'll sit in pieces on the floor of the den. It's not that he's not handy. It's just that things slip off his priority list pretty easy. He's got like about a million projects half-finished around the house. Carburetors he's rebuilding. Parts soaking in gasoline in the sink. Alternators he's rewiring. He's got flies half tied sitting everywhere, like those dead bugs that collect on your dash. But like I said, it doesn't make any sense to nag.

The dark's coming on quick now, so I head straight across toward Kineo. I pick out the McMillans' cabin in the clearing by the shore and use it as a beacon. When I get close, I'll veer north, toward Farm Island, so I'm head on into the wind. The cabin, the only building on Kineo except for the abandoned fire lookout on top, is closed up tight already. They're summer folks, from Boston, but nice, not like some you get up here. They come over to our camp now and then for supplies, gas or propane, or to moor their boat while they go into town. We let them park their Blazer at the camp, too. They're older, mid-sixties, I'd guess, with grown children who come and stay sometimes. Mostly it's just the two of them. Before he retired the husband was a lawyer down there and now they have plenty of time on their hands. But he's not snooty at all, neither are. They're just down-to-earth people. They even invited us over for supper once, wanting to pay us back for our help. Yet Eddie doesn't like going places, especially not in a boat. Besides, he said, what the hell are we going to talk about with them? Just talk, I said. Like people do. Oh, yeah, Eddie said. Like how he could've gotten more money if he'd had some big-city shyster who knew what he was doing? Eddie jumps to conclusions about people and there's no getting him to see it otherwise.

But the McMillans are nice really. A sweet old couple. They're what I used to picture being old together would be like. Like matching salt and pepper shakers, or an old vaudeville team: George and Gracie Burns, sitting at the breakfast table practicing one-liners. One night a couple of summers ago, I was in the boat coming back from Greenville with supplies. Sometimes I do that instead of taking the truck in. I like the long boat ride. It clears my head, blows the stink off. I was swinging past their place and could see a light on in the window and hear music spilling out over the water. This old big band stuff, the sort you picture navy boys dancing to after World War II. I cut the motor and drifted for a bit, not trying to be nosy or anything, just kind of curious. I could see them through the window. They were in the kitchen, moving fast, their arms swinging, their hips twirling like crazy. At first I thought something was the matter, maybe they were having a fight. You don't see that sort of stuff up here too often. But then I could see they were dancing. That's all it was. The husband was twirling his wife around, both having a good time but serious about it, too, the way they used to dance back then—a lot of showmanship and pride involved. A real skill. Not just getting up and throwing your ass around like they do nowadays. I floated out in the water in the dark, watching for what must've been ten minutes. I started crying, and I'm not the blubbery sort. My heart ached watching them, ached *for* them, alone out there on Kineo, knowing, as they must have known, that in a couple of years one or the other would be left all alone, and that that one, the survivor, would probably sell the place and wait out his time down in Florida. But for that moment they had each other and it was all they needed. Then I felt kind of guilty, spying on them like that, so I waited till the current had taken me past a ways and then I started the motor and headed across to camp.

I'm close enough now I turn and head toward Farm Island and the rock off Hardscrabble Point. It's a tricky spot. You have to pass between the point and a rock about fifty feet out and no more than six inches under water. Every year we warn our guests about it and every year some jerk grinds up one of the fifteen-horse Johnsons pretty good.

When I get around to the north side of Kineo I can make out the old fire lookout sitting on top like an antennae. In the old days, before they had planes, they used it to watch for fires up in the logging country north of here. But it's been abandoned for years now, its iron girders and stairs rusting away. People, mostly kids, still like to hike up the two miles to the summit and then climb to the top of it. It's seven stories straight up, all of it open and rusted and creaking like the whole thing'll collapse any minute. I've been told that from up there, on a clear day, you can see Quebec. I wouldn't know. You couldn't get me up there if you paid me. I've always been afraid of high places, even as a kid. Before Lyman came and with Eddie laid up, I used to have to force myself to do things I'd have never done: replace a lightbulb at the top of the signpost out at the road; in winter get up on the cabin roofs and push the snow off. I've always hated to be off the ground. Sometimes Eddie'll say why don't we take one of those sightseeing planes, see what everything looks like from up there. Not this girl, I say. I can see everything just fine down here.

I had been up as far as the second-story landing once, with Lyman. In fact, he'd talked me into it. This was a few years ago. A beautiful spring day. Me and Lyman had been working pretty hard getting the cabins ready for the ice-off rush. Eddie said why don't we knock off and go over to Kineo and have ourselves a little picnic. I said fine, thinking he meant *all* of us. He'd gotten pretty pale and I thought he could use the fresh air and sun. But he was meaning for me and Lyman to go. I said nonsense, he could come along too. Lyman even offered to carry him up on his back. But Eddie said he didn't want to piss on our parade—that's one of Eddie's favorite lines. So we packed a lunch and went by ourselves. I remember looking back as we headed across and there was Eddie on the dock, sitting in his chair saluting us with a beer can. He kept getting smaller and smaller until you couldn't even tell it was a person anymore, just something fixed on the dock.

Lyman had just dropped out of the university the fall before he came to work for us. We'd tried to run the place by ourselves for the first few years, hiring somebody part-time now and then to help out when it got busy. But after a while we started doing better than we could've hoped. More people began coming to the camp, telling their friends and so on. Finally we decided we needed somebody full-time, at least from ice-off through hunting season. Lyman showed up. He was this tall, rangy kid, with droopy eyes that fool you into thinking he's slow. He turned out to be a good worker. He's dependable, never complains, and knows his way around fishing and tracking. He's a good enough guide that guests will ask for him each year, to show them where the togues are running or where they can get a shot at a black bear. We were lucky to get him. He slept in the spare bedroom downstairs until we were able to fix up the toolshed behind number 1. Now, except for April when it's pretty slow and he heads south to visit his family, Lyman lives there all year. Eddie likes him around. He says it's to give me a hand but who's he kidding? He looks at Lyman as a sort of kid brother, even though he's young enough to be his son. They'll sit around at night drinking beer and playing poker. Sometimes the two of them will even take off fishing together, which surprises me because Eddie doesn't really feel comfortable in a boat anymore. Says he doesn't like the idea his legs wouldn't be of any use if something happened out there. But he trusts Lyman.

I take it easy going past Hardscrabble Point. Twenty feet off to the left I know the rock's sitting there under the water, waiting like some sort of monster ready to take a bite out of the propeller. After I make it through I open it up again. The wind's stronger now and there's ice crystals in it: gritty pieces that sting your face like gravel. I'm just hoping the kid's got brains enough to get it in to shore, not be out in this with just a pair of oars. Somebody's always drowning. It's a big lake and things can turn on you pretty quick. Down-staters come up here, thinking they know how to handle a boat, and they end up doing something stupid.

Take last fall. Two people died—a father and son. They weren't our guests, thank God. I say thank God not so much because it'd be bad for business—although it would—but because I feel responsible for our guests. Even the assholes. I'd feel bad if something happened. These two, the father and son, had gone out to North East Carry to troll and were coming back when a storm came up. Instead of turning around, they tried to make it back. Their boat capsized and even though they both had life jackets on, the water was cold and neither made it. Lyman says you'd last about twenty minutes in water this cold.

I keep busy. Judy Provost says that's the name of the game, and I have to believe her. There's always something. The cabins got to be cleaned, sheets and towels and whatnot. Food and supplies to pick up. And if it's not one thing, it's another. Eddie's always got something on the burner. Last year we put in new leach fields, and replaced the stoves in all but number 4, which already had a new one. Next year he's saying we should paint all the cabins and put in a new bulkhead down at the dock. The old one's slowly breaking apart. He's got other plans, too, big plans, but like everything else he'll get bored with them and go on to something else. Even talking of putting in a sauna and a swimming pool for the guests. A swimming pool, I say, when they got a forty-mile lake right outside their door. He says that's not the same thing. That's it's too cold for swimming even in August. Says Whispering Pines up Route 15 has one and we got to be competitive. No harm thinking big, I guess. Besides, it keeps him busy. Me, too.

Monday nights there's bingo. If anybody'd ever told me ten years ago I'd be playing bingo Monday nights I'd have said they were crazy. I could never stand the game and even now I'm not big on it. After about three calls my mind starts to wander, and Judy will give me an elbow in the ribs. "Irene! Get with the program. You're missing I-16." It bugs her I don't concentrate. She says, "What do you come and waste your money for?" But it's something to do. After bingo, while I'm not much of a drinker either, we'll stop at Marty's Place on the way home. I'll have something sweet, with Sambuca or Grand Marnier in it. Judy calls me the tutti-frutti girl, because I like little-girl drinks. But we sit and talk and eat the pretzels Marty puts out, maybe watch a little Monday Night Football, and generally unwind. That's the real reason I go out. Not for the bingo. That's just something I can tell Eddie and feel like it's the truth.

Judy's good to talk to. She's a little older than me, pushing fifty with a couple of grandkids on her Christmas list, but not like any grandmother you've ever seen. She's a hot ticket. I can open up with her since she knows the score. She's divorced. Her husband was usually just two drinks shy of falling down, and sometimes not even that. He lost four toes one winter when he fell down outside their trailer and nobody found him till morning. He was hell to live with, Judy says. But she wasn't a doormat, one of those sit-at-home-martyr type of women. Not Judy. She calls herself "one tough broad."

And she is. She'll down a shot of cognac—that's the only thing she drinks, says she could drink them all night and still know who she's bringing home—and tell me I should open my eyes.

"What would it hurt?" she says, her own eyes opening wide, searching Marty's Place for possibilities.

"*Who* would it hurt, you mean?" I reply.

"Who then? It's not like it'd be any skin off his nose."

She means Eddie. That if I were to do what she does, Eddie wouldn't mind.

"It wouldn't be right. You know that."

"It wasn't your fault, Irene. It wasn't anybody's fault. It's just rotten luck, that's all. He was just plain unlucky."

"We were, Jude," I say. "*We* were unlucky. Not just him."

"That's exactly what I mean. Just because he's got no use for it doesn't mean you got to put away your feelings in cold storage."

"I haven't put my feeling away anywhere."

"I mean *those* feelings. You'd probably be doing the guy a favor."

"Some favor."

"No, I mean it. If you're not satisfied what sort of wife can you be?"

"I manage all right."

"Yeah, manage. Managing's not living. When was the last time?"

"I don't know. I don't keep score like you do."

"Since before the accident, right? Am I right?"

I don't usually think about it, but when she puts it like that it's kind of hard not to. Eight years. It doesn't seem that long, you're going along, day by day, until you say it to yourself: *eight years.* Then it stretches out like a string of those lousy, breathless, late-winter days, when you feel like your skin's too tight and there's insects inside trying to get out.

"You're still a good-looking woman, Irene," says Judy. "You could have some fun." I know, I feel like telling her. I'm not stupid. It's not like I haven't had the opportunity. There've been men, guests mostly, who have said things. Sometimes it's just playful, something to pass the time. Just innocent flirting. But sometimes it's more. I'm not a nun or anything. I like my fun as much as anybody. I can't say I don't notice the way they'll look at you when you bring them clean sheets. You can see the gears turning as if their heads were made out of Plexiglas and the insides no more complicated than a wind-up toy. If I'd wanted to I could've had my fun. It would have been easy. But flirting's one thing, following through another.

Judy says, "You think I sat home and twiddled my thumbs while that zero of mine was out killing brain cells?"

"That's different," I tell her.

"Why's it different?"

"Because Eddie didn't mean for this to happen. He's a good man. Besides, it's not everything," I say.

"Maybe not," she says, looking over my shoulder at some new guy who's just bellied up to the bar. "But you got to admit, it sure helps pass the time."

Judy's situation is different. She was married to a jerk and so you can't really blame her for fooling around. But Eddie was a decent man. Is, I mean. It's not his fault. He had nothing to do with it. We were just unlucky. With some people bad luck follows them around and keeps happening to them day after day. But with me and Eddie it was just the one thing. One bad moment. Judy tells me he's not a quadriplegic, he could still do things if he really loved me. Sometimes Judy's downright pushy. She talks as if I should live my life according to her rules. I've tried to tell her it's not even that part I miss so much anymore. It's the warmth of another body on cold nights, the being held, the touching of hands. Before, we used to hold hands through an entire movie. In some ways I miss that more than the other stuff. I don't expect much anymore. I'd settle for the salty taste of Eddie's mouth after he'd had a few beers.

This happened a few months ago: Eddie was lying there, watching some Chuck Norris thing on TV. Even without the sound you knew ole peace-loving Chuck had been messed with and now he was out for blood. I'd just taken a shower and came out in my bathrobe. I got Eddie a beer and I lay down on the lounge chair with him, curled right up against him. I hadn't done that in a long time. We waited there like kids on a first date, wondering who was going to make the first move. Finally I turned and kissed Eddie on the cheek. He didn't look away from the TV, so I leaned over and kissed him on the lips. They were dry and cool as wallpaper in a room you've shut off for the winter. I pushed my tongue into his mouth and was surprised to find that warm, moist place I hadn't known for so long. He looked up at me then and kissed back, hard, like he meant it, like he'd been holding back so long he couldn't stop himself even if he wanted to. I don't know why I did what I did next. I scooted up over him, so I was straddling him. I opened my robe and placed my breast against his lips. I shivered. Eddie started to kiss me there and I could feel my whole body stiffen. His, too, at least the half that could still stiffen. But then the damn radio came on, interrupting us the way my mother used to when we'd sit in Eddie's T-Bird out in front of our house. I got up quick as I could and went over and flipped it off. I came back and tried to pick where we'd left off. I don't know, maybe I tried to rush things too much. Maybe I wanted too much, too soon. I don't know. But pretty soon Eddie was wheezing, pushing me off like I'd been trying to hurt him, saying he couldn't breathe. You could see the terror in his eyes, like someone clinging to the gunwale of a capsized boat, wondering if he'd make it. Course I never told Judy that.

I'm on the other side of Kineo now, heading toward North Bay. The rain's really coming down, blowing right into my face. I have my lights on but there's no boat in sight. I'm looking for a flare, thinking maybe he's smart enough to light one of those Eddie keeps in the emergency kit in the boat, but no such luck. Up toward Folsom Farm there's a couple of small coves, where someone could put in and you wouldn't see him from here. But now I'm getting worried. I don't like the looks of it. I get on the radio and call Eddie. There's no answer though. I try again but still nothing. Now my mind's going in two directions at once: worrying about the guy out in the boat and wondering where Eddie is. Finally I decide to call Rog at his auto body shop. He lives right above it and he's usually home.

"That you, Irene?" he says.

"Yeah, it's me, Rog. We got a call about some kid over in North Bay, couldn't start his motor. I'm over here now and I can't see a thing. You hear anything?"

"Nope. If I do I'll get right back to you."

"Do me a favor, Rog? Give Lyman a call and have him check on Eddie."

"Anything wrong?"

For a moment I sift through that one. It strikes me as funny. If I were a comic I'd think of some line, some good comeback. But I'm never able to think of jokes, or if I do I always screw up the punch line. Instead I just say, "Nobody's answering at home."

"Sure thing. Looks sloppy out there, Irene. You'd better get your butt in."

"I'm all right," I say, though I grab a life jacket out from under the seat and throw it on to be on the safe side. Still, this cold out it wouldn't do you much good.

I happen to glance back over my shoulder and way off in the distance, in the bay behind Kineo, I catch a silver gleam of something, like the momentary flash of a salmon as it hits your line. It could be nothing, just the shine off the water, but since there's nothing in sight toward North Bay, I decide to take a chance. I turn around and then gun it south. The closer I get, the more it looks like a boat. I can't make out anybody in it and I start praying *please, no, please, no,* chanting it like somebody doing yoga.

On this side, the cliff face of Kineo shoots straight up, a rock eight hundred feet high. Even after all these years it still scares the hell out of me just to look at it. Sometimes climbers will come up here to give it a try. It's supposed to be one of the best in the Northeast. They'll stop at camp and rent a boat, and you'll see them up there with their ropes and their helmets. Or some crazy high school kid'll risk his neck to write Tom Loves Sue in spray paint. I got this screwy dream. I have it every once in a while since we moved here. It wakes me up cold. In the dream I'm on the side of Kineo. Don't ask me how I got there, it's just a dream. Anyways, I'm up there and I'm petrified to go up or go down. I just cling to the side of the cliff like a treed cat. Sometimes, if I'm lucky, I wake up before I slip. Other times I'm in free-fall for what seems like years before I land with a thud in bed.

The time Lyman got me up there on that fire lookout. I say he got me up there but it was as much my doing as his. In fact, I'm older and should've known better. We'd had our little picnic up there, in a small clearing where there used to be a cabin that the rangers had lived in. The clearing was about thirty feet from the edge of the cliff but since I couldn't see over I didn't mind. Me and Lyman had finished eating and we lay for a while on blankets, enjoying the newness of the sun as it warmed our bodies. Lyman even took off his shirt. He's skinny but he has the young, lean body of a greyhound. After a while, he took out a joint and lit it. Eddie didn't like that stuff around but Lyman guessed I wouldn't mind. He even got me to take a couple of hits. Who would know, I figured. We started talking. He was usually pretty quiet. We'd work all day together, cleaning the boats or fixing a toilet in one of the cabins, and he wouldn't say two words. He'd just sort of look at me every once in a while, and smile in that way he had. But this day he went on about how he was thinking of going back to school. He said he had an old girlfriend at Orono who wanted him to come back. I told him if that's what he wanted he should go for it. I told him he had to think about his future and that there wasn't much keeping him here. I wanted to be honest with him. I didn't want to lead him on at all. He was just hired help, and in ten years that's still all he'd be.

Then he leaned toward me and put his arm around me. My heart froze but I didn't do anything because the truth is it was kind of nice having his warm, naked arm over me. Lyman smiled at me then and said why don't we climb the tower. He said it as if that had something to do with his future, with his deciding to go back to school or not. He said there was a nice place up top that was private and the view would turn my head. I remember he said that: *the view would turn my head.* I should've just said no. I should've said he was crazy, *me* up that high. But I didn't. It might have been the joint or the spring day, or just that I didn't want him to think of me in a certain way. I don't know. But I let him take me by the hand and lead me over to the fire tower. We stood at the base and looked up. It pointed straight up into the air, like what I imagine the Eiffel Tower looking like, only much smaller. At the top there was a small room where the ranger used to stay during his watch. The whole tower was in bad shape though. The girders and rivets were all rusted. The wood steps were rotted and chipped. Even the guy wires attached to concrete pylons in the ground were pockmarked with rust. You could just picture one of those things snapping and the whole shebang tumbling down.

"Come on," Lyman said, pulling me by the hand. "Don't be a chickenshit." And when I hesitated to take that first step, it became a sort of game, him tugging, me pulling back, both of us laughing nervously like a couple of kids on a playground. Finally he put his arms around me and picked me right off the ground. Like I said, he's a skinny kid but his strength fools you. He lifted me up and set me down on the third or fourth step. "There," he said, like we'd decided something.

I stared at his droopy eyes, his blond hair almost orange in the sun. He was smiling up at me. Maybe I figured if I tried it once, got over that fear I had, I would be all right. I could then do it again anytime I wanted. I just had to try it once. "OK," I said. "But you go first. And don't be an asshole."

He promised he wouldn't. I was a little surprised how easy it was, at least the first dozen steps or so. Pretty soon I was up over the treetops and could see the surrounding country. It *was* beautiful. I'd never seen it from up this high. My head felt suddenly light, not dizzy light, but the way it does when you take off a helmet after riding a motorcycle. Kind of swirling, without gravity. We kept going. One step after another, moving toward something that wasn't clear to either but was there at the top waiting for us. Lyman was up ahead of me, egging me on, excited about some new thing he could see from just a few steps above. *Look at that,* he kept saying. *Wow!* He kept telling me not to glance down, to look out, to look far away. And I could remember Eddie saying that very same thing when he used to work construction. For a while it worked, too. I thought I could make it, go all the way. There didn't seem much to stop me. Just Lyman and me and one step at a time. I kept thinking how I'd tell Judy about it over a drink at Marty's Place. I kept wondering what it'd feel like up there. Wondering in what way I'd be a different person once I got over this fear.

But when I reached the second landing something happened. I didn't even look down. I just froze. Lyman came down and tried to help me, but I'd latched onto the metal railing and wouldn't let go. He put his arms around me and pressed his shirtless body into mine. I could hear somebody's heart chugging away, his or mine or both of ours—I don't know. I remember he kept saying, "It's all right, Irene. It's going to be all right." I think I'd have started crying if I wasn't so scared, and so ashamed, too. Here I was this middle-aged woman, scared shitless because of some stupid dare, being hugged by a kid young enough to be her son. I kept saying to myself, what did it matter, after all, if I made it up or not. It wasn't important. There were other things in life. Yet I knew then, that of all the things I could overcome in this life, this was sure not going to be one of them.

After that I never come near anything I have to use more than a stepladder to get to. That's my limit. For anything higher needs doing, something high up like the sign out front or a shingle needs replacing, I let Lyman do it. Eddie says to me, let Lyman do it. That's what he's here for.

At about a hundred feet, I see it's one of ours. And there's something covered up in the boat. It looks like one of those rain ponchos, but even with my lights on it's so dark now it's hard to tell. Maybe I'm just hoping. I cross my fingers and back off on the throttle so I won't swamp the smaller boat. He must feel my wake because the poncho comes off and this head pokes out.

"Jesus Christ," he curses when he sees me. I shine a flashlight at him. His eyes glow red, like the eyes of dog. His hair is matted and he has the look of someone who's afraid enough to try to hide it under anger. I can see he's been under his poncho trying to work on the motor. The cap is off and the fuel filter's in his hand.

"Started to get worried about you," I say, trying to play it down.

"Fuckin' great," he replies. "Why the hell don't you people make sure your equipment works?"

"Does normally."

"Normally, hell," he says, but his voice breaks with the cold. He's shivering now. The fingers gripping the poncho look ghostly white, like dead shiners floating in a bait bucket. He thinks of going on with this, but I can see the fight has drained out of him. He's half froze and scared, and he just feels lucky now someone found him out in this. He had a glimpse of something he doesn't like having seen, and he's smart enough to keep his mouth shut. "Fucking cold out here," is all he says. I give him a hand up into my boat and I get out a blanket and wrap it around him.

"We'll have some hot coffee when we get back, OK. Did you eat yet?" But he just looks at me and shivers. He won't be watching a girly film. Not tonight. Tonight he'll call home and tell his wife he loves her. Then I hook a tow line to his boat and head back. I call home again and this time Eddie answers.

"Where were you?" I ask. "You scared me."

"On the floor."

"On the floor? What happened?"

"I fell asleep and must've rolled off. I don't know. I heard you call but I couldn't get to it in time."

"You OK?"

"Of course," he replies. "You find what's-his-face?"

"Got what's-his-face right here," I say, smiling. What's-his-face—Andy, I remember now—looks over at me, smiles sheepishly, and blows out air. He doesn't look at me the way he did the other night. Full of hunger and the cockiness of youth. Now it's the drained look of a little child who's had a close call.

"Hurry up home," Eddie says. "I don't like thinking of you out in this."

"I will," I say. I consider saying something more, to give Eddie something to chew on till I get back, but then, blaming it on the fact that we're not alone, that Andy is sitting there listening, I just manage, "I will," and open the throttle full-bore toward home.

## About the Author

Assistant Professor of English at Fairfield University in Fairfield, Connecticut, Michael C. White has written more than forty short stories, which have appeared in publications such as *New Letters* and *Redbook*. He is also the founding editor of the yearly anthology *American Fiction*.